THE CURSED DAUGHTER

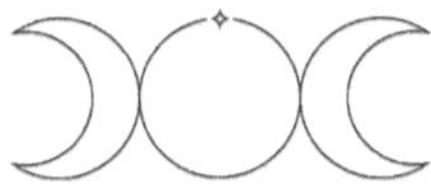

THE LOST COVEN BOOK TWO

E. O'MEAGHER

ISBN: 979-8-9883605-2-0 (paperback)

ISBN: 979-8-9883605-3-7 (ebook)

Lori,
For igniting my love of all things spooky.

"In the old days, if a witch betrayed her coven, they would kill her."

—Nancy Downs, "The Craft"

Chapter 1

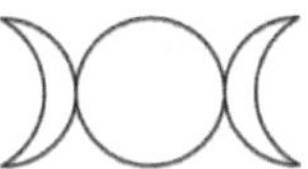

Slick cobblestone held up my rushed panic; the dampness hadn't frozen solid yet, but as the night grew colder, it would. I brushed a loose strand of gray hair out of my face and stuffed my hand back into the pocket of Selene's coat. As the wind whipped around my ears, I glanced down the street, waiting for shadows to follow. Hurrying up the front steps, I knocked on the door and waited. A few agonizing seconds ticked by, and my breath puffed out small clouds in the freezing air. Selene had bought us time, but I had no idea how much. Impatience getting the best of me, I knocked again.

Ian opened the door a few moments later, yanking a sweatshirt over his head. His face fell after he gave me a once-over. "Uh, hi," he said. He ran a hand over his hair. "Thanks, but I've already found Jesus."

I blinked at him. "What?"

"I'm good on information," he said, the fake smile he used for placating strangers on his face.

"It's me," I said.

He shook his head. "I'm sorry, ma'am, I think you have the wrong place."

"It's Em," I persisted. A gust of wind swept up the street and I scrunched down in the coat to protect my already freezing ears.

He opened his mouth, closed it, and blinked a few times. "You're...what?"

I pushed by him, desperate to be less exposed to the cold and any potential Emissaries who had followed me.

"Look, I don't think—"

"I just look like Lyra's grandmother right now," I said, dropping my duffel—still disguised as the carpet bag—on the couch.

His eyes went wide, and I could practically see him processing. "You—she—what?" He shook his confusion away. "But you don't *sound* like you." He always caught on quick.

Rubbing my hands together to get feeling back into them, I headed for the kitchen. "I guess Selene Tsipras has perfected her glamour."

"So...they caught you?" he asked.

Turning on the single-serve brewer, I opened the top and tossed the used coffee pod out. "Sort of." I grabbed a mug out of the cupboard. "Lyra'll be here in a second."

"You brought Lyra?"

I shook my head. "She brought herself."

"Ah."

I pulled the coat tighter around me, an involuntary shiver running up my spine. The cold had seeped into my bones. Lyra had dropped me off three blocks away before heading off to ditch the car.

I dug around in the kitchen drawers, finding the only tea bag left of my stash. I hadn't been over in so long, a restock was needed.

"You want to head out now?" he said, eyeing the door.

I shook my head and ripped open the package, sticking the bag into the mug. While adjusting my plan and leaving before Lyra got here was smart, I couldn't. Not until the burning question that lodged itself in my brain on the drive over had an answer. I watched the water spit out of the machine, hoping that answer wasn't going to eliminate Sandusky altogether.

"Can you , like, turn that off?" Ian said.

It took me a second to register he'd said anything. When I looked over at him, I frowned.

He gestured to me as a whole. "It's kinda freaky."

I glanced down at the hands that weren't mine and shook my head. "I'm hoping Lyra can," I admitted.

He nodded. "Whelp, I'll go grab your stuff." He headed out of the kitchen as I added a little honey to my tea and took my time stirring it in. I hadn't run a cycle of water through to get the stale coffee taste out of the water, but I was more concerned with warmth than taste right now.

Curling my fingers around the hot mug, I moved over to a seat on the other side of the kitchen counter. A stack of papers caught my attention.

Train schedules, next semester's calendar, and events in Boston, Philadelphia, and Chicago. Ian's scribbled notes next to each of them and messy highlighted lines showed just how busy he'd been. Busier than I realized—considering he'd finished his semester.

None of our plans, however, had accounted for Lyra or her grandmother's involvement. They'd helped me get out of my Collective-infested house, but I wasn't ready to reveal *everything* yet.

Lyra walked through the door without knocking, just as Ian came out of the bedroom with the bag of things we'd stashed a few weeks ago.

"We need to get clear soon," she said, tossing her backpack next to the carpet bag on the couch and pulling her hair off her neck into a ponytail. "Even though Gram brought us extra time." She walked over to the counter and eyed the papers in front of me.

"How much?" Ian asked.

She shrugged. "Half an hour, if we're lucky."

He nodded.

I took a deep breath and hoped I wasn't about to add more trouble to my night. I pulled my magic to the surface just in case. "Lyra?" I started.

She looked up.

"How did your grandmother know what I was planning?"

Lyra shrugged. "She didn't."

I frowned at her. "There's no way—"

"Not like, the *plan*-plan," she corrected. "I asked some hypothetical questions about things, and, yeah..."

Ian caught my eye. "What things?" he asked.

She pulled the sleeves of her jacket down and looped her thumbs through the holes. "What *might* happen if I helped a witch miss their appointment with the Council."

"So, you told her." I watched the steam swirl up from the hot tea between my hands. It wasn't the worst answer I could have gotten. But Lyra ratting me out to someone *on* the Council still stung a little.

Lyra shook her head. "I wasn't even sure you were going to run," she admitted. "Especially after you and Jax got all romantical. It was a hunch."

Heat crept up the back of my neck and I was thankful her grandmother had chosen to wear a high-neck sweater.

"Pretty solid hunch," Ian said.

Lyra picked up one of the event schedules for the Boston Garden. "It's not my fault Gram is a fucking genius and figured out my hypotheticals weren't so hypothetical."

Ian kept his eyes on me, and I nodded. That was either the complete truth or Lyra was a better liar than I ever gave her credit for. I forced my magic to settle, content for now that Lyra wasn't a threat. To me, anyway.

"Can you do something about that?" Ian asked, nodding to me.

She shook her head. "Gram's spell. Can't fuck with it unless we want to risk...issues." She replaced the event schedule and picked up the printed-out train tickets. "Philly?"

He nodded and circled around to the other side of the counter, leaning on it as he spread out the other items he'd printed.

"That's where Sasha and them are from, so I figured it would throw your people off for a bit."

"Smart."

He smiled. "Bought those with my card," he continued. "Em's with a friend's. Hopefully, it'll take them a minute to figure it out." He nodded at me. "Only bought one though..."

Lyra waved the comment away. "All good."

She didn't elaborate, and I didn't ask. "Are you sure you want to do this?" I asked Ian instead. "Getting involved is dangerous."

Lyra tapped a blue painted fingernail on the ticket. "He's already involved," she said. "They're coming for him either way."

"Comforting," Ian muttered.

She gave him a playful punch on the arm. "Jax'll make sure you're good in the long run." And *that* thin hope was the only reason I was willing to let Ian out of my sight.

"What's the plan for cameras? Only thing I got doesn't last too long," she said. "And once we split up..."

Ian shrugged. "We're the same height. I throw on a wig and hope for the best."

Lyra crossed her arms. "A wig and hope? That's your plan?"

"Pretty much."

Lyra looked over at me and her eyes widened "Shit. You look like you again."

I glanced down at my hands to see them returned to the paler, less lined ones I knew.

"Thank God," Ian said.

Lyra shook her head. "That means Gram looks like her again," she said. "And they'll notice Em's gone."

"Shit." Ian checked his phone. "Jada won't be here for another fifteen minutes, and your train doesn't leave for an hour."

Lyra moved to the bags on the couch. "Looks like we're going to have to modify the plan."

Ian hurried out of the kitchen and came back with his own bag. Lyra was keying away on a laptop behind us. The sudden rush and urgency tightened the nerves nestled in my gut. I took a sip of tea to try to settle it, but all that did was leave a strange mix of chamomile and watered-down coffee taste on my tongue that made me want to gag.

"You good?" Ian asked, voice low as if he didn't want Lyra overhearing.

With shaking hands, I set the mug on the counter. "I just—" I took a deep breath. "I didn't think I'd have to do this. Leave."

Sure, I'd planned for it. For years, the possibility was there, like a bad dream I couldn't shake off. I'd taken out cash, stashed supplies, and made sure the wards at the Sandusky house were set and strong. But I'd wanted it all to be paranoia. Ultimately, a waste of time and energy I'd laugh about one day.

Wes was with Selene's friends and Chad was with his mother, separated from each other. Ian was risking too much. All because of me. Leaving—running—was selfish, and second thoughts were creeping in. But the need to run had been ingrained in my mind, passed down from too many generations to outright ignore. I wrapped my hand around the ruby.

"You'll be back," Ian said. "They can't keep you away forever."

"Don't underestimate them," I reminded him.

He put his hands on my shoulders and gave them a tight squeeze. "Don't underestimate yourself," he said.

I tried to smile, but forcing it took more energy than I had to spare.

"Okay," Lyra said, closing the laptop. She slid it back into her bag and hopped over the back of the couch to come stand next to us. "It's not pretty, but we got a little more than wig-hope," she said.

"How?" Ian asked.

"It's—you know what? I'll explain later. Maybe." She glanced around the small kitchen. "You got sage?"

He waved his hand at the space. "Whatever you find is what I got."

She mumbled a curse under her breath before moving to dig around in his cupboards and drawers. Each time she pulled something out, she'd give a head shake or nod, grouping items on the counter. I found a thicker sweater in my bag and pulled it on, hoping to get as warm as I could before we had to go back into the cold.

Ian and I watched as Lyra mixed a bowl of herbs she'd found. She whispered over it, giving the bowl a faint glow for a second. She then spooned the mixture into two mugs and slid them over to Ian.

"Mix with hot water and drink no more than half an hour before you head to the station," she instructed. "Any security footage will have a twenty-second lag on your faces."

He eyed the contents of the mug. "Only twenty seconds?"

She nodded. "Anything more and I'd need to be on site." She grimaced. "If they put Jax or Leander on lead though...well, then this was completely pointless."

"Completely?" I asked.

She shrugged. "Unfortunately, I was cursed with intelligent brothers."

Ian nodded and sniffed at the mug again. "What's in it?"

"Whatever I found is what it's got," she teased. "Nothing weird, swear."

Lyra looked over her shoulder to check the clock on the oven. "We need to be as close to our final destinations before they figure out the disruption is magical." She went back to the papers on the counter. "So, Em and I need to be..."

"Sandusky," I said.

She looked up at me. "Ohio is the *final* stop?"

I nodded.

"But..." She let out a huff. "Fucking *Ohio*?" It came out as more of a whine than a question.

"I have a house." I shifted, pulling at the ends of my sleeves. "It's...protected," I added lamely.

She raised her eyebrows. "I get that," she said. "But if we're going to be all fugitive-y, or whatever, can't we go somewhere interesting?"

I pinched the bridge of my nose and let out a long breath.

"Like, Siquijor has this amazing healing festival. Or, like...Bolivia?"

I sighed. "We can't go international. You said it: your brothers are smart, they'll be watching for IDs."

She made sure the bags were all zipped up. "Yeah, we're going to have to correct that particular fuck-up in your plan."

I crossed my arms. "We should be able to get to Sandusky without fakes," I said.

She nodded. "True. But I'd rather drop the *should* from that." She slung her bag over her shoulder and picked up my two. "I'll get a car, and we'll make a teensy pit stop."

"What?"

"Don't worry about it." She opened the front door and nodded to Ian. "Stay smart."

"You too," he said with a small wave. She closed the door with her heel, and I realized too late I'd just let her take everything I had with her. If this were one big trap, I'd just completely screwed myself over.

Swallowing hard, I turned to Ian and as soon as he smiled at me, I had to press the side of my hand under my eyes to keep the burning tears from falling. The last thing I wanted was for our goodbye to be a blubbering mess.

I took a shuddering breath. "I should have made you something," I said. "Protection, a charm bag, or—"

"Em," Ian said, pulling me into a hug. "I'll be fine."

My stomach tightened. "But there's something..."

"Probably wouldn't work on me anyway," he said, voice rumbling in his chest against my cheek. I shut my eyes, and the tears rolled out. He stroked my hair and let me sob against him as the goodbye I never wanted to say hit me.

"It won't be forever," he said again.

I nodded. He was confident of that, but I wished I could say the same. Despite his confidence, the plan, and Lyra's help, I couldn't drown out the uncomfortable nagging in the back of my mind telling me this was the last time we'd see each other. It was strong enough I wanted to chuck all the plans and drag Ian to Ohio with me.

When we broke away, I wasn't the only one with tears. "Don't," I said with a watery chuckle, wiping tears away with my sleeve.

"I'm trying not to," he admitted.

A honk from outside told us time was up. For the first time in eight years, he wasn't going to be a phone call or a short drive away. This was it.

Another honk. We gave each other one last squeeze before he walked me to the door. Lyra was waiting, double parked. I pulled Ian into a final—tight—hug and jogged to the car before I changed my mind.

Climbing into the passenger seat, I gave him a final wave before Lyra pulled away. Barely buckled in, Lyra turned the corner a little too quickly, I took in the dash in front of me.

"This isn't your grandmother's car," I said.

"We're not taking the turnpike in a car rented by the fucking Collective, *Circe* Em."

I sighed. "You stole it?"

She shrugged. "I left a note."

I angled the air vents to warm my hands. "No, you didn't."

"No, I didn't." She pressed on the accelerator, hitting a speed far from legal and whipped around a car going too slow for her.

I leaned my head against the seat and watched the lights of Portland blur by. "Where is this pit stop?" I asked, anything to take my mind off the sinking feeling in my gut the further from Ian we got.

She smiled over at me. "Salem."

Chapter 2

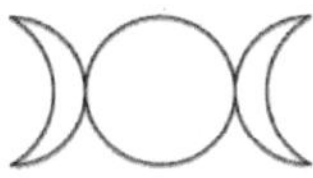

We'd left our stolen car a block from the Ropes Mansion, and from there Lyra had led me up Essex Street, her long strides hard to keep up with. I'd been thankful we crossed the street to avoid walking directly in front of the dark house of one of the trial judges. Tragedy could leave a haunting mark on a place, and Salem was no exception. Negative energy would only slow our progress and I didn't need that. After we'd cut through a small snow-covered park that housed the "Bewitched" sculpture, Lyra had dumped me at O'Neill's—a local Irish pub—and quickly left without explanation.

I'd managed to get down a few bites of the shepherd's pie, but it mostly remained untouched, and my tea had long gone cold. Every time the door opened, a gust of cold air ushered in a new arrival. The chill that lingered only bothered me. Everyone else was happy, draping coats over chairs, greeting each other with smiles, and ordering rounds of drinks.

Plenty of witches called Salem home. They'd set up mystic shops, read palms and tarot, and used the history of the town to market their craft in a way other places rarely welcomed. An apothecary here, a metaphysical shop there—magic was out and thriving. Three centuries of superstition rolled into a tourist attraction.

The fact that we could run into a witch with unwavering loyalty to the Council at any turn, combined with our proximity to the Collective's post in Boston, made me uneasy. Lyra had been so vague about what she was up to that it left room for doubt to creep in. I kept waiting for Leander, Kane, or even Sebastian to walk in laughing at my pathetic attempt at escape. I had to remind myself that backstabbing wasn't Lyra's style. If nothing else, I knew that for sure. She'd punch me in the face and drag me back herself before giving anyone else the credit.

I clutched the ruby for comfort. It was warm, humming, wired, as if the magic stored inside sensed where we were. Amity's birthplace and the place her coven met its end. The place this all started.

My server brought a fresh pot of hot water with an attempt at a consoling smile. I'm sure they, along with everyone else, assumed I'd been stood up and was in denial. I'd rather that than the truth.

The next frosty gust brought in small flurries and Lyra. She hurried over to me, rubbing her hands together. She didn't say a word; instead, she grabbed my fork and went straight for my abandoned pie. She got two forkfuls down before she swallowed hard with a grimace. When the server circled over, Lyra ordered her own food and a hot whiskey.

"So?" I prompted.

She pushed the plate of cold food away. "We're good," she said. "Or as good as we can be." She put her hands on the hot pot of water and let out a relieved sigh. "Z will meet us tomorrow."

"Tomorrow?" I asked. "Why not tonight?"

"Because—" She paused when her drink came. She gave the server a wide smile and waited for them to engage a couple three tables down before continuing. "Even magical fake identities take time. Tomorrow's a rush as it is. Z is doing me a favor." She wrapped her hand around her own glass and took a sip. "*Circe*, that's good. It's fucking freezing out."

I stabbed at my unfinished meal. "Hope you got a car with a big back seat."

She shook her head. "Got a room at the Hawthorne."

"Lyra you—" I lowered my voice when two people at the bar looked over, thanks to my outburst. One of their gazes lingered a little too long. Flinching as the ruby sparked hotter than it had in a while, I went to grab it—but the sensation left as soon as it had struck.

I made sure their attention returned to their drinks. "They've definitely figured out we're missing by now," I said. "We need to get out of here."

She rolled her eyes. "Relax. Ian's trail is good, they'll follow that first."

I opened my mouth to argue.

"Then, they'll have to fix the corrupted footage, *then* the Council will have to call in a D.R.U." She took another drink. "By then, we'll be long gone."

I blinked at her. "What the hell is a D.R.U.?"

She stirred the lemon floating on top of her drink in slow circles. "Dissenter Retrieval Unit."

"Seriously?"

She shrugged. "And you thought 'Emissary' was bad."

I crossed my arms and sat back against the booth. "And what happens if this Z decides to tell them we're here?"

"They wouldn't do that," she said. "They hate the Charlevoixs more than you."

I snorted. "Doubt it."

She shook her head. "Sebastian did a number on them a few years ago, trust me."

"Of course he did." I watched a bundled couple hurry outside. The few interactions I'd had with the guy after regaining consciousness didn't make me doubt he was capable of being a complete ass. His sense of entitlement alone was—

"Sebastian's a Charlevoix?" I blurted as it clicked.

"Yup." She took a long drink. "Grandson of the Councilwoman herself. Talk about nepotism..."

"But, if he's...wouldn't that—no—but that means we're..."

She lowered her glass and pursed her lips like she was trying not to laugh. "Cousins," she confirmed. "That's great."

"Shut up," I mumbled. I was going to need something significantly stronger than tea. There went the fraction of a hope that Lenore was the exception and my father's side of the family wasn't completely full of assholes. When I was younger, I'd always wondered what it would have been like if I had been raised around them. Now, I was glad that never happened.

I sulked for another hour while Lyra ate her own dinner. We stayed long enough for the beginning of a trad session that brought in a lot more people, leaving nothing but standing room. Finally, I convinced Lyra we should head out after occupying a table for almost three and a half hours.

The Hawthorne was barely a ten-minute walk from O'Neill's. It was a large place in a great location for historic Salem. Our room was comfortable with two queen beds, a nice bathroom, and a wonderful view of Essex. It was also way too expensive.

Lyra shrugged out of her coat and tossed it onto a bed. "Not bad, huh?" she said, pulling her hat off.

"For the price, it should be better than 'not bad,'" I mumbled, stripping off my top two layers. Despite not being thrilled with the choice of pricey accommodations Lyra had made, I *was* looking forward to a hot shower to wash off the chill in my bones.

"Now," Lyra started, climbing onto the bed and crossing her legs under her, "I need you to have an open mind about tomorrow."

I kicked off my shoes. "I don't like the sound of that."

She rubbed her hands over her thighs. "Z already had plans, so we're sort of putting them out."

"What kind of plans?"

Lyra cocked her head at me. "New Year's Eve kind of plans."

Tracking the days after dropping out had been difficult; almost dying had made it impossible. Christmas felt years ago, not a week. And now, in less than forty-eight hours, I was facing a new calendar year.

Lyra continued. "So, I told them we'd meet at a party."

"Okay…"

"At a popular nightlife establishment."

I groaned. "A *club*?"

She nodded.

I fell onto the bed. "Can't you just go?"

She yanked the hair tie out of the end of her braid, ran her fingers through her hair, and retied it into a bun on top of her head. "Nope. They have to see you to finish."

"What—"

"Don't ask me," she said, holding her hands up in mock surrender. "Scribes are weirder than the rest of us."

I rubbed my face and laid back to stare at the ceiling. "Fine," I muttered. "But I'm not going to enjoy it."

"That's the spirit."

○

Lyra's quiet, steady snoring filled the air, distracting me from unfamiliar sheets and the too-clean smell of the room. Falling into an uneasy sleep, my dreams were a confusing mix of past and present. I'd be running from Lenore and Sebastian, but the streets would turn from pavement to dirt and the lights would vanish, replaced by torches.

Amity and another woman with red irises made appearances but were no help as I ran, and ran, and ran, never getting far enough away. The ruby burned so brightly it lit the woods.

Old Salem became more vivid as I tried to hide from my family, but those visions held their own dread. Witches hunted and murdered. Amity's anguish as her coven was ripped away.

The shift I'd felt as we came into town followed me into my dreams. A heavy presence pressing against my mind and stirring my magic like a cat uncurling from a long nap.

The living weren't the only ones hunting me.

○

The sound of the TV woke me, and the bedside clock told me it was almost noon. I'd managed to stay mostly asleep for almost seven hours.

If only I'd felt like it.

Lyra was sitting on her bed, watching some old action movie Ian would have known the name of. I sat up and rolled the stiffness from my neck.

"You good?"

I rubbed my sore eyes. "Didn't sleep great."

After absently staring at the movie for a few moments, I forced myself out of bed and to the bathroom. Ignoring my reflection as much as I could, I waited for steam to fill the room before climbing under the showerhead's stream. I turned the water cold for the last minute to shock my groggy brain awake. Time really had ceased to mean anything. It had barely been a day since I'd woken up surrounded by Emissaries in my own home, not even a week since I almost died, and mere hours since I let Ian lay a trail for them to follow instead of me. I didn't even know what day of the week it was anymore.

Walking back into the main room, I dreaded whatever the plan for the night was. Lyra was halfway through unloading way too many shopping bags for the health of my budget.

I pulled a sweater on and sat on the bed, folding my knees up. "What's all that?"

"Options," she said, spreading out a variety of sparkly tops. She held one up, gold and black, and looked at me. She shook her head and put it back.

"When did you go shopping?" I asked, stifling a yawn.

"You were asleep," she said. "I had to do something to kill time." She dumped out a bag of monotone—though mostly black—bottoms. "Oh, that reminds me." She pushed aside all the other clothes to reveal a black box with a large red ribbon on it and offered it to me.

"Happy birthday! Or Solstice, or Christmas. Or...just pick a holiday. Happy that."

I slid the ribbon off and opened the box. Wrapped in black tissue paper was a deep red leather jacket, soft to the touch and matching the shade of the ruby around my neck.

"Like?" she asked, returning to sorting her pile of clothes.

"It's..." I took a breath. I couldn't decide *what* it was. "Too expensive" came to mind first. "Perfect" was next. Then back to being too expensive. I'd always wanted one, ever since I saw pictures of Grandma Geri with a red leather jacket. The idea had stuck with me. Mom promised I could get one when I stopped growing so fast.

There was no way Lyra could have known any of that. She was, however, the type to splurge on something she thought looked cool. I couldn't stop the tears from leaking out. I wiped them away quickly.

"You hate it," she said.

I looked up and realized she'd been watching me. "No, it's great. I just...the...it's too much."

She shook her head. "It *is* great and would look fucking amazing with..." she trailed off as she moved some clothes around. "This!" She held up a black mini dress with a touch of sparkle to it.

I shook my head. "Too cold."

She frowned. "But it has little stars on it," Lyra whined.

"So you wear it."

She sighed. "They didn't have it in my size."

"Then it gets returned," I insisted, hoping she'd kept all the receipts.

"Right," she said, tucking the dress away. "'Cept I sorta stole it."

"You *what*?"

She shrugged.

I glanced down at the leather jacket in my lap.

"I paid for *that*," she said. "Hence the need to steal the rest."

I rubbed the spot on my chest where the ruby touched skin, the light shock leaving an irritating itch behind. "You shouldn't steal so much."

"You're the one all obsessive over the budget or whatever," she said. "Only way to stick with it is to steal."

"No," I said, my annoyance at both the ruby acting up and Lyra making it come out harsher than I meant. "You do that by not buying things we don't need."

She rolled her eyes. "You're a super boring criminal."

"And you're a little too comfortable with it."

Lyra waved the comment away and went back to outfit planning. She'd gotten us a few things that would come in handy, like toiletries and a larger backpack to consolidate all my stuff into.

I transferred everything I needed and double-checked I hadn't forgotten anything in the pockets. After a quick spell, we used the room phone to try making a quick call to Ian.

He didn't answer, not that I expected him to. It was a random number, and we'd agreed not to contact each other until day three. That way, even if they were able to find me, I'd already be in Sandusky and they couldn't get to me.

I dozed while a docuseries on ancient conspiracy theories spun tales on the TV. I was tired, but I didn't want to fall asleep again, not fully. I had no desire to let my brain finish the dreams it started.

I wasn't sure how long I laid in bed, but only a few short hours after the sun dipped and the lights came on, Lyra stirred and I forced myself up. She ordered room service—I didn't have the energy to argue. And after we ate, it was time to start getting ready.

Lyra went to work on her hair and makeup like it was any other night out. Music, a bottle of wine, the whole production. I had to wonder if the nonchalance was real or for my benefit.

She pulled her hair out of her face, braiding the top half away. Her black, cat-eye liner got dusted with gold to match the gold sequined jacket. Under the sparkle, her outfit was simple: black faux leather leggings, a strapless black corset top, and black heeled boots.

I let her curl my hair and add more eyeliner than I'd already put on. I pulled on black velvet pants, a black and silver sequined tank top with a deep V-neck, and the red leather jacket. It was a splurge, but I didn't want to give it back.

Two hours and a bottle and a half of Moscato later, we were ready. I slipped our room key, some cash, and my ID into my pockets as Lyra skipped into the hallway. I took one last swig of wine, a deep breath, and followed her.

Chapter 3

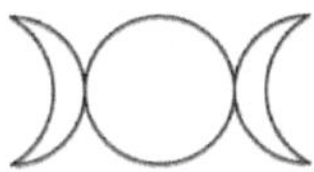

We faced the sliver of an old stone wall. Not a door, or anything that resembled one. It wasn't even its own building. It was an inlet nestled between the back of a closed tattoo shop and office suites. Laughter and loud conversations echoed up the street as partygoers made their way through town. Two months ago, that had been me. Out for the night with my friends, excited about where things would take us. Now, the idea of not knowing terrified me.

I stomped my feet to get the feeling back into my numb toes. Lyra watched a group pass on the other side of the street before stepping up to the wall. She motioned me forward, putting us awkwardly close to it. She tapped one of the stones with a knuckle, three times, counterclockwise.

"Widdershins," she said.

Where Lyra had tapped, a stone disappeared, then another, and another. Darkness opened in the space, creating a moving shadow large enough for a few people to walk through. A lean man in a silver suit, with dark hair pulled into a bun at the back of his head and eyes as dark as the shadows behind him, appeared in front of us.

He gave me a quick appraisal before turning to Lyra and putting his hands in his pockets. "And what do two powers seek from us?" he asked, accent hinting at an Eastern European background.

"A dance in the waning light of mother moon and sister night," Lyra said with half a smile.

He returned it. "Malen'kiy yastreb," he said. "It's wonderful to see you."

"Vadim." She gave him a once-over. "New look?"

"Boss wanted something special for the night," he said, straightening the lapels of his suit coat.

She shook her head. "I prefer you in black."

Vadim tilted his head towards her. "Me too," he said with a wink before turning to me. "And you?"

I couldn't remember all the words Lyra had said. "I'm, uh, with her," I said, jerking my thumb at Lyra.

He cocked his head at Lyra. "You vouch for her?"

"Until the day I die."

I hoped that was another part of the password.

Vadim nodded and moved to the side, motioning for us to step into the void. My ears popped like I was climbing through the air too quickly, and my whole body tingled as if every nerve had fallen asleep and woken up at the same time.

The sensation vanished and the wall was replaced by large black double doors with lightning crackling across them. The handles were shaped like bolts and a neon sign hung above them.

I gaped at the sign. "*Sabbats*? Really?"

Lyra shrugged. "I think it's supposed to be funny," she said, walking through the doors when they opened for her. The club was loud, dark, and warm. Feeling was coming back to my nose and fingers. To our right, dim booths offered more privacy than the large open bar to our left. Above the bar top, storm clouds brewed as light flashed through them. Below us, a sunken dance floor crammed with bodies that swelled with the music. A haze of magic hung in the air, electrifying the atmosphere.

Lyra pulled me over to the bar where half a dozen employees served drinks that bubbled, smoked, and changed colors. A few of the bartenders had the bright gem-like eyes of sprites—like Krinae. If they were half as good, we were in trouble.

Sprites tending bar, a magically concealed entrance, and any number of witches that could report back to the Council that two rogue witches were out in Salem. I grabbed Lyra's arm before she could order a drink.

"What the hell?" I hissed.

She gently pried my hand from her arm. "What?"

"This place is full of witches."

"No shit." She turned back to the bar.

I ducked in front of her. "What if someone recognizes us?"

She laughed. "Em, relax. This is an Outliers club."

"Is that supposed to make it better?"

Lyra nodded. "Vadim isn't going to let any Emissaries in."

"He let you in."

She sighed. "For, like, the hundredth time, I'm not an Emissary," she said. "And I'm a regular. So...drinks!" She scooted around me to get to the bar and ordered. Faster than any mortal bar I'd been to, she handed me a drink with swirling gray fog on top; I downed half of it without asking what it was.

"Where's your friend?" I asked after the burning in my throat subsided.

"Downstairs, probably. They love to dance."

"Then why are we up here?"

Lyra chuckled. "Someone's tense."

I shook my head at her. Being back in a place like this, with the heavy music, too many people, and oscillating lights reminded me of Onyx, and I did *not* like it. The drinks—and company—may have been better, but that did little to squelch the memories of that night.

"Fuck."

"What?" I glanced around for faces I recognized but didn't see any.

"Thea," she muttered and downed the rest of her drink.

"I thought you said—"

"She's not an Emissary," Lyra said quickly. "Just annoying as fuck." She reached over to grab a fresh cocktail and gulped that one down too. "Don't say anything," she told me.

A tall woman with long legs, light auburn hair that fell to over her shoulders, and perfect skin made her way over to us. I felt too short next to both her and Lyra.

"Lyra," Thea said. "What are you doing here?"

"It's a club," Lyra said. "Take a fucking guess."

I raised my eyebrows at her. I'd heard her and Leander fight before, but the angry irritation that laced the few words she'd spoken to the woman had me wondering what this Thea person had done to earn it.

Thea's gaze shifted to me, and I was grateful for the one pair of contacts I still had. They didn't cover my red irises as well as before, but in the dim light of the club, they were better than nothing.

After giving me a quick once-over, Thea refocused on Lyra. "I thought you were on assignment?"

"Was that an independent thought, or did my dad put it there for you?"

Thea frowned down at me, and I resisted the urge to make sure the ruby was tucked out of sight. She flipped her hair over her shoulder. "Where's your brother?"

Lyra cocked her head to the side. "Which one?"

Thea scowled and crossed her arms.

"Right, the one who dumped your ass. Not here."

Thea let out a long breath. "I get we've had our differences," she said. "But you don't have to act like you don't like me."

"It's not an act, Thea, I *don't* like you."

Thea pulled her lower lip into her top teeth and for a moment I swore she looked like she was about to cry. "Is he in town with you?"

Lyra laughed. "Do I look like his fucking babysitter?"

Thea eyed me again, eyebrows drawing together. "Can you just tell him to call me?"

"No."

"Lyra, please." It felt like Thea was begging. She may not have actually gotten on her knees, but the tone was there. I wondered if she could her the desperation in her own voice. "This assignment has his head all messed up." She turned a small purple gem ring around her middle finger. "He's not acting like himself. I think this witch you've been dealing with did something to him."

I bristled and the ruby heated.

"He's a big boy, Thea. He can take care of himself."

"Not if the rumors are true."

Lyra looked casual enough, but she shifted slightly in front of me, her back tensed. "What are you smoking?"

Thea took a step closer, as if worried she might be overheard. "You found a Blood Witch."

Shit.

"Hadn't heard that one yet," Lyra said like we were in high school discussing who was hooking up that week.

My heart, however, was thudding in my ears, drowning out the music around us. I scanned our way to the doors in case we had to bolt for it. I knew they'd have a tough time squashing rumors of a living Blood Witch after a second unit of Emissaries had been dispatched to Portland, but I'd hoped the rumors would have stayed in a closer circle. If Lyra was right and Thea wasn't an Emissary, then the magical community at large had already heard about it—and that would make staying under the radar a lot harder.

Thea's eyes narrowed as she looked between us. "We all know what they're capable of."

I balled my fists in my jacket pockets and my magic itched under my skin, all thoughts of keeping a low profile shoved to the side by the anger that shot through me.

Thea continued. "If she did something to him—"

I could do something to *her.*

"Oh, fuck off with that *'we all know'* bullshit," Lyra said, stepping up to Thea. The other woman took a half-step back. "There hasn't been a Blood Witch in centuries." Lyra added another step, sending Thea back another one. "But *if* there is a Blood Witch around, saying shit that would piss them off is just stupid."

"You—"

"And *if* we'd met a Blood Witch on assignment, you wouldn't get to know," Lyra said. "Because despite all your pathetic attempts to use my brother to get in good with dad, you're *not* an Emissary."

Thea's face flushed and she clenched her fist. I thought she was about to take a swing at Lyra. "Neither are you," she said quietly.

Lyra smiled, but it was anything but friendly. "Then I guess I don't know anything."

Thea raised her hand slightly and my magic flared out in Lyra's defense. The brief contact left me cold and a rotting taste in my mouth. Her magic—whatever it was—was icy, bitter, and rancid, like death. But as my magic tried to dig deeper, there was a flicker of warmth. A flame trying to break through and connect with my own magic. I had to physically take a step away to rein it back in as it brushed with Thea's power.

Thea blinked, clearly unsure what the feeling had been. I pulled behind Lyra, shutting my eyes and trying to get my power to stay where it needed to.

Thea righted the ring on her finger. "You're being impossible," she muttered, before striding away. She stopped at the doors to shoot us one last look that Lyra returned by flipping her off.

Lyra handed me another drink.

"She's..." But I wasn't sure how best to describe the woman without being mean. Sure, she insinuated some not-nice things about me, but that wasn't exactly her fault. No one spread the happy stories about Blood Witches. I took a drink to cover my lack of descriptor.

"Yeah, no idea what Jax ever saw in her."

I choked on the sip I'd taken.

"You're absolutely an upgrade," Lyra said.

I coughed up the liquid I'd inhaled, and my throat burned. "That was *Jax's* ex?" I wheezed.

She nodded. "Shockingly, she's trying to find any reason besides her total lack of redeeming qualities for their breakup." She patted my shoulder. "Don't get into trouble. I'm going to find Z."

She left me at a seat on the far end of the bar, away from anyone that might try to talk to me. One of the bartenders—a sprite by the name of Serael—delivered another drink without a request. None of their drinks were too strong, as if they knew I wasn't here to party.

My spot in the corner did its trick and kept people away. But, after almost twenty minutes on my own, I felt the prick of eyes watching me. When I found the woman, she was directly across from me, not even trying to hide her staring.

She wore a black, long-sleeved mesh top. Her dark hair was chopped to just above her shoulders and streaked with red. The heavy eye makeup only made her stare more intense, and there was something oddly familiar about it.

The ruby sparked and sent another shock through my skin. I instinctively reached for it and her gaze followed, widening when my fingers curled around the stone.

"Hey!"

I started when Lyra jumped in front of me. I glanced around her, but the woman was gone, leaving nothing but her half-empty drink. Lyra followed my gaze.

"What-'cha looking at?"

I shook myself out of the odd feeling. "Nothing. Did you find them?"

She nodded. "Em, this is Z. Z, Em," she introduced.

Z had bright green, pixie-cut hair, tattoos covering the dark skin of both their arms, their neck, and what I could see of their chest. They had a pierced eyebrow, nose, and lip, and large gauges in both ears. Their lids were covered in green eyeshadow, and their lips were dark with flecks of bright green that glowed in the dim light.

Z handed Lyra a package. "Rush jobs are stressful," they said. "But the phones are set with the contact list you gave me and nearly impossible to trace."

"Nearly?" I repeated.

They smiled at me. "If they got someone with skills like mine, they could crack it in a year. I don't want to make guarantees and find myself cursed."

Lyra glanced up from the package. "IDs?"

Z nodded. "Now that I got her face, they'll be ready tomorrow."

Lyra pulled out the two phones, tucked one into her pocket, and handed the other to me. "What do we owe?"

Z nodded at me. "Ounce of her blood."

Lyra frowned. "Why?"

"Witch blood is powerful," Z said. "Boswell blood is better. A Boswell Blood Witch? The best."

"You think she's a Blood Witch?" Lyra asked, although her covering laugh was far less convincing than it had been with Thea.

"I hear things and I'm not stupid, Ly," Z said.

"Not going to happen," I said before I could stop myself. Z was right, and that's why giving up my blood was not an option, not to just anyone.

Z looked at me. "You want my help, I need to cover my ass if the Collective comes calling."

"I can get you protection," Lyra said.

Z shook her head. "Blood protection is the strongest."

True.

Lyra glanced at me. "You're asking a lot, Z."

"That's the fee. Pay up or find another Scribe."

Lyra leaned against the bar. "Your call," she said to me.

I bit the inside of my cheek. We could risk using our own IDs, but that would make this whole thing a waste. If, for some reason, our path to Ohio was cut off, it would be smart to have another option. It was risky either way.

My magic coaxed me to another idea. Force Z to give us what we needed. Keep them under control until we get it and leave. They'd have little time to prepare, and Scribes—witches that specialized in magical documents—probably wouldn't put up much of a fight anyway.

I swallowed that down. Thea's suspicions played over in my head like a bad song. If I did a fraction of what my magic was itching to do, I'd only be proving her right.

"Half an ounce," I countered, and they started to argue. "That's enough for a basic protection spell," I said. "Keep you safe for at least a year."

Z frowned. "And if I need more than that?"

I took a deep breath. "You won't."

Lyra looked at me curiously while Z played their teeth along their lip, pausing to tease at the piercing.

"Deal." They glanced over their shoulder. "Meet me back here tomorrow at nine."

"That long?" I blurted.

"Sloppy work gets you caught," they countered.

"Fine."

"Tomorrow. Nine. I'll meet you back here." Z gave Lyra's arm a gentle squeeze. "Don't be late."

"Am I ever?" Lyra said, and both Z and I shot her a doubtful look.

Z nodded to my jacket. "My number's in both phones. Use that and *only* that to contact me."

"Nervous?" Lyra teased, bordering on flirting.

Z's smile was absolutely flirtatious. "Your brother will be at my door by end of week."

Lyra glanced at me. "Week and a half."

"Losing his touch?"

Lyra shrugged. "Just finally met his match."

Z placed a hand on Lyra's cheek and their smile turned sad. "Lucky him." With that, they turned, and I watched their bright green hair get swallowed by the crowd.

"You two..."

Lyra sighed. "Long time ago," she said, half-heartedly. She stared after Z long after they were out of sight.

Serael appeared, leaving a shot for each of us without a word before gliding away. Lyra cleared her throat and picked up the glass.

She raised it to me. "Let's have some fun!"

I shook my head. "We came to meet Z, not party."

She downed the shot. "*I* came to do both," she said, setting the small glass on the bar. "But you do you." She gave me a wink and followed Z's path to the dance floor. I squeezed the hotel key in my pocket. I could head back myself; it wasn't far. But it was cold and dark, and I wasn't entirely comfortable wandering back without her.

I wasn't in the mood to celebrate like everyone else here. New Year's Eve had never been a huge deal growing up. Wes didn't even consider it a real holiday. Ian and I would watch the ball drop and eat too much junk food. Senior year, we went to Tommy Dalton's parents' cabin for a party. That's when I learned I hated Fireball.

That nagging feeling that something was off came back, pushing me to pull out the phone Z had given me. Sure enough, Ian's number was there, one of the few. My thumb hovered over the call option for his name.

My eyes caught the next name in the list. Jax. It had been a little over twenty-four hours since I'd lied to him and left. A part of me wanted to call, wanted to hear him tell me everything was going to be okay and we'd figure it out. Sighing, I stashed it back in my pocket.

Catching Serael's eye, I asked for the bathroom before I headed out. Lyra could have her fun; I'd ring in the new year back in a comfy bed.

I headed down the stairs and hooked a left, avoiding the throbbing hoard of dancers as best I could. It felt like I was the only one not drunkenly enjoying themselves. A year ago, I would have been.

My skin pricked. Someone was watching me again.

The strange woman from the bar swam in my memory and I glanced around, looking for her. But she wasn't there. People danced on, two women near the bathroom hall were making out, a couple on the edge of the floor were fighting, but I didn't catch any wandering eyes focused on me—until I did, and my breath caught.

Jax.

Chapter 4

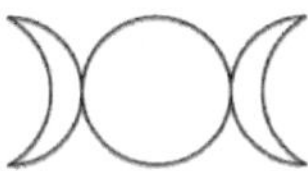

I blinked a few times to ensure I wasn't seeing things, but there was no mistake. Jax stood in an archway at the edge of the dance floor. My heart pounded as I scanned the rest of the space, looking for the others.

Jax nodded to the space behind him. Minutes ago, I'd thought about calling him to hear his voice, and now here he was. He stuck his hands in his pockets and smiled at me. I took a few deep breaths before making my way over, my guilt for leaving without a goodbye overriding any logic.

The archway led to a set of stairs. Jax was halfway down by the time I reached them. This level blocked the noise of the dance floor, nothing but the steady bass reaching me. There were rooms off the main hall with thick black velvet curtains drawn over the entrances. Jax ducked into the third room, and I paused just outside, unsure.

I tentatively reached out with my magic. When only the edge of one energy registered, some of my unease lifted. Unless they'd figured out a way to mask themselves from me in the last twenty-four hours, Jax was alone.

Bracing myself, I pulled the curtain back and stepped inside. Candles lit the small room. Two round nest chairs faced me, and the slight woody aroma of vanilla mixed with the rich sweetness of jasmine filled my nostrils, the heaviness making it difficult to take a full breath.

"Jax?" I let the curtain fall behind me, but he'd disappeared. I moved further inside, and he shifted behind me, close enough to touch. I sucked in a breath as his hands brushed the back of my neck. His fingers curled under the shoulders of my jacket and slipped it off.

"Jax," I started, but froze when his fingers trailed up my bare arms to move my hair from my neck.

I shivered. "How—how did you find me?" I asked breathlessly. It was hard to focus, especially when his lips feathered across my skin. He wrapped an arm around my waist and pulled me closer, tongue caressing my jaw.

Something wasn't right. "Jax."

"Shhh," he whispered, breath tickling my ear. The faint stench of rot hung in the air after he spoke. I tried to pull away and his grasp tightened, his fingers digging into me with unnatural strength.

His nose grazed my neck and I let out a small gasp as a sharp pain stung my skin. As I struggled against his inflexible grip, the stinging grew worse.

I drove my elbow into his gut with as much force as I could. Breaking free, I rounded on him and pressed a finger to my neck to find sticky wetness that could only mean I was bleeding.

"What the—"

"So sweet," he purred.

My magic lashed out instinctively. It found something to latch onto: blood, not magic, and *not* mortal. Whatever it was, it hurt. When I tried another burst, I went toppling over one of the chairs behind me.

Gasping, I pulled myself to my knees and looked around. We'd been flung away from each other, repelled like the wrong side of magnets. An inhuman grin spread across its face and its eyes burned bright white.

I scrambled for the exit, but it—still wearing Jax's face—lumbered into my path. Knowing I was going to regret it, I let out another flare of power. Enough to stop it in its tracks. It let out a hair-raising screech and the next thing I knew my face was pressed against the fabric of the chair, the taste of cut grass and burnt popcorn coating my tongue and a blazing pain at the base of my skull.

Pushing myself up, I stared at the thing on the floor. Its body was bright moss-green and its arms a grotesque disproportion to the body. Pure white eyes to match the two large fangs protruding from its upper lip. Its fingers were long, spindly, and seemed to go on forever. Its lanky red hair spilled out around it, slick as oil.

A vaibit.

I found it hard to swallow through the fear lodged in my throat. A vampiric creature that changes forms to lure victims. According to Amity's book, they usually stay deep in the forests where they feed off wayward travelers.

"Em!"

"Here," I called, voice hoarse. I sat down on the edge of the chair and rubbed the back of my neck, not wanting to take my eyes off the thing in front of me. It twitched. I tried to stand to put distance between us, but the room spun, and I sank back down onto the chair.

Lyra ripped the curtain open. "*Circe*," she cursed, stepping over the vaibit. "What did you do to it?"

I shook my head, and my stomach swam. "I don't know. But it hurt."

She crouched in front of me. "Did it get you?" she asked, tipping my head to the side to look.

"I don't think it's deep," I said.

"It's deep enough," she muttered, poking at it.

I sucked in a breath. "Ow."

She rolled her eyes.

"She should get some sauthern milk," a man said, stepping into the room. "Just to be safe." He wore an all-black suit with silver accents and a silver silk tie. His black hair was smoothed back to expose shaved sides, and his beard was shaved close to his jaw. He stood with one hand in his pocket, a curious smile playing around his mouth.

"Didn't ask for your help," Lyra said, not looking around.

"Only a suggestion, Little T."

"Don't call me that," she snapped, standing to face him. I'd seen much larger men back off when she looked like she was ready to kick their ass, but he only seemed more amused.

"Besyn," he called, and a woman with short pink-tipped curls and a silver dress appeared at his side. "Find out how it got in," he said.

She nodded and scooped the creature up, slinging it over her shoulder like it weighed next to nothing and carried it out of the room. The pain at the base of my skull was getting worse, and the taste left in my mouth was not helping the nausea.

I opened my mouth and my jaw popped, followed by my ears. The candles were too hot. I pressed my palm to my forehead. Way too hot.

"Get her upstairs," the man said. "Serael will get something."

Lyra glared at him but didn't argue. She pulled me to my feet, and I clutched her arm when the room spun again.

Lyra helped me back into the hallway. "Birch tree stakes work better," she teased. Vaibit venom was potent and fast-acting. If too much got into the system, it eventually would cause paralysis, which makes it easier for them to feed on their prey. Driving a birch stake—blessed in salt water under a winter's full moon—between its eyes would be the only way to kill it.

We slowly moved back up the wobbly stairs to the bar. Lyra deposited me on an open seat and Serael set a tall glass of what looked like purple milk in front of me.

"Drink," they ordered. I tentatively gave the drink a sniff. It had no scent—like water—and warmed the glass it was in. The last thing I wanted was something hot, sweat already coating the back of my neck.

A small sip of the milk brought my temperature down a little, and the throbbing in my head eased. The aftertaste was like Fireball and coffee, something that did not mix well with the grass already in my mouth. I tried to scrape the taste off my tongue with my teeth. I was going to need an entire bottle of mouthwash after this.

"Not the smoothest in my collection," the man in the silver-accented suit said. He handed me my jacket. "But it will have you feeling like yourself soon enough."

I took the jacket and draped it over my lap, forcing more of the drink down. Now that he was closer, I could see the stormy gray of his eyes and slightly crooked nose. Four of the five fingers that held his glass had rings on them. One on his middle finger in the shape of a lightning bolt covered the length of his first knuckle to his middle one. His index finger had one that looked like one of those old-fashioned signet rings.

"Vadim thinks it could have snuck in with the Kolgrim party," Besyn said, returning. "When it wakes up, we'll find out for sure."

"When it wakes up?" the man asked, raising an eyebrow.

She nodded at me. "Whatever she did knocked it out cold. I gave it something, but that didn't work."

"Interesting," he said. "Thank you, Besyn."

She nodded and left.

"You have some real fucking bad luck with clubs," Lyra said.

I glared at her.

The man offered me his free hand. "Rez Dorsey," he said.

I nodded to him instead of taking his offered hand. "Em."

He smiled and took his hand back. "I must apologize, we have a strict policy against creatures with uncontrollable vampiric tendencies."

"Policy does shit after the fact, Rez," Lyra said.

He snapped his fingers and a new sprite with diamond eyes and fire-red hair appeared. "Ginger Howlers for my guests, if you would, Dasa."

Dasa flipped two glasses over in their hands and in less than a minute set two steaming mugs on the bar. Rez circled the rim of his glass with a ringed finger, regarding us like we'd given him some deep philosophical dilemma to solve.

His gaze shifted from me to Lyra. "You're doing a terrible job of laying low," he said and took a drink.

"Who says we're trying to lay low?" Lyra countered, taking a sip of her own drink.

He inclined his head. "The two D.R.U.s the Council has looking for you."

I squeezed my mug tighter.

"Only two?" Lyra asked.

He swirled his glass, the single ice cube moving inside with the motion. "Harboring two dissenters will bring them here," he said. "And the last thing I need is your brothers bothering me."

She leaned closer to him. "Trust me, they don't want to deal with you either." She swept her hair over her shoulder. "And we're not dissenters."

I didn't like his knowing smile.

"I have my sources, Little T."

She clenched her fist and her nostrils flared.

"You harass all your customers?" I asked, before she could throw a punch and draw more attention.

He smoothed his already slicked hair. "Only Blood Witches and the Tsiprases."

Lyra and I exchanged a glance.

"Rumors are like wildfire, spread quickly and hard to stop," he said. "Whatever you're doing to hide those eyes," he pointed to my face, "isn't working."

I forced myself not to look away, even though I knew he was right. I was sure when I'd tried to use my magic on the vaibit it had burned through the contacts. They'd been my last pair, and there was a slim chance of getting more.

Lyra finished her drink. "In the know as ever," she said, pulling cash out of her pocket.

Rez held up his hand to stop her. "It's on the house."

She gave him a disingenuous smile as she slapped three twenties on the bar. "Always a pleasure, Rez."

He inclined his head to her again. "You too, Little T."

She tapped the bar with her finger. "Call me that one more time and I'll break your nose again." She turned to me. "Let's go." Her mood had significantly darkened since we'd met with Z.

I took another gulp of my drink and hopped off the seat. "It was nice to meet you," I said. He raised his glass to me. "Have a wonderful evening." His glass refilled on its own and the countdown to midnight began. I slipped my jacket on as we weaved through the crowd. The clock stuck twelve just as the doors closed behind us.

Chapter 5

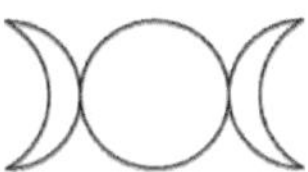

The vaibit attack replaced the dreams of running through Old Salem. I wasn't sure which was worse; my own grandmother hunting me while a long-dead ancestor watched from the darkness hadn't been enjoyable, but trying to sleep through Jax's comforting smile warping into the face of the creature that attacked me was impossible.

I was still groggy when the alarm went off and wished I could have spent the rest of the day in bed. Unfortunately, we had to check out or put another large dent in the budget. Somehow, Lyra managed to pack away all the clothes she'd bought and still zip her backpack closed. I folded the leather jacket and put it with the sweaters and warm socks.

Once we packed, the only thing left for us to do was perform a makeshift blood draw in the bathroom. It was the first time either of us had used that spell, and there was a lot of trial and error—mostly error—before we managed half an ounce. We spelled the vial to keep it both magically and physically viable and tucked it into my coat pocket until we met with Z.

We checked out as late as possible. I waited in the lobby with our bags while Lyra found another car. Her ability to steal without an ounce of guilt was its own magic. Despite my warnings that a string of stolen vehicle reports might tip off her brothers, she insisted on spending the day giving me a tour of Salem.

She gave me the highlights. Not the haunted graveyards, or the house that held the trials most tourists came for, though. I got the site of Mary Boswell's original home before it had been burned to the ground by hunters using the trials for their own ends. The coffee shop that was a front for the first Emissarial Academy—now a museum, as the current one was in Boston. According to Lyra, there were training posts all over North America and parts of Western Europe.

A part of me wanted to hike the Salem Woods, to the spot where Amity's coven met its end. Even with the nightmares sticking in my mind after I'd woken up, I was drawn there. But not knowing why it was pulling me, I was too scared to suggest a visit.

We stopped at the Salem Witch Trials Memorial and left on a gift on each of the snow-covered benches. None of the known victims had been witches, but their deaths were senseless all the same.

We returned to O'Neill's for dinner, and I swore I saw the same woman with the short red-and-black hair from the club. But when I came out from the bathroom, she was gone.

After we left the pub, Lyra ducked into a metaphysical shop—Hex—on Essex Street while I waited outside. She wasn't clear on what supplies she needed or for which spells, but I was too tired to care.

If the vaibit dreams weren't forcing me awake, the ruby was. The last couple of nights hadn't been great for sleep. I'd woken up sweating like I'd actually been running, and the ruby burned hot enough against my skin to leave a mark.

None of the grimoires could explain why it was acting up. Well, none of the ones I had. For all I knew, the answer was in the pages of Amity's book. The book that currently sat on the shelves in my living room back in Portland—at least, I hoped it was.

Running the ruby along the chain, I watched the street for Lyra. She'd left me, alone with my backpack and nervous energy, in the alcove that led to Sabbats. The sun had set hours ago, and the dark street felt too much like the ones from my dreams. At least this time I wasn't freezing to death in my jeans, thick sweater, and warm coat. I'd also put on the best running shoes I'd packed, just in case.

I dropped the ruby when it shocked my fingers and I shook my hand out. It was getting worse the longer we were in Salem.

Lyra jogged around the corner and tapped the wall the same way she had the night before. Vadim—silver suit replaced by an impossibly black one that did look better on him—let us in without asking for any kind of passcode. We found seats at the bar. The place was far less packed than it had been last night.

Serael was working again and gave us drinks before I shrugged my coat off. I passed the vial of blood off to Lyra to make the trade when it came time.

A drink came. Then another. Lyra rolled the vial back and forth on the bar top and kept looking between the time on her phone and the door. Her nerves didn't help ease mine. The next drink that came was herbal tea.

Lyra lit up her phone screen to check the time again and I knew why she was on edge: Z was almost twenty minutes late. The last time someone was late for a meeting with me, it didn't end well. I tried not to picture Z like that, eyes cold and lifeless. It was hard not to. Not after Phoenix and Raven.

Lyra's sigh of relief came moments later, and I turned to see Z rushing through the door. Their green hair was covered by a gray beanie and the only tattoos visible now were the ones wrapped around their hands and neck. They also had a large backpack with them. Spotting us, they hurried over and stood on the other side of Lyra, not bothering to sit.

"You're late," Lyra said, concern edging into her tone.

Z nodded and ordered a boiled chili tonic before turning back to us. "I was packing. A friend ran into a D.R.U. passing through Lynn."

"When?" Lyra asked.

"Ten, fifteen minutes ago."

"Fuck."

They downed the drink in one gulp when it came. "I'm clearing out. Suggest you do the same." They pulled out another package and slid it to Lyra in exchange for the vial of my blood.

Z pocketed it before taking Lyra's face in both hands. "Be careful," they said before placing a soft, quick kiss on her cheek.

Lyra nodded when they broke apart. "Always."

Z looked around her to me. "Don't know what you did to piss them off, but keep it up."

I didn't have time to come up with a response before they hurried out of the club. Lyra opened the package and handed me a fake driver's license and passport. I looked them over and groaned. I wanted my blood back.

"Is this a joke?" I asked.

"Partly," Lyra said, stowing hers in her pocket. "But they'll stand up to any mortal agencies and the names won't flag any of ours."

I held up the one with my image on it. "Sabrina LeFay," I read. "How is *that* not suspicious?"

"Hey, if we could trade, I would," she said. "I'm *so* not a Morgan Sanderson."

I turned back to my tea. "Not sure these were worth it," I mumbled. Finishing the tea that managed to stay the perfect drinking temperature the entire time, I pulled out cash. "Can we go now?"

She shrugged on her coat.

"What are you two up to now?" Rez asked, walking up behind us before we could leave.

Lyra pulled her hair free from her coat collar and pulled it into a ponytail. "Nothing but a friendly exchange of bodily fluids," she said.

He glanced at the doors. "I thought you two broke up?"

She tossed a pretzel at him. "Shouldn't you be upgrading your security or something?"

"I have," he said. "Which is how I know your brother and a rather testy Sebastian Charlevoix are attempting to force their way in."

Lyra grabbed her backpack. "You got a back way out?"

He nodded to Serael. "Are you asking for my help?" he said with a smile.

"Rez."

A glass of amber liquid appeared in front of him. "Just say the word, Little T."

I grabbed her arm before she could finish the swing. "Help or don't," I said. "But if you don't, there *will* be a fight."

Lyra wrestled her arm free but didn't try to hit him again.

He sighed. "They have the back covered." He took a sip. "Vadim will see you out."

"It would be my pleasure." Vadim appeared at my side, and I started. He inclined his head to us both and turned, hands in his pockets, to lead us away.

Rez caught my arm as I shoved it into my coat. "Careful with your trust," he said. "A Tsipras will betray you at the first offer of something better."

I yanked my arm away. "And I suppose I should trust you?" I countered.

He held my gaze. "Trust that I have good reason to keep the Council from getting their hands on you."

A shiver crawled down my spine as he released my arm and returned to his drink. Scooping up my backpack, I jogged to catch over to Vadim and Lyra. He took us down the stairs the vaibit had lured me to. We ducked into one of the curtained-off rooms and Vadim shoved the chairs away from the back wall.

He muttered something in Russian while moving his hand over the wall, tracing whorls over it. Where his fingers touched the wall became a black ripple. This explained why he was the chosen bouncer. As a Shade, he could manipulate shadow into anything. Creating doors out of nothing but darkness. Exceptionally skilled Shades could even use shadows to cross distances.

I zipped my coat up and slung my backpack on. Vadim extended a hand to each of us, and we stepped through the ripple together. My head was pressed between two boards, and I had no idea where my fingers or toes went—not fully confident they were still attached. In half a second, we were standing on a dark street.

"Be safe, malen'kiy yastreb," he said and stepped back into the side of the building. I tightened the straps on my pack while Lyra snapped hers into place over her chest. It took us a moment to get our bearings, but once we did, we took off in search of a car.

Lyra's head swept up and down the street. Once she decided it was clear, we jogged left. She stopped at a Grand Cherokee and put her hand on the driver's side door handle.

"Without a doubt, need a way out. No way to get a key, door unlock for me."

I raised my eyebrows. "That actually work—" The lock clicked, and she pulled the door open with a smirk.

The window blew in with a crash and I yelped.

Lyra jilted forward, her knee buckled, and she fell against the car. I bent over to help her as another shot clipped the side mirror.

Glass shattered, raining down on us. Lyra scooted around to the other side of the car, clutching her arm. I followed, tripping in the snowbank.

"They fucking *shot* me?" Lyra said, gripping her upper arm tightly. Blood pooled under her fingers. She glanced over at me. "I can't believe they fucking shot me."

I slid to the end of the car and peered around it. Another shot went off, and I ducked back next to Lyra. A cold that had nothing to do with the weather swept over me.

"It's Sasha."

Chapter 6

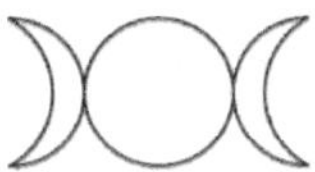

Lyra elbowed the car door with her uninjured arm. "Fuck." She let out a groan. "Hunters never come to Salem."

I crawled to the end of the car, risking another peek to try to count how many were in the street. "Yeah, apparently if you piss them off enough, they do."

"Now?" she hissed. "You chose to have a sense of humor *now*?"

Voices replaced gunshots. I knew better than to think Sasha had given up. Her brother was lying in a coma because of me. She wasn't going to stop until I was dead.

It was too dark to make out faces, but the streetlights gave me enough light to discern six shapes. At least six hunters and who knew how many Emissaries. I leaned back against the car and glanced at Lyra. Her eyes were closed, and she was taking slow breaths, clutching her arm.

There was no easy way out of this. If we could get back to the club, maybe Rez would let us hide until the hunters moved on. The others would be a problem we could deal with if we survived.

I secured my backpack. "Can you walk?"

Lyra nodded, eyes still closed.

"Get ready then," I said. I took a deep breath. It didn't need to be a big distraction, just a long enough one. My power rushed forward, and I had to rein it back before it tried for every energy near us. I only needed one...for now.

They weren't ready and went under my control within a second. Their fight started not long after that, but it was barely a brush against the power that pulsed under my skin. I grabbed Lyra's arm and pulled her around the car.

I knew exactly which one I'd taken once I saw them. The dark figure wasn't moving the same as the rest of the group. Letting out a long breath, I forced him to raise his gun and squeeze a shot out. It landed just above Sasha's head and threw the group into chaos.

"She's close!" Sasha's head whipped frantically around, looking for me.

"Go," I hissed, pulling Lyra up and tearing off across the street. We just had to make it back to the club.

A shot hit the brick above us as we rounded the corner. It was barely three blocks away, but the hunters were getting closer and the effort of keeping one under my grip was slowing us down. I tossed off control and put all my strength into running.

Lyra stopped short. Sebastian and Jax were interrogating Vadim outside the entrance. They had our only way in blocked.

"What now?" Lyra asked, leaning against the building next to us.

I glanced over my shoulder. "You about to bleed to death?" I huffed.

She shook her head. "I got some time."

"Then we find another car and get out of here," I said, nudging her towards the other side of the street. Before we could get out of sight, Sasha's shouts drew Jax's attention. We ducked quickly, but there was no way he hadn't seen us.

"We should go back," I said as the distinct sounds of fighting broke out.

Lyra shook her head. "They'll be fine. We—we need—" She swayed, and I grabbed her arm to keep her upright. She swallowed hard. "We need to go."

"You're bleeding too much."

"I'm okay." It was far from convincing. I slung her good arm over my shoulder before she could collapse. We needed to stop the bleeding before anything else. Shouts, the dull pop of gunshots, and the flare of magic followed us as we stumbled through the darkness, over icy sidewalks.

The pedestrian mall opened in front of us. A parking garage wasn't far and would have more than a few cars to choose from.

Icy air clung to my lungs as I panted for breath. We were halfway there, and my muscles ached from the strain of holding Lyra up. Shadows moved between buildings.

More figures came at us from behind. We were trapped. Trapped between death or capture. I knew which one I'd prefer given the choice. Lyra doubled over, leaning against the shop behind us.

I gathered my power, and it came as if it had been waiting for me to finally give in. My vision blurred red, and heat flared in my veins.

The door behind us opened and I jumped—my shock made worse by the massive jolt the ruby gave me.

"Get in," a voice hissed.

Lyra frowned at the doorway.

"Now!"

I only allowed myself a moment of hesitation before helping Lyra over the threshold and stumbling in behind her. A young woman shut the door behind us and drew a shade over it. My magic blazed defensively.

Inside was significantly warmer, and the shouting from outside grew louder as the stranger made sure all the curtains were pulled shut. I watched her in the dim light, struggling to find anything recognizable about her. And there was *something*. I just couldn't put my finger on it.

A few low lamps with dark shades and a line of LED grow lights over a shelf holding small potted plants on the back wall lit the shop. Other shelves around the room held books, crystals, herbs, and other odds and ends a local witch might need. Another wall had what looked like generic souvenirs for any tourists that stopped by.

Once I was sure the room itself wasn't hiding anything—or any-one—threatening, I turned my attention to the person who'd let us inside. She had to be around my age, taller than me but shorter than Lyra, and her black hair—pulled into a messy half-knot at the back of her head—was streaked with red. Her straight nose was familiar, even with the stud in the left nostril. Piercings covered her ears, and tattoos peeked out from the slouchy black sweater she wore.

Despite the dim room, I could have sworn I'd seen her before. I tried to recall exactly where, but my mind was drawing a blank. I was still trying to place her when a door at the back of the shop opened, spilling in light from the street.

I clenched my fists, digging my nails into my palm, to hold onto the thin control on my power to stop it from lashing out at the new arrival. Lyra went into a fighting stance but faltered and held onto a bookcase for support.

"They're out front and won't be stalled for long," the new girl said. Her black hair fell out of a loose braid, and her warm brown skin had a slight pink flush from the cold.

"Shit," the one with black-and-red hair said.

"Not to sound ungrateful," Lyra said, breathing labored, "but any chance you got some yarrow?" She tried to stand up straight again. "Or some fucking painkillers?"

I barely managed to catch her before her knees went out completely.

Someone pounded on the front door.

"Blythe, get them upstairs," the one with the braid said, moving towards the front door.

"Sofia, don't," Blythe started.

Sofia shook her head. "They can't come in without good reason." She nodded to us. "But if they're out here in the open..."

"Fine," Blythe said. "Let's go."

I hoisted Lyra to her feet and followed Blythe to a set of stairs at the back of the shop. We were halfway up when I heard Sofia greet someone at the front. I paused on the step to listen, seeing if I could recognize the voice.

"Get your ass up here," Blythe hissed.

Sighing, I helped Lyra up the last of the steps into a small apartment. Like the shop downstairs, it was lit with lamps. A set of string lights surrounded the living area, thick curtains blocked the street from view, and a gray couch covered with mismatched throw pillows and unfolded clothes sat against the wall. A mix of dryer sheets and the waxy aroma of burning candles hung in the air.

I deposited Lyra into the only open spot on the couch and helped her out of her jacket. Blood stained the inside lining and the sleeve of her sweater. It still seeped from the wound in her arm. I took extra care not to get any of it on my skin. She was too pale from the blood loss already, the last thing she needed was me taking more of what little energy she had.

Blythe waited by the cracked door, listening to whatever was happening downstairs. Seconds felt like hours as we waited.

Footsteps hurried up the stairs and Sofia came through the door. "We're good for now," she said.

"You sure?" Blythe asked, locking the door.

Sofia nodded. "They can't come in without mom's permission and she won't give it."

Lyra snorted. "Bet they loved that," she said, but her normal energy was missing as her eyes fluttered shut.

Sofia rushed over and examined her arm. "They shot her?" she asked, looking at me.

"Hunters," I explained.

"Merda," she breathed.

"Of course," Blythe muttered as Sofia made her way to the small kitchen and gathered supplies. She opened the cupboard by the refrigerator.

"You have any moon water left?" Sofia asked.

Blythe shook her head. "Used it up with the last..." She tugged at the hem of her sweater sleeve as she looked at me. "Spell."

"Of course you did," Sofia said under her breath.

"Tap's fine," Blythe and Lyra said at the same time.

Sofia rolled her eyes. "I'll be right back." She left and returned within a minute with a small vial of moon water. She ripped the purple price tag off with her teeth and grabbed a towel off the counter.

I moved out of her way and stood across from Lyra, double-checking I hadn't gotten any of her blood on my hands. I caught Blythe watching me and quickly stuffed my hands into my pockets.

Lyra swore loudly as Sofia used a spell to remove the bullet still lodged in her arm.

"Sorry," Sofia muttered. She wrapped the towel around Lyra's arm before going back to the kitchen to mix ingredients for a poultice. I'd seen Wes do it enough to know one when I saw it.

"What are you doing here?" Blythe blurted.

I stared at her. "I—we—what?"

She rolled her eyes. "In Salem."

"Oh, uh…" I swallowed and glanced at Lyra. "We were just passing through."

Blythe raised her eyebrows. "And you brought the Collective and hunters with you?"

"Blythe," Sofia warned.

Blythe pursed her lips and crossed her arms.

"I didn't know they'd find us," I said quietly. *That*, at least, was the truth.

Blythe snorted.

"Tea," Sofia offered. "Valerian, please." Her stare was focused on Blythe, and something passed between them. Blythe sighed but went to make it.

"There's gauze and wrap in the bathroom," Sofia said, nodding to me. "Second drawer on the left."

I hurried into the bathroom. It was in a similar state to the living room and kitchen. Whoever's place this was, they weren't one for organization. I found the supplies buried under half-empty lotion bottles and an odd amount of travel-sized mouthwash.

Once back in the living room, Sofia applied the poultice, placed a piece of gauze on top, and wrapped the bandage around it. She placed her hands over it and whispered a spell, brow creased and mouth moving quickly.

Blythe came to stand next to me, a steaming, chipped mug in her hand. I wrinkled my nose against the pungent smell of dirty socks. Pure valerian tea would help anyone sleep through the night, but it reeked. Sofia finished her spell and took the mug from Blythe, forcing it into Lyra's hand.

Lyra's eyes opened and she wrinkled her nose against the smell. "Whiskey would work too."

"Drink," Sofia ordered. "And get some sleep."

Lyra blinked slowly a few times but didn't argue and downed the tea. She pinched her face as she swallowed against the taste and handed the mug back. Leaning her head on the back of the couch, she was asleep in minutes.

"Is she…" I wasn't even sure what to ask.

"She'll be fine," Sofia assured me, even as fatigue etched its way into her face. She took the mug to the kitchen. "But I'd try to avoid any more excitement like that for a while. Stay put for a bit."

I bit the inside of my lip.

"How long?" Blythe asked.

Sofia sighed. "A day, at least."

"Seriously?" Blythe seethed.

"Tu és impossível," Sofia muttered. She rinsed out the mug and stacked it on top of the already large pile of unwashed dishes.

Sofia pulled out her braid. "I'm going for food," she said, redoing the plait.

Blythe nodded and shifted on her feet. Sofia muttered something under her breath and left the room.

A steady drip of water from the sink filled the space she'd left. I watched Lyra sleeping on the couch, wondering if it would be better to find Jax. She'd be safe with him.

Blythe moved away without a word to the bedroom. She came back with two pillows and a couple of throw blankets.

"You can stay until tomorrow," she said, handing them to me. She went back to her room but stopped just inside the doorway. "Don't touch anything."

She shut the door, leaving me alone with questions running through my head, too fast to stop. I was going to need my own dose of valerian to get any sleep.

Chapter 7

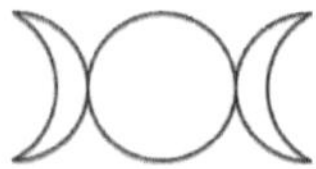

Lyra slept through the night. I did not. I'd made a spot for myself and curled up under a blanket, knowing I needed sleep. But every little creak from the shop downstairs and voice from outside sent my heart into my throat.

After a few hours, I gave up and tried calling Ian. It was late, and he still wasn't expecting it, but I needed to know the reason they'd found us wasn't because they'd caught him first.

He didn't answer, and I convinced myself it was because he was sleeping.

I managed a light doze that Sofia interrupted when she came back in the early morning, bringing news the Emissaries were nearby waiting for the shop to open—and breakfast sandwiches from Red's.

Blythe was unconcerned. She insisted the protections on her place were strong enough to keep anyone out. I kept my doubts to myself; anything short of a blood ward wouldn't stop them.

Sofia checked Lyra's arm while Blythe got ready for work. Once Sofia was certain Lyra was going to make a full recovery—a scar inevitable—Lyra inhaled her food before crashing again. I picked at the sandwich Sofia had been kind enough to get me, but worry and lack of sleep left my stomach churning and appetite nonexistent.

Once Blythe and Sofia left, I tried Ian again. Still no answer. This time, I risked a quick voicemail, letting him know I'd try again in a couple of hours. I wasn't desperate enough to leave the number of my new phone...yet.

Next, I tried to find something to keep myself occupied until we could leave. Flipping through Blythe's streaming options, nothing held my attention for longer than a few minutes. The apartment wasn't huge. One bedroom, small bathroom, kitchen with minimal storage, and a living room large enough for the couch, TV, and an overloaded bookcase.

I tackled the kitchen first. There was no hint at a system to follow. Glasses and plates mixed together in cupboards, mugs were inside bowls, and the utensil drawer was a disaster. The spices were even worse.

After scrubbing the dishes, I dried and put them away in a more practical arrangement. Blythe didn't have any dividers for the drawers, so I did the best I could. Once I alphabetized the spices and wiped the counters down, the space felt larger.

The project hadn't expelled enough of my nervous energy. With Lyra still sleeping and no way to know if the clothes on the couch were clean or dirty, I opted to leave that alone—for now.

Instead, I went into the bathroom. It wasn't terrible, it just lacked organizational...anything. I wiped out the drawers and grouped all the items by type as they went back in. I found a practically empty bottle of glass cleaner and used it to shine the mirror and wipe down the surfaces.

I moved the clothes out of the living room and put them in her room where they might be least in the way. I left the bedroom alone. Even with my itch to tidy up, *that* felt too personal.

Once the clothes were out of the living room, it really opened up the area. I dusted off the TV stand and the altar space next to it. The rug needed a good vacuum, but Lyra was still sleeping, and I had no idea where Blythe kept it—if she even had one.

Checking the time, I decided to try Ian again. This time it didn't ring, just went straight to voicemail. I wasn't sure if that was better or worse.

Sitting down in front of the bookcase, I crossed my legs and read the spines. If she had a system, I couldn't figure it out. Books were stuck on top of other books, spines and pages were facing out at random, and a small stack was on the floor. Nothing in this girl's place had any semblance of a system.

Pulling off books and piling them next to me, I wiped the dust from the shelf and made sure their spines were facing out and alphabetical by author when they went back. A well-read copy of *The Yellow Wallpaper and Other Writings* was the first book on the second shelf. A thin leather string was stuck in the pages, dragging out a leather-bound book with it. It landed on the floor with an unnatural heaviness.

Staring at the leather cover, I slowly picked it up and ran a hand over the pressed symbol on the front. Identical to the grimoire sitting at my house, the Triple Moon stared back at me. A coincidence, surely.

Hands shaking, I moved to open the front cover.

"You cleaned?" Lyra croaked from the couch.

I tossed the book off my lap and slid up next to her. "How are you feeling?"

She shifted and glanced down at her arm. "Like I never want to be fucking shot again." She rubbed her face. "You *cleaned*?" she repeated.

"I needed something to do."

"You need a hobby," she mumbled. She yanked the tie out of her hair and let it fall loose from the ponytail. "Where are we with a plan?"

I looked down at my hands. "We need to get out of town," I said. "That's as far as I've gotten."

She stretched. "Accomplishable."

I let out a nervous laugh. "They know where we are," I said. "It's not going to be easy."

"The hunters or the D.R.U.s?"

I thought it over. If Sasha knew we were in here, they wouldn't have knocked. "The D.R.U.s," I concluded.

"Well, fuck," she said.

"Yeah." She yawned. "You heard from Ian yet?"

I shook my head. "Tried a couple times, though."

"He's probably sticking to the original plan," she said.

"But..." I bit the edge of my thumbnail. "The original plan kind of went, you know, to shit."

"That it did," she agreed. "Just means we need a bett—new one."

I slouched back against the couch.

Lyra stood and stretched, arms, leg, back. "Are you sad because there's nothing left to organize?"

I pulled my knees up to my chest and eyed the bookcase. "No," I mumbled. "Just thought I'd be in Sandusky by now."

She rotated her torso from side to side. "Right, about that—"

"We're not going to Bolivia."

She rolled her eyes. "I got that," she said. "I was just curious what we're doing once we get there."

I stifled a yawn. "What do you mean?"

"I mean," she started, walking to the kitchen, "what are we doing *in* Ohio?" She opened a few of the cupboards until she found a glass and pulled out a pitcher of water from the fridge.

I rested my chin on my knees. "Hoping this all blows over quickly."

She poured herself a glass of water. "I don't follow."

"They can't chase me forever," I said. "I'm sure Lenore will eventually give it up."

She gulped down half the glass. "Hiding?" She finished the rest of the water and wiped her mouth on the back of her hand. "Really?"

I let out a frustrated sigh. "What?"

She leaned against the counter and crossed her legs at the ankles. "Nothing."

"Lyra."

"Fine." She crossed her arms. "You gave the Council the middle finger," she said. "You faced Armin *fucking* Scholz and lived."

"But—"

"And now you just want to pretend like you haven't totally changed the game?"

"What do you want me to do?" I snapped, springing to my feet. I was too tired and frustrated to discuss this right now. The worry clawing at my gut didn't help, either.

"Just thought this was the start of, you know," she said with a shrug. "Fixing some shit."

"Don't put that on me," I said rounding on her. "I just wanted to be left alone."

She shook her head. "We both know you were meant for more than that."

"Don't start with that."

"Why not?"

"Because I don't need another person throwing that stupid prophecy in my face!"

She frowned. "I wasn't talking about—" The door opened, and Blythe, Sofia, and a third girl walked in. Sofia looked between us, and Blythe's gaze swept across the apartment.

A smirk played at the edges of Lyra's mouth as Blythe's frown deepened.

"What the fuck did you do?" Blythe snapped.

"She cleans when she's stressed," Lyra offered.

"You litt—"

"Let it go," Sofia said, setting a bag of takeout on the counter. She moved to Lyra. "How's it looking?"

Lyra glanced down at her arm. "Doesn't hurt, so...good?"

Sofia unwrapped the bandage to take a look while Blythe slid onto her couch. The third girl gave me a small wave.

"I'm Devya," she said. She'd pulled her deep brown hair half up, and her warm brown eyes were lined with bright blue eyeliner. Under a denim jacket, she wore a black T-shirt that read "Witch Please" paired with a geometric skirt over leggings and short black ankle boots.

"Em," I said. "That's Lyra."

"Definitely going to scar," Sofia confirmed, taking a towel from the drawer to wipe away what was left of the poultice.

"Thanks," Lyra said.

"Try not to get shot again," she offered.

Blythe let out a snort of frustration before getting up to grab a sandwich out of the bag of food off the counter. "They don't clear out, we're all getting shot."

"Just need a car," Lyra said, going for the food herself.

Devya nodded. "And we're here to make sure no one follows you."

"And if I get to smack Sebastian in the process, even better," Sofia added.

"Go for the nose," Lyra said through a mouthful of hot ham. "Probably still tender."

"Nice," Sofia said with a chuckle.

"Em," Lyra said, nodding to the sandwiches on the counter. "You should eat."

I nodded, but eating wasn't on my mind. Blythe and her friends seemed nice enough—well, Sofia and Devya were anyway—but that didn't mean I wasn't wary of what exactly they were doing. Helping complete strangers take on both hunters and the Collective wasn't exactly the same as a ride to the airport. I swallowed and braced myself for the worst.

I cleared my throat. "How did you know we were in trouble?" I asked.

Everyone looked at me.

"You mean other than the gunshots?" Blythe said, tone dripping with sarcasm that could rival Lyra's.

"Yes," I said, trying to keep my tone even. "No one else came to help, and I'm sure they heard it."

"Em," Lyra said slowly. "What are you getting at?"

"I just want to know what made you help *us*," I said.

Sofia, Devya, and Blythe exchanged a tentative look before Sofia set her sandwich down and wiped her hands on a napkin. "We were told to."

"Sofia," Blythe said with a shake of her head.

Sofia ignored her and moved to the altar. She lifted the cloth that covered it and slid out a folded piece of paper.

Devya looked down at her hands instead of me.

Sofia held out the paper for me and I took it carefully. Tears pricked my eyes as I recognized the spell copied onto the page. Lyra leaned over the counter to read it upside down.

"That looks like your tattoo," she said.

I took a deep breath. "That's because it is." The copy of the sigil spell Phoenix had taken hours before we'd found him dead on the floor of his parlor. The paper trembled slightly in my hands the further I read. Scrawled in dried blood at the bottom of the spell were two words. *Help her.*

"Hazel got that the day he died," Blythe said.

I looked up to find her watching me with an accusatory stare.

"Hazel?" Lyra asked, looking between us for the answer.

"Chase. Phoenix's daughter," I reminded her.

"Oh." She stepped back from the counter and paid more attention to her half-eaten sandwich than the people in the room. To say I had a full memory of experiencing his last moments wouldn't have been fair to him, but I did have a vague sensory memory of him trying to get something away from the people who murdered him. To get it away and safe. This had been what he'd been trying to hide. My spell and one last message for his daughter. His death was horrible enough; this made it so much worse.

I crumpled the page in my fist and turned away from them all. Without asking, I slipped into Blythe's room and closed the door on the quiet conversation starting in the kitchen. I sat on the edge of the bed in the dark room and unclenched my fist, staring at the page. He'd died because of me, and the last message he was able to get to his daughter was about me. She didn't even get a goodbye.

But her friends had this. She'd given it to them. Despite her completely justifiable anger at me, she'd honored him in helping me. They were still willing to help me, and I was suddenly afraid it was because they were expecting the same thing Lyra was and I couldn't give that to them. His sacrifice was for nothing.

A nagging in the back of my mind pulled me back to the present and I pulled out the phone and quickly hit Ian's number. It rang twice, three times before he finally picked up.

"Hello?"

The relief at hearing his voice didn't ease the ache that something was still wrong. "It's me," I said. "Are you okay?"

He was quiet for a moment. "Sorry," he said. "Who is this?"

I swallowed. "Can you not talk?" I asked. "I just need to know they haven't found you."

Another too-long pause. "Look, I think you have the wrong number."

My stomach dropped to the floor as relief turned to dread. "It's Em." Tears welled in my eyes. "Boswell," I croaked, hoping he'd give me a laugh and tell me he didn't know any other Ems.

"Yeah, sorry. Definitely have the wrong number."

A hot tear ran down my cheek. "Right. Sorry."

"No problem."

The call went quiet, and I closed my eyes against the brimming tears. He hadn't ended the call, and I couldn't bring myself to either. That would make it real, final.

A shuffling on the other side sprouted a seed of hope that nestled in my chest. I thought Ian was going to come back on and tell me he'd been faking—that it was a lie to make sure we weren't overheard.

"You could have prevented this." Kane's voice, where Ian's should have been, made me angrier than I thought possible. "It really is a shame."

I took a few breaths, trying to steady myself, but they did nothing to stop the tinge of red from creeping into my vision. "You—you didn't—" The words wouldn't come.

"You've made an enemy of the Council, Emaleth," he said. "This is the consequence."

The ruby sparked with heat and angry tears replaced the despair. "You'll regret touching him," I said, voice low.

"Turn yourself over," he ordered. "And we won't have to find anyone else." I ended the call before he could add anything to his threat. Gripping the phone so hard it hurt, my hands shook, trembling with fury.

Everything was too hot. Burning. Kane's voice rang in my head. There was no stopping the flood of power that surged through me. And for the first time, I didn't care if it took over.

Chapter 8

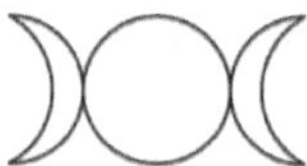

Blythe's bedroom disappeared in a flood of red as hot rage coursed through my veins and Kane's voice rang in my ears. He'd blamed me for what they'd done. But it wasn't my fault. It was theirs. *Hers.*

She was the reason for all of this. She told them what to do and they blindly followed those orders. And they were going to hurt for it. They took him. It would only be fair for me to take one of theirs.

Before the thought had finished, my power was searching for someone to hurt. There were plenty of options just outside. Regret was painful, and they were about to find out just how much.

Sweat dripped down the back of my neck as anger and the surge of power overheated my body. I moved for the door. My hand was half an inch from the knob when it swung open from the other side.

Blythe shut it behind her. She was vivid against the haze of the rest of the room. She stepped close to me, blocking my way out.

"Get it together." Her voice was muffled like we were underwater. It was amazing I heard anything over the rush of blood in my ears.

"Move," I growled, voice deep and unnatural.

She didn't.

I lashed out. Her magic was right there, close to the surface. Easy to take.

Only I couldn't. I could feel her magic, but it wouldn't take. She was stronger than me. No—that wasn't it. She wasn't stronger, her magic was...like.

The ruby heated, knowing what I wanted before I spoke the words. "*Nostri sanguinis, viribus m—*"

"*Ní ó mo chuid fola,*" Blythe incanted, and the ruby cooled at her words.

A sharp bite across my face brought the world back. I fell against the bed, holding my stinging cheek. I stared up at her, her eyes glowing a faint red in the dim bedroom.

She crossed her arms. "You good?"

I blinked at her. "Did—did you just hit me?"

She shrugged.

I straightened, rubbing the warm spot on my face. "Your eyes...what the hell was that?"

"I could ask you the same thing."

Flattening a hand to the dulled ruby, I felt nothing but cool stone. "How did you do that?"

"Open, flat palm," she said. "Leaves a more lasting sting."

"That's not what I meant."

She sighed. "Doesn't matter," she said. "You were losing it, I stepped in."

I shook my head. "Your magic, it's..." The realization was struggling to break through the cement block in my mind that was what I—what everyone—had been told for years. But there was no other explanation that made sense. Why my power reacted the way it had to hers, her eyes, and why she *knew* her wards were unbreakable. The impossible was standing in front of me.

"You're a Blood Witch."

She tensed. "All the Blood Witches are gone," she said. "Except you."

"I know what I felt."

She let out a harsh laugh. "You were completely out of control," she said. "You can't trust yourself." She was trying to be harsh, but there was doubt in her tone.

"Just admit it."

"Why?" she snapped. "Because a *Boswell* wants me to?"

I frowned. "What?"

"Just keep your theories to yourself," she said, moving to the door.

"Wait—"

"We're leaving soon," she said quickly. With that, she left me standing alone in the room, reeling.

I sank onto the bed and put my head in my hands. The room was spinning, and it had nothing to do with my magic. My chest tightened.

Ian's memories were gone. Blythe was a Blood Witch. Everyone I'd ever tried to hide from surrounded me.

How had my life gotten so incredibly off track?

I pressed the ruby hard against myself, hoping the pain of the rough-cut gem on my skin would ground me as the world spun out of control. The room wasn't tilting, and my head cleared enough for a singular thought to come through: I'd have to turn myself in.

I'd make them give Ian his memories back. They wanted me, and I wanted him. They'd have to listen.

Except they wouldn't. Even if I agreed to every term they laid out, they'd never give me that. It was a punishment, and crawling to them in surrender wouldn't change that.

Lyra squeezed into the room. "Hey, you okay?"

I shook my head.

She knelt in front of me.

"They go—" I swallowed and shook my head again.

"You're freaking me out here, Em."

I managed to get past the lump in my throat. "They got to Ian."

Her eyes widened.

"He has no idea who I am." I bit my bottom lip to keep it from trembling.

"Fuck," she breathed.

I glanced at the door. Blythe hadn't confirmed it, but Lyra and I needed to be on the same page if we were going to get through this. "And..." I took a deep breath. "I think Blythe's a Blood Witch."

Lyra stared at me, eyebrows pinching together. "But...they're all dead."

I raised my eyebrows.

"Not you, obviously," she said. "Or her—are you sure?"

I ran my hand through my hair. "She didn't admit it, but I'm pretty sure."

"Well shit, neither would I," Lyra said. Then grimaced. "Sorry."

I waved her unneeded apology away. I wouldn't have admitted it either. The only reason I had was because it was the fastest way I saw to help get Wes back alive.

I stood and paced the length of the bed. The plan had been to be in Ohio by now, but maybe Lyra had been right. I'd tried hiding, tried running, and I'd told myself it was to protect my family. They'd found Ian—taken him from me. Protecting the rest of my family would mean fighting.

I stopped pacing. "Chad."

"What?"

I faced her. "They know where Chad is."

She started to shake her head but stopped and sighed. "We need to get there first."

We hurried out of the bedroom to find Blythe sitting on her counter, tapping away on her phone. She looked up when we made our way out.

"Sofia and Devya will make sure they're clear so you can get out," she said.

"You sure they can?"

She shot a glare at me.

Lyra balled up the wrapper her sandwich had come in. "What happens if they get caught?"

Blythe set her phone on the counter. "They won't."

"Cool," Lyra said. "But if they do?"

Blythe sighed. "Neither of them are part of any Collective coven, they don't answer to the Council." She scratched her nose. "And all they know is you're headed to Logan Airport, doesn't exactly give anyone much to go on."

"Providence," I said.

She glanced over at me, frowning. "Why are you changing the plan now?" I was surprised at the slight panic in her voice. Changing our destination shouldn't have meant anything to her.

I caught Lyra's eye. "The Council is targeting my family," I explained, running the ruby along its chain. It was still cool and dormant after the clash with Blythe. "And I need to get to them first."

Lyra shoved her arms into her bloodied jacket. "I'll go find a car."

Blythe raised a pierced eyebrow. "You stealing another car is only going to draw more attention."

Another? Lyra mouthed to me. Blythe's casual mention that she'd known what Lyra and I had been up to the last couple of days only made her point for her. Clearly, we hadn't been as subtle as Lyra thought.

Blythe typed a quick message on her phone. "We'll take my car."

"*We?*" I blurted.

She hopped off the counter. "We'll you're not getting my car without me," she said before leaving the kitchen for her bedroom.

I looked over at Lyra. "Stealing a car would be easier."

She laughed. "No, it wouldn't."

I bit my bottom lip.

"If you want to get to Chad before them, you're going to have to accept the help," she said, tying her hair up.

"It's not that," I said, dropping my voice to a whisper.

Lyra picked at the bread of the sandwich I never ate. "Then what is it?"

"Are you sure we can trust her?"

Lyra cocked her head at me with a slight smirk. "Even if I didn't, you kinda just told her where we were going."

Dammit.

Blythe *was* offering a quick way out. One that could give us back the small head start we'd lost. It should have been an easy answer. But Blythe wasn't easy to read. There was a reluctance to her actions that left me with doubts. It *could* be explained away by wanting to keep what she was a secret, but something told me that wasn't it. I'd been burned by believing people had decent motives before, and I wasn't about to risk my family doing it again.

Lyra glanced at the bedroom. "I get it," she said. "But something tells me keeping the only other Blood Witch around is better than having our friends find her."

Blythe came back out of her room with a small bag and went to the shelves to grab a few of her books. She stuffed them inside and zipped the bag up as she moved back to the counter. Her phone screen lit up and, after a second of reading, she scooped it up and stuffed it in her coat pocket.

"They're ready," she said. "We good?"

Lyra raised her eyebrows in question.

I grabbed my coat and backpack. "Yeah, let's go."

Lyra nodded and swung her own pack over her shoulder with her bad arm, wincing slightly. Blythe locked the apartment and led us out the back door at the base of the stairs. Lights blinked at us from a black 4Runner squeezed between a Fusion and a Mini Cooper. It wasn't fully dark yet, but the sun would set in less than an hour.

"Huh," Lyra said.

Blythe tossed her bag into the back seat. "What?"

"Nothing," Lyra said, cocking her head at the car. "I just expected something, I don't know, sportier."

Blythe rolled her eyes. "Corvette's in the shop." She shut the back door.

Lyra chuckled as she opened the door behind the passenger seat and tossed her bag in. I climbed in after it and clicked the buckle into place.

As we waited for the heat to kick in, I shoved my hands in my pockets. Despite not sleeping well the last few nights, the surge from earlier left me wired.

It was odd. A few months ago, something like that would have left me completely drained. Magic was a lot like building physical stamina, that's how mom had always described it. Starting was the hard part, but work at it enough and you could hold a spell longer or draw on more power and it would take longer for the aftereffects to kick in.

By the time the car warmed to the point where I didn't need to keep my hands in my pockets anymore, nerves had replaced the cold. We still hadn't heard from Blythe's friends, and her anxious grip on the steering wheel—tight enough her knuckles blanched—didn't give me much confidence.

Lyra tapped the center console. Indiscernible sounds came from the low music. I tried not to breathe too loudly in the uncomfortable silence.

Two shrill beeps interrupted our waiting. Blythe hit the text-to-speech option on the screen in the dash.

"Go," the feminine robotic voice said.

Blythe threw the car into gear and backed out of the spot, whipping around fast enough to send me crashing against the door. Within seconds, we were flying through town. I wrapped a hand around the ruby, hoping we weren't too late.

Chapter 9

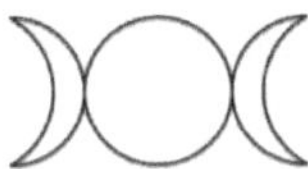

Mama Bell's place was a large Georgian Revival on the east side of Providence. I'd spent a couple Christmases, the occasional Memorial Day, and two weeks one summer there when I was younger. She, like Chad, hadn't even blinked when she found out my uncles were taking me in. Neither had Chad's five sisters. It had been just mom and me for so long, then I was thrown into the largest family I'd known. Overwhelming, but nice.

She was nice, expecting me to call her Mama like I was one of her grandchildren, never missing a birthday card, and insisting I never needed an invitation to visit. We were about to test that.

I should have called ahead and warned them I wasn't coming alone, but until I was absolutely convinced that my calls to Ian hadn't been the reason they found him, I wasn't going to risk it. The Collective might know where I was headed, but I didn't need to help them by confirming it.

Blythe parked in front of the garage and turned the car off.

Lyra clicked her seatbelt off and turned to me. "Chad's rich?"

I shrugged. "They're comfortable." I unbuckled my seatbelt and grabbed my bag.

"That's what rich people say," Blythe muttered.

I slid out of the car and hurried to the back door, tapping my boots against the jamb to clear the little bit of snow that had collected. I rang the bell, thinking Lyra and Blythe should've waited in the car until I could give Chad and Mama a heads-up.

The door opened, and I went to give an explanation, but Chad pulled me into a crushing hug before a sound could make its way out of my mouth. I wrapped my arms around him, embracing him back, tears working their way into my eyes.

"You're okay," I breathed when he let me go.

"Gained a few extra pounds since being cooped up," he said. He held me at arm's length, a frown creasing in his forehead. "You look tired. Are you sleeping?"

I nodded.

"Who is it?" Mama demanded from somewhere in the house.

"It's Em, Mama," Chad called back. "Get inside before you freeze," he added to me, stepping aside.

I jerked my thumb over my shoulder. "I, uh, have friends."

He glanced around me, eyes widening as if he'd just noticed I wasn't the only one standing at the door. He nodded and motioned for us to come in. We'd have to quickly figure out how to explain to Mama who they were and why we were showing up on her doorstep without warning.

The back entrance led to a narrow hallway with hooks for coats and hats and a mat for shoes. I kicked mine off and put them next to another pair before hanging my coat up. Lyra and Blythe followed suit before we followed Chad to the end of the hall where it opened to a large kitchen.

A small pot simmered on the stove, smelling faintly of lime and pears. Empty pie crusts in pie plates were on the island, ready for whatever Chad had on the stove.

Mama looked up from the breakfast nook, her narrow glasses hanging on the tip of her nose. She marked the place in her book and took her glasses off, letting them fall around her neck, held by a red and purple chain—one I'd made her years ago.

She stood, using the back of one of the chairs to steady herself, and opened her arms to greet me. I stepped into her hug, and she gave me an extra-tight squeeze.

She frowned when she let me go. "You look tired," she said. "Are you sleeping?" She turned to Chad. "Is she sleeping?"

"She's fine, Mama. Stop fussin'," Chad insisted.

She refocused on me and took my face in both of her soft hands. "You need sleep."

"I'm okay, Mama. Promise."

She dropped her hands and put them on her hips, clicking her tongue. I knew she didn't believe me, but if I told her I couldn't remember the last time I got a full night's sleep she'd never let me leave.

"These are friends," I said quickly, hoping for a momentary distraction. "Lyra and Blythe."

She gave me the same look I'd gotten when I'd snuck out one summer and I'd lied about it, badly. She wouldn't be pacified by guests for long.

"Hello," she said.

"Hi," Lyra returned.

Blythe gave her a weird, awkward half-wave.

"Are you girls hungry?" Mama asked, turning towards the kitchen, a slight hitch to her step thanks to a knee surgery she still hadn't fully recovered from.

"Starv—" Lyra stopped when I shot her a warning look. "Nope," she corrected.

"We were just passing through and wanted to stop and check in," I said, voice a little higher than I wanted it to be.

Chad raised his eyebrows behind his mother's back.

Mama drummed her fingers on the counter.

"You have time for dinner," a new voice said at the entrance to the kitchen. "And I wouldn't mind hearing what you've been up to." Supported by a cane and looking a little gray was Wes.

I let out a small cry of relief and flung myself at him, not caring about the cane. But he didn't topple or protest when I hugged him so tight I could have cracked a rib. A sob escaped and I held him.

"How?" I wiped wetness from my cheeks. "I thought you were with Selene..." I stopped before I said too much in front of Mama. She only knew the bare minimum when it came to Wes's and my relationship—and nothing about my abilities.

He nodded. "I could have let you know if you answered your phone." His tone was soft, but it still felt like a scolding.

I grimaced. "Sorry," I said. "I had to get a new one."

He frowned.

"Mama, don't you have book club?" Chad asked.

Mama eyed her son. "I do," she said slowly. She scooped her book off the table and stopped next to me on her way out of the kitchen. "Take any of the guest rooms you want." She gave my arm a squeeze and bestowed a comforting smile before leaving.

Lyra took a seat at the island. "We staying the night?"

"Can we risk it?" Blythe said, slipping into the chair next to Lyra.

Wes took Mama's vacated seat, hooking the cane on the back of another chair. I sank into the chair next to him.

"How bad?" he asked.

I swallowed hard. "Pretty bad."

"We've got at least one D.R.U. and some pissed-off hunters on our tail," Lyra offered.

Chad glanced at his husband. "Do I want to know what a D.R.U. is?"

Wes shook his head. "I'll explain later," he said. He placed one of his hands over mine. "Stay the night, you all look too tired to drive anymore tonight."

"I'm fine." The lie didn't sound as convincing to him as it should have. His knowing smile told me he wasn't about to accept it either.

He looked over at Lyra.

"Not sure we have that long," Lyra admitted.

He sighed. "We'll cover what we can now, then."

"I'm off," Mama said, poking her head into the kitchen. "Chad, make sure the girls eat."

Chad nodded. "Have fun." He opened the fridge and pulled out containers of leftovers. While he busied himself making plates, we all waited quietly until we heard the front door close.

The microwave beeped as Chad punched in the cook time.

"Now," Wes said, giving my hand a squeeze. "Start from the beginning."

I took a deep breath. There was a lot to cover, and I wasn't even entirely sure what the "beginning" was. So, I started with the tickets

Raven had given me. Ignoring that warning—in a way—had started all of this.

Alex's attack and learning I was able to tap into the ruby's power without really trying. Meeting the Tsipras siblings, Kane, and Sadiki. Them essentially moving in. The police interview.

He let me talk uninterrupted and kept his face neutral. I went on because no one was stopping me. How we—Jax—convinced Kane not to drag me to the Council. How I found out the hard way Raven had been using me the whole time.

When I got to the part where Jax and I learned I could use my power on other witches, Wes's passivity broke for the first time. It cracked more when I told him about Armin.

I almost stopped there. Admitting I'd been stupid enough to run headfirst into a hunter's trap took a lot. But I did it. To his credit, he managed to keep his composure when I got to the part where I got stabbed. I left out the bit where I'd put Alex in a coma. Wes was pale enough; I didn't want to stress him out even more.

I took a final breath. "And that's when we headed to Salem."

He stared at me, nodding slowly. "That's it?" he said with a shaky laugh.

I shrugged.

"You left out the vaibit," Lyra piped up over a mouthful of the spaghetti Chad had given her.

I shot her a glare.

"When did you run into a vaibit?" Blythe asked, looking between us.

"What *is* a vaibit?" Chad asked.

"You don't want to know," Lyra and Blythe said at the same time.

"I need a bourbon," Wes said.

I faced him again. "I'm sorry," I blurted. "I know I should have told you what happened at Onyx that night, I just thought—"

He put his hand up to stop me as Chad set a drink in front of him. "Focusing on that is useless," he said. "What happened, happened. There's nothing we can do about it." He took a sip. "What we need to figure out is what happens now."

I bit my lower lip. "I—" I didn't want to start crying, but it was hard thanks to my lack of sleep. "I need you to go to the Sandusky house."

Wes lowered the glass before he could take another drink and glanced at his husband.

"The wards here are fine," he said.

"I know, but…"

Lyra set her bowl down and wiped her mouth with a napkin. "They got to Ian," she said. "His memory's gone."

I looked down at the scuffed tabletop. A deep mark still remained on the surface from when one of the cousins tried to teach us how to play pinfingers. We all got in massive trouble for that one.

Wes sighed. "Okay."

My head snapped up. I wasn't sure why I'd expected him to argue. But when I saw his drawn brow aimed at Chad, I figured it out.

"You think Mama will miss us too much?"

Chad shook his head. "She's got a trip south planned to visit Sherri and the kids anyway." He glanced at the clock. "But she'd never forgive us if we sneak out in the middle of the night."

Wes nodded. "We'll leave in the morning." It was clear from his tone he meant that for me too.

I shook my head. "They've got to be right behind us—"

"You need to rest," he insisted. "Does anyone other than these two know this address?"

I thought it over. "Ian," I said quietly.

"If he'd given it up, we wouldn't have gotten here first," Lyra offered.

"Good," Wes said. He finished his bourbon and stood. "Then they won't be able to find it."

Lyra sat up straighter. "A shrouding charm?"

He nodded. "We'll start packing, and you get some sleep."

I wanted to argue, wanted to help them pack and leave tonight, but that would only take more of Wes's strength. And maybe he was right. A night in a familiar place might help me get some sleep. Salem had been nothing but one nightmare after another.

I showed Lyra and Blythe the spare rooms they could use and found the one I usually stayed in. Falling onto the bed I stared up at the plastic glow-in-the-dark stars on the ceiling. The sheets had hockey pucks and sticks. A kid's room that never got to grow up.

Tears spilled over and ran down either side of my face. I didn't bother to try stopping them. Gulping down air, I sobbed until I had a headache and no more tears would come. The last time I felt this empty had been the day mom died.

I forced myself off the bed and stripped out of the clothes I felt like I'd been wearing for a week to take a hot shower. Letting the warm water run over me, I found myself unable to stop from crying again.

After getting out, I washed my face with the supplies under the sink, but no amount of moisturizer could hide my reddened eyes. I braided my wet hair out of my face and pulled on sweats. Despite feeling more drained than I had in a very long time, I wasn't sure I wanted to try to sleep yet.

I headed out of my room to the upstairs den to find that Lyra had made herself comfortable there already. She and Blythe were on opposite ends of the couch, curled up under throw blankets while a horror movie played on the TV.

I climbed onto the couch next to Lyra and watched a few minutes of the movie without retaining any of it.

"You look like shit," Lyra said.

"Thanks," I muttered, rubbing at my sore eyes. I glanced over at the book in her lap and recognized it as one of my grimoires. Maggie's, I concluded, thanks to the sketches in the margins of the page Lyra was reading.

"What's that for?"

She closed it and stretched. "Trying to see if there's anything in there on memory spells."

My chest tightened. "Oh."

"Nothing, sorry." She put the book on the coffee table. "Gram might be able to convince them to give it back, though."

"Not likely," Blythe muttered.

We both turned to her.

"I just..." She sat up. "Memories are tricky."

"What do you mean?" I asked.

She pulled her knees to her chest. "Taking memories is a hack job. Putting them back is precise. It can get complicated."

Lyra's gaze flicked between Blythe and me. "Are memory spells a Blood Witch thing?"

Blythe's eyes narrowed. "Not that I'm aware of," she said.

"So, it's a you thing," Lyra prodded.

Blythe's jaw tightened. "No."

Lyra yawned with a stretch. "Then what's with the metaphors?"

"Can we just drop it?"

"That's not *her* thing," I offered, staring at the TV screen.

Blythe rubbed her face. "I just know someone who specializes in it, or whatever."

"You do?" Lyra asked, rolling over to face her. "Do I? Wait, who are you talking about?"

Blythe shook her head. "No one, forget it."

I tore my eyes away from the exploding car and focused on Blythe. "You know someone that could help?"

"That's *not* what I said." Blythe curled herself tighter under the blanket. "He's not an option."

"Who?" Lyra pressed.

Blythe turned a ring around her finger.

"Blythe," I insisted.

She let out a frustrated huff. "Martin Foster, okay?"

Lyra sat up and leaned over me to get closer to Blythe. "You know *the* Martin Foster?"

Blythe twisted the ring faster and stared ahead of her at the movie without a word. If Lyra was looking for confirmation, I doubted she was going to get it without a fight.

Lyra settled back into her seat and nudged me with her elbow. "Do you know Martin Foster?" she asked me under her breath.

I shook my head. "I don't even know who he is."

"He's the head of the Eris Coven," Blythe muttered.

Eris wasn't one of the Collective covens, I knew that much from mom's history lessons. My faded memories, however, couldn't recall which of Mary Boswell's daughters it was founded by. One of the triplets probably.

I looked over at Blythe. "But you do know him?"

She sighed. "Technically."

I wasn't even sure how to take that non-answer. She knew of him, and if she was right, he specialized in memory spells and was part of a non-Collective coven. It wasn't much, but it was enough. A plan to help Ian started to take form.

"Don't you have any more of those?" Blythe asked, waving a hand at Maggie's book on the coffee table. "You're a Boswell after all."

"Amity's book might have something," Lyra suggested.

I pulled my sleeves down past my knuckles and grimaced. "Yeah, I don't have that with me."

"Why the fuck not?" Lyra demanded.

"Seriously?" Blythe added.

I kept my gaze on the bloody mess on the screen in front of me. "I had to leave it in Portland."

"Why in the ever-loving fuck would you do that?" Lyra asked.

"I looked like your *grandmother*," I reminded her. "Going through my shelves would have been super weird."

"Gram does weird shit all the time," Lyra said.

"Well, excuse me for not picking up on that for the whole five minutes I knew the woman," I snapped.

Blythe rubbed her forehead. "Are you telling me that Amity Boswell's book is currently with the Council?"

I shrugged. "I'm hoping it's still on the bookshelf."

"Fantastic," Blythe muttered.

"If Charlevoix gets her hands on it…" Lyra didn't need to finish the thought. We all knew Lenore getting ahold of Amity's grimoire would be bad. It held spells unique to my family, my bloodline, and my power. She already had the force of most of the Council behind her, she didn't need another advantage.

Blythe let out a long breath and ran a hand through her hair. "I guess it's good Portland's on the way, then."

"To where?" Lyra asked.

She threw off the blanket and stood up. "Martin's."

"I thought you—" I started.

"I know," she groaned. "But at least this way, I know you're not going to run off and do something stupidly dangerous again."

Chapter 10

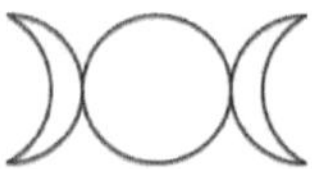

Someone had turned off my alarm and I slept longer than I'd planned. By the time we'd all gotten up and ready, packed, and eaten the large brunch Mama prepared, it was a little after two o'clock—far later than I wanted to leave.

Lyra helped Chad put the few bags they had into the taxi's trunk. I watched them from the front steps, my heart speeding up every time a car slowed down too much for comfort.

Wes limped out of the house, helped down the icy steps by Blythe, and came to stand next to me. He wrapped one arm around my shoulder and pulled me into a hug.

"Lyra gave me your numbers," he said. "I'll check in."

I leaned into his hug. "Let me know when you get there."

He kissed the top of my head. "Of course," he said. "Stay safe and—" he glanced over his shoulder where Blythe had gone back into the house before adding, "be careful with Martin." Wes hadn't liked it when I told him we weren't coming to Sandusky with them, but when I explained why, he at least understood. He admitted he had a cousin who knew Martin Foster but didn't know enough to tell me much more than that.

"I will," I said, forcing my voice through the lump in my throat. I hated this; I'd finally gotten him back and now he was leaving again. Just like Ian had.

All I had to do was make sure they made it to the Sandusky house, that way I *knew* no one could get to them unless I was dead. And if I were dead, no one would be coming after them anyway.

Chad and I helped Wes into the car.

"I love you," Wes said from the back seat.

"I love you, too," I replied.

Chad closed the door for him and turned to give me a hug I didn't want to end.

"Take care of yourself, kid," Chad said as we released each other. "And give 'em hell."

I choked out a laugh. "I'll do my best."

"Good." He walked to the other side of the car and slid in next to Wes. I waved as the taxi pulled away.

Tears chilled my cheeks, but I couldn't bring myself to go inside yet. Instead, I watched the car until I couldn't see it anymore.

A piece of me wished I hadn't gone to the club that night. Wished that, instead of watching them leave, we were all back home recovering from a New Year's party. Laughing in the kitchen at Chad's newest leftovers experiment, teasing Ian about some conspiracy theory rabbit hole he'd fallen into, planning for what came next.

But wishing was useless. This was my life now, and it was impossible to go back. We'd never be like that again, not really. I wasn't going to accept Ian was gone forever—not until I'd exhausted everything I could get my hands on to fix it.

Lyra stepped up next to me. "They'll be fine," she said, giving me a gentle nudge with her elbow.

I rubbed my arms against the chilly air. "They better be."

She sighed. "We'd better rescue Blythe from your grandmother."

"Do we have to?" I grumbled.

Lyra put an arm around my shoulders and steered me back into the house. "She has the car keys."

Mama had Blythe cornered in the kitchen and was trying to shove more food at her for us to take. We'd already turned down the cooler she'd tried to give us.

"You'll need carrots with your sandwiches," Mama insisted, head in the fridge. "And I've got some cheese in here somewhere."

"We're good, Mama. Promise," I said.

Blythe took our arrival as her opportunity to slip away. "I'll be in the car," she said on her way by, our sandwiches in her arms. "Hurry it up," she hissed.

I nodded.

"Are you sure? How long of a drive is it?"

"A few hours." I wasn't sure if Chad told her exactly where they were going, or that I wasn't going with them, but I decided the less she knew, the better for everyone.

She ducked out of the fridge and closed it. "Well, alright then. You drive safe now."

I stepped forward to hug her goodbye. "I will."

"And visit more often," she chided. "I never see enough of you these days."

I nodded against her shoulder.

She gave me a gentle pat on the back before letting go to pull Lyra in for her own hug. "You too," she said. "Any friend of Emmie is a friend here."

Lyra recovered from her surprise quickly. "Oh, okay," she said, then mouthed to me, *Emmie?*

I shook my head. Mama was the *only* one who got to call me that. And only because I didn't want to hurt her feelings by telling her I hated it.

Almost five minutes later and we managed to convince her we were indeed all set with the amount of food we had, and she handed me a twenty-dollar bill for gas—with a wink—and we were able to leave.

Blythe had the car heat turned up and drummed her fingers impatiently on the steering wheel. It was just under a three-hour drive back to Portland, which meant we had exactly that long to come up with a halfway decent plan on how to break into my own house.

○

We'd been sitting in the parking lot of the Greek Orthodox Church across from my house for almost twenty minutes to get a good count of how many Emissaries were still in the place. Only, not a single person had come or gone the whole time.

"So, once we get the ward—"

"We've got it, Em," Lyra reminded me, tying her hair up.

"I know, I just feel like I'm forgetting something."

She pulled off her tight black sweater and replaced it with a loose blue one. "And if you did, we'll deal." She laid down on the back seat and wiggled out of her jeans. "There's not a whole lot anyone can do about it between the three of us anyway."

Blythe snorted.

"What?" I asked as Lyra pulled on the too-big jeans we'd picked up earlier.

"Just wondering what happens when this goes to shit," Blythe said.

"It's fine," Lyra said. "What are they going to do against two Blood Witches?"

Blythe glared at her in the rearview mirror.

"And with a Binder, this is going to work perfectly," Lyra continued.

I looked over at Blythe. "So, you'll admit it to her?"

"I asked nicely," Lyra said.

Blythe pressed the knuckles of a closed fist against the bottom of the steering wheel. "It was the only way to get her to shut up."

Lyra chuckled from the back seat.

I rubbed my forehead with my knuckles. Knowing Blythe was a Blood Witch was one thing, but Lyra was partially right. Blood Binders were known for a lot more than their designation suggested. What we knew about them was that they were experts at bindings, unbindings, warding, breaking through wards, and in rare cases, binding entire bloodlines.

That would help with the wards on the house, but that didn't mean there weren't other issues that needed addressing. "What if someone wants to talk to you?" I asked.

"Then we're fucked," Lyra said simply.

Blythe turned to me. "Why?"

Lyra added brown leather boots to her ensemble. "Haven't worked out that part of my glamour yet."

"So, we're already fucked." Blythe crossed her arms and slouched against the driver's seat. "Why bother then?"

Lyra poked her head between the two front seats. "You are a very negative person."

Blythe glanced at her. "So?"

A smile played at Lyra's lips. "It's weirdly hot."

I pinched the bridge of my nose. "Can you focus, please?"

With a shrug, Lyra ducked into the back seat.

"Let's just get this over with," Blythe said, a slight blush creeping into her cheeks.

"You won't have to distract them for long," I said, more for my own comfort than theirs. In the mirror, I watched Lyra shrug on the jacket and close her eyes. Her mouth moved soundlessly as she moved her hand over her face. Within seconds, she changed: a perfect copy of Jax sat in the back seat.

"Here we go," Lyra-Jax said. She took a deep breath and opened the door. "Let me know when." She shut the door behind her and jogged across the street.

I counted to five and opened my own door. Zipping up my coat, I led Blythe up the street, around the back of the row of townhouses, and down the back alley.

Using a stick, I flicked the latch open on the back gate and let it swing open. Undisturbed snow met us, as no one had used it since Christmas. No lights were on in any of the rooms overlooking the yard.

We came to the patio, and I jumped to grab the freezing metal of the bottom rung on the emergency ladder.

"Break into your house a lot?" Blythe whispered.

"It's become a necessity recently," I admitted, pulling the ladder down as quietly as I could. We both waited a couple of heartbeats to see if the noise had drawn anyone from inside to investigate.

When no one did, we climbed to the ledge outside the main bedroom's window. It was locked, as usual, for the winter. I placed my hand on the outside of the glass, my skin tingling from the cold.

Rippling just behind the pane, the energy of Wes's ward was palpable. It wasn't just his, though; there was something different and stronger there. Jax had said he—or someone—had used Wes's as a foundation. We just had to hope our magic was stronger.

I dug into my pocket and removed the small bottle. It wasn't a tried-and-true method of removing a ward—by anyone—but it was better than trying to get through the thing without any help.

Crushed bay leaf and nettle mixed with horsetail oil. All traditionally used in creating protections, not stripping them, but we were working on the theory that intention would outweigh the literal.

I poured it across the window's ledge. It sparked and glowed a bright green, illuminating our faces in the dark, and ran down the length of the window and around the corner of the house. No one thought that it would get rid of Wes's ward completely, the idea was to simply weaken it.

Now, we had to deal with whatever additives the Emissaries put in place. I replaced the empty bottle and nodded to Blythe. She uncapped a liquid chalk pen and drew a circle on the glass.

Voices in the alley pulled my focus. They were just cutting through, but I didn't like having anyone else out where they could see us.

"This is going to work, right?" I asked for what was probably the hundredth time.

Blythe added a second, smaller circle in the center of the larger one and tilted her head to examine her work. "I've done this spell before," she said.

"That wasn't a yes."

"Wasn't a no." She drew a rune in the smaller of the two circles. I recognized it: two vertical parallel lines connected at the top by crossed lines. *Mann*—something. I couldn't remember the name or meaning. Rune work hadn't been prevalent in my magical education. Neither mom nor Wes worked with them much.

She added four more runes to the circle. A sort of lightning-shaped S to the right of the first, and then something that looked like the less-than symbol at the bottom. The one she put to the left I did know. *Uruz*. A rune for courage, bravery, and—as Wes put it—stubbornness.

Finally, she drew a straight vertical line at the top of the circle and recapped the pen.

"Now what?"

She shot me a glare that I felt more than saw. She dug back around in her pocket and opened a safety pin, pricking her finger. She took a deep breath and used the bead of blood that gathered to connect the four runes at the edge of the circle, muttering under her breath. I caught a few words but understood nothing. It wasn't English, or Latin, or any language I knew.

She traced over the line she drew one more time before flattening her palm against the center rune. "*Lúb nó briseadh ní cúram liom, ach tá mo thoil níos láidre.*" The runes glowed a bright red, matching the reflection of her eyes in the glass.

The ruby sparked angrily against my skin, and I sucked in a breath against the burn. I'd never seen another Blood Witch work like this before. Mom hadn't used her power in front of me, she never needed to.

Still burning, the ruby grew uncomfortable, and just as I was about to pull it out, it stopped. The circle of runes dimmed, and Blythe's eyes stopped glowing.

She turned to me. "As good as we're going to get."

I put my hand on the base of the window, visualizing the lock on the other side. Using Lyra's unlocking spell, I waited a second and pulled.

The window slid open without issue. Now, for the real test. I let out a breath and slipped inside. Nothing happened. No alarms, no magical hook tried to yank me back outside. Just my own breathing in an empty room.

Blythe climbed in next to me and closed the window. I could hear faint voices from downstairs but nothing indicating they'd heard anything. Creeping into the hallway, Blythe behind me, I made it to the landing and strained to listen. The TV was on, plus two other voices. Neither one I recognized.

I nodded to Blythe, and she shot off a text to Lyra. Now, we just had to wait for her to make sure whoever was in the living room was out for us. She wouldn't be able to pass as Jax for long—less if anyone wanted to actually talk to him. Timing was everything.

The front door opened and Lyra-Jax walked in with a nod to us.

"Jax!" one of them said. "We weren't expecting you for a couple of days."

Shit.

Lyra grunted with a shrug and headed straight into the kitchen.

"Guess the reunion with the girlfriend didn't go well," one of the couch crashers said, earning a chuckle from the other. But they didn't move. They didn't follow him for an update.

I glanced behind me at Blythe. We couldn't get to the shelves if they didn't move. Blythe tapped my shoulder and jerked her head over her shoulder. We snuck back down the hall and ducked into my room.

"Can we get to the kitchen?"

I shrugged. "Maybe, but if they're not completely focused on something else, they'll see us at the bottom for sure."

"Avoid the bottom of the stairs then," she said. She placed both hands on my shoulders. "*Déanann cosa chiúin éacht chiúin*," she muttered, repeating the phrase three times. My spine itched from the point of contact all the way down, making me fidget.

She placed a hand on her own chest and did it again. "Should be good." She didn't wait for me to ask any questions before striding out of the room and down the stairs. I reached to grab her before she got too far. She didn't know about the damn step.

"Skip th—" but my hissed warning was unnecessary. At the fifth step, she leapt over the banister and landed silently on the floor below, hidden from the living room.

My mouth hung open for a second before I realized she expected me to do the same. I shook my head.

She rolled her eyes and walked into the kitchen like she honestly thought me jumping over this thing was going to work. I hovered on the step, debating if I could swing around the bottom step quickly enough to miss the notice of the living room. It wasn't likely.

I hurled myself over the banister before I could talk myself out of it. Trying to mimic Blythe's movements as best I could, I was shocked when I landed upright. Wobbling slightly to the side, but I had come out of it unscathed. My landing hadn't made a sound. Whatever spell Blythe had used worked perfectly.

I hurried to the supply pantry and squeezed inside with Blythe and Lyra.

"What now?"

Lyra shook her head. "Desmond and Felix are, like, the laziest people I know," she said. "They're not getting off their asses unless absolutely necessary."

"Lazy Emissaries," Blythe mumbled. "You down on recruitment quotas or something?"

Lyra peeked out from the pantry. "Probably just figured Em wouldn't come back here so soon. Especially after Salem," she said. "Put the best resources into finding her."

"I'm flattered," I muttered.

"Jax, grab us some beers, would ya?" one of the men called.

Lyra rolled her eyes. "See, won't even get their own fucking beers."

"Go," I said, looking around to see what we still had in stock.

"You got a way to get them out of there?" she asked. "If I—Jax starts going through your stuff, they're going to have questions, and I only have a few grunts to choose from."

I'd already started going through drawers, pulling out what I needed. "I do." Unlike the little rune schooling I'd had, the lessons on what could become volatile if mixed incorrectly had stuck with me.

Blythe's eyes widened. "You're not serious."

"You got a better idea?"

Lyra took in the ingredients I'd already set out. "This is going to be fun." She closed the door behind her, and I heard the fridge opening. We didn't have too much time before Desmond and Felix started asking questions.

"Grab me some muslin bags," I said, pointing to the cabinet next to Blythe.

She pulled one out and handed it to me. "Don't make it too big if you want a house to come back to," she warned.

Into the mortar I tossed everything Wes had always told me not to. Basil with sage, spearmint and rosemary, chamomile with mint, thyme, and parsley. There were good reasons they shouldn't be planted together. A pinch of Solomon's seal and yarrow for that extra punch. Garlic followed by black salt turned it into the most pungent thing I'd ever made.

Blythe wrinkled her nose as I ground everything into a fine powder. Tipping it all into the open bag in her hands, I added a long wick and tied the bag shut, keeping the top of the wick exposed.

Scooping up a lighter from the countertop, I headed out. Blythe's usual scowl had turned into something closer to surprise, my turn to spontaneity unexpected for the both of us. But I had come here for the book that belonged to me and I wasn't leaving without it.

I tried the lighter a few times, but it wouldn't take. Frustrated, I pulled my magic to the surface with one intention at the ready and lit the wick. "*Ardeat*," I commanded. The wick lit like a detonating cord and burned quickly towards the powder inside the bag.

"Get the car," I told Blythe, not bothering to whisper anymore.

She nodded and bolted for the door at the same time the two men in the living room turned their heads to the kitchen. I tossed the bag at them.

The contents let out a high-pitched whine when they ignited, and I rushed for the shelves. The sound grew louder and louder until it exploded and knocked the now standing men into the opposite wall.

"The fuck did you put in that thing?" Lyra yelled over the whining that was still filling the room as sparks exploded like mini fireworks.

Yanking Amity's grimoire off the shelf, we sprinted for the front door as the two men tried to collect themselves. We jumped the steps to the pavement, and I spotted Blythe pulling the car out of the lot and turning towards us.

Something heavy clipped my side, sending me sprawling into the snowbank and the book flew from my grip. A clay pot lay smashed next to me, potting soil scattered around it.

Lyra—back to herself—skidded to a stop in the street. Rolling onto my back, I groaned as pain lanced up my side. Sebastian stood on the sidewalk, smiling at me like I'd done something mildly entertaining.

His gaze flicked to Amity's book, lying open a few feet from me. He flicked his fingers at the same time I lunged for it.

I flattened myself on top of the book as it lifted into the air—exasperating the pain in my side—and glared up at Sebastian. He closed the distance between us quickly and I kicked out, catching his shin. He let out a hiss of pain and I scrambled to my feet, clutching the book.

"You can't escape this," he said.

Hot anger bubbled inside me. It was ready and aimed at the man in front of me. "Watch me."

He raised his hand at the same time I harnessed that anger into power. Our magic clicked into place and his arm dropped to his side. His face screwed up as his own power tried to come to his defense. It pounded against my control like a battering ram.

I sent a surge of magic forward, driving his defenses back and sending him to his knees. He let out a grunt and tried to stand again, but I wasn't going to let him.

Tires slid to a stop behind me. "Get in!" Lyra called.

Not yet. He needed to understand just who he was dealing with. I sent another wave and his scowl turned to pain. Good.

"Boswell!" Blythe's voice cut through everything, numbing the current of power that had taken over my thoughts. It brought me back to what we came to do—this wasn't it.

I backed into the car and yanked the back door open before releasing my hold on him. I tumbled into the back seat and Blythe sped off, the momentum closing the door. Breathing heavily, I slumped against the leather, hugging the book to my chest.

Chapter 11

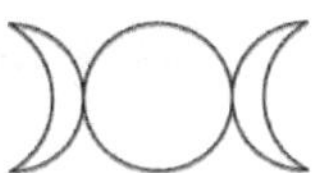

Wolfe's Bend was half an hour northwest of Crawford and straddled the Maine River. Lyra insisted it was better to stay out of the way in case Sebastian was already following us.

I'd wanted to cross the border as soon as we could, but we knew they'd be watching the crossing points carefully in case we did just that. As much as I hated it, it did make more sense to stop for the night. Lyra won out, and we agreed to stay in the small town.

It was a town off the map for most of the year. Their one claim to fame was their annual Fall Festival. Every October, they'd put on weeklong festivities—falling around the full moon to add to the mysterious legend behind the town's founding.

Seven families from Germany settled sometime before the Revolutionary War and built their new home. And it did feel like an old European town, if nothing else. Snow capped the brightly colored buildings, and iron lampposts lit the narrow main street.

The stone bridge connecting the two sides of town had recently been cleared of snowfall, and large wolf heads of carved stone stood sentry on all four of its corners, lending to the old-world Gothic feel.

This particular aesthetic wasn't the reason Lyra had been so keen on staying. Everyone in the magical community knew the lore of those founding families—to varying degrees. They'd fled their homes near the

Black Forest because of hunters. They weren't witches in the sense that we were, but a magical people with the ability to change into wolves. Werewolves, essentially. This, apparently, drew hatred from the religious fanatics of the day, and so the families left to avoid death.

Lyra was hoping the rumors of the seven bloodlines were true. That had been the draw for her, especially since the invite to her Solstice party had gone unanswered. She assumed it was because they'd been busy. I didn't have it in me to tell her it was probably because the rumors were just that.

Wolfe's Bend Inn wasn't far from the bridge and looked like a gingerbread house. Combined with the recognizable German fairytale lettering, it almost felt fake—or like a trap.

The woman at the front desk looked up when we walked in the lobby and smiled at us with unsettlingly perfect teeth.

"Hello," she said. "What can we do for you?"

"Just need a room for the night," Lyra said.

The woman nodded and uncapped a pen with her teeth. "Shouldn't be a problem," she said around the cap in her mouth. "Don't get too many visitors this time of year." She added the last part with an eyebrow raise.

Lyra shrugged. "We're headed north," she explained. "Thought we'd check it out."

The woman took the cap out of her mouth and clicked her tongue as she made a note in the logbook on her desk. "Just need an ID and a credit card, please."

My heart jumped and beat a little faster. Her eyes flicked to me. I tried to rearrange my face. Ian always said I had a terrible poker face.

Lyra pulled out her fake from Z and a credit card I didn't recognize like it was no big deal. The woman looked them over, her smile widening.

"Lovely." She keyed in the information on the card and handed it back to Lyra. "Just going to copy the ID." She waited a moment as if expecting Lyra to argue. When no one said anything, she turned and moved into a room just behind the check-in area.

The way the woman watched us, as if calculating our every move, made me nervous. Lyra trusted Z and their skill. But it occurred to me—a little too late—that if her brothers knew about her connection to Z, they'd know how good the IDs were.

I tried to shake the feeling from my mind. I'd grown up looking over my shoulder, so it was second nature at this point. But it was worse now. Every black SUV made my heart race, or whenever a stranger looked at me too long I wanted to bolt. Even that woman's too-wide smile made me jumpy.

The woman returned with the ID, passing it and two golden keys on large wooden keychains engraved with wolves back to Lyra.

"Room one-thirteen," she said. She pointed to our right. "Stairs are at the end of the hall," she continued. "Wi-Fi password is in the information packet in the room." She counted out three slips of paper and slid them over. "These are vouchers for the diner across the way. We're remodeling our restaurant at the moment."

"Thanks," Lyra said, scooping them up. She hefted her bag over her shoulder and headed down the hallway.

"Enjoy your stay," the woman called after us. Her voice made the hair on my arms stand.

The room was decently sized, with two queen beds, a desk, a mini fridge, and a microwave. A sliding door opened to a balcony. The bathroom had a standing shower, a large soaking tub, and wallpaper with more wolves.

Lyra dumped her bag on the bed by the balcony doors and yanked the tie out of the end of her braid. "We need drinks," she said, shaking her hair out.

"Food," I suggested.

"Both," Blythe said, flopping down on the end of the other bed and kicking her shoes off.

"I'll see what they have down the street," Lyra offered, grabbing one of the room keys and stuffing it in her pocket.

I went to the bathroom as she left and carefully pulled my sweater off. The pot Sebastian had hit me with managed to get me pretty good, but thanks to my coat and other layers it hadn't broken skin. It was red and irritated and would turn into a nasty bruise, though.

After cleaning it up with a warm cloth, I changed into sweats and went back into the main room. Curling up on the empty bed, I stared at the

TV program Blythe had turned on. I wasn't sure how long I sat like that, but eventually the sound of turning pages caught my attention.

Blythe was sitting up, legs crossed, and thumbing through Amity's book.

"What are you doing?" I asked.

"She really wrote *everything* down," she marveled, not looking up.

"How'd you get—"

"It's a basic concealment charm," she said, rolling her eyes. "Anyone with half a brain could get in."

I stood up and moved to grab it back. "Doesn't mean I *want* anyone getting in."

She didn't stop me from taking it. "Besides, there's nothing in there about Binders," I said.

She stared at me.

"There wasn't one in the family until later," I continued, clutching the book like it might jump out of my hands.

Blythe stood and faced me. "I don't need to know how to practice my own magic," she shot back.

"Then why—"

"You done in the bathroom?" she asked, pushing past me without waiting for any answer. She closed the door with more force than necessary. I sat back down and ran my hand over the now-exposed cover.

I shouldn't have snapped. Knowing where I came from and the magic inside me was something I was still working on. Questions I never got to ask mom, questions she may not have even been able to answer and that weren't going to go away. But now another Blood Witch was here, and I *still* couldn't let go of my paranoia.

I let out a long sigh and tossed the book to the side. Before I could settle in, I got a text from Lyra telling me to get ice for the wine. Grabbing the bucket and the room key, I set out to find the machine. According to the map in the packet, the closest one to us was near the lobby.

It was tucked in a small inlet, and I frowned at it. It wasn't making any noise. I set the bucket under the dispenser and pressed the button. Nothing happened. Of course. Rubbing my forehead, I turned to ask the woman at the front where I could find another machine.

"Three of 'em," she said. "Said they were passin' through."

I crept closer to the entrance and peered around the corner. Her back was to me, and the coiled phone cord wound around the computer.

"Cres should know."

Did the Collective have spies in a place this small? Did hunters?

"Whatever *she* decides." There was venom in her tone I hadn't expected given all the friendliness from earlier. I waited another moment, but either the call was over or whoever was on the other end was carrying the conversation.

Ducking back into the inlet, I grabbed the bucket and turned to leave. Starting, I dropped the bucket when I came face to face with the woman.

She caught it before it could hit the ground. "Hello, dear," she said. "Lost?"

I shook my head. "I think the ice machine is broken," I said, pointing at it lamely.

She gave me a slow smile. "I have some in the back room."

I took the bin back. "We're fine," I said a little too quickly. "Thank you." I took a few steps away and walked as casually as I could back down the hall, resisting the urge to look back and see if she was watching me.

I took the stairs back up two at a time while racking my brain to see if there was anything we did to tip her off about who we were. There was no way she could have known, unless Lyra's fake hadn't done its job. We couldn't stay here.

Locking the door behind me, I found Lyra opening the first bottle of wine.

"Ice?"

"Machine's broken," I said, tossing the bin back on the counter.

"Then we'll start with the red," Lyra declared, pouring it out into the plastic cups. She offered me one.

I shook my head. "We have to go."

Lyra cocked her head. "Why?"

I grabbed my coat off the bed. "The lady at the front desk just called someone and told them we were here."

Blythe clicked the TV to a new channel. "Who'd she call?"

"I don't know."

"And she told them we, *specifically*, were here?" Lyra asked.

I draped my coat over folded arms. "I don't know."

Blythe set the remote on the table between the two beds. "What *do* you know?"

I sighed. "She told them three people showed up and told her they were passing through," I said. "Which is exactly what we told her."

Lyra put her hands on my shoulders. "That's what anyone who shows up this time of year is going to say."

I shrugged her off. "How many people could that possibly be?"

"Enough to keep the place open in the offseason," Blythe offered, scooting off the bed to pour herself a cup of wine.

"But—"

"Have some wine, snacks, and sleep," Lyra said. "Things will seem less paranoia-y in the morning."

"She mentioned someone named Cres," I offered.

Lyra frowned. "I don't know anyone named Cres." She looked over at Blythe.

Blythe shook her head. "Nope."

Lyra turned back to me. "See."

I bit the inside of my cheek to keep myself from screaming. We were barely four hours from Portland. Four hours was nothing for someone determined enough. "What if you're wrong?" I asked.

"Oh, for fuck's sake," Blythe said, setting the cup of wine down. She dug out the safety pin from her bag and pricked her index finger before striding over the door.

"What are you—" But the answer came seconds later as she drew an intricate rune above the door's lock. The static of magic in the air made the hair on my arm stand as the rune glowed red. It seeped into the wood as if it had never been there and the air returned to normal.

Blythe turned back to us. "There. No one uninvited is getting in. Can we drink now?"

Lyra pursed her lips to hide the smile and raised her eyebrows at me. I sagged onto the bed; I clearly wasn't going to win this one. Blythe's ward did make me feel better about it, though. If I trusted blood wards enough for the Sandusky house, I had to trust them now.

Lyra once again offered me a cup of wine, and this time I took it, then she raised her own cup. "To us and our fucking awesomeness."

Blythe snorted, but the small half-smile gave her away.

I tipped back almost half the cup before Lyra had finished her toast. She grabbed her phone and turned on some music, and before I knew it, we'd gone through a bottle and half of wine and three bags of chips.

After Blythe and Lyra had started a round of bashing mutual connections—Sebastian prominently featured—I grabbed the half-empty bottle of Riesling and stepped out onto the balcony overlooking the river. I slid the door closed on Blythe's nasally impression of someone I didn't know—but which Lyra found hilarious.

Wrapping my sweater tighter around myself, I took a deep breath of the fresh air. Below, the river wound by, and somewhere overhead an owl called. It was peaceful here, distant, somewhere it would be easy to forget the last few weeks.

Ian would like it here. He was a lot more adventurous when it came to the outdoors than I was. We'd gone camping a couple of times in high school, hiking and everything. I preferred my nature a little closer to indoor plumbing.

Wiping away a tear that escaped, I pulled out the phone Z had given me. Just like they said, all the contacts were there. My thumb hovered over Ian's name. He didn't remember me. That didn't stop the ache to hear his voice, his laugh. It didn't stop the impossible hope that maybe hearing *my* voice would be enough to break the spell.

I set the wine on one of the snow-covered patio chairs and held my hand up, open palm towards the river.

"*Sonus removere,*" I whispered. It silenced the rush of the river and creak of the woods. All I heard was my own breathing. Taking a swig of wine, I scrolled until I found the name I was looking for. Lyra had contacted Z, and they'd assured us my calls to Ian hadn't been traced that easily. Lyra trusted them and, for once, the reputation of Blood Witches didn't bother me if it meant Z would be less likely to lie.

It rang three times before he picked up. "Hello?"

"Ian was off limits."

Jax sighed. "I know," he said. "I'm sorry."

"You're *sorry*?" I practically yelled, glad the spell also meant Lyra and Blythe wouldn't be able to hear me.

"I told them that wasn't..." He paused as if trying to come up with the right words.

"If they wanted any kind of civil end to this," I started, hot tears spilling over, "they shouldn't have taken my best friend."

"Em," he said softly. "No one wanted that, but—"

"No," I said, gripping the neck of the bottle so tightly my knuckles whitened. "*You* could have made sure he was safe. But you had to come after me."

"You ran," he countered, harsher than I expected. "They wouldn't have sent anyone if you had just stayed and met with them."

I let out a bitter laugh and wiped the tears off my cheeks with the back of my sleeve. "How'd you even know where we were?" I asked instead. His own grandmother had told me to run, a member of the Council herself. I had enough of my own guilt, but I wasn't about to be scolded into thinking it hadn't been the right decision.

He didn't answer right away, and I thought he wasn't going to. A faint clicking on the other side told me he wasn't stalling for words but for someone to try to figure out where I was. Time to find out if Z was worth what I paid.

He sighed. "Thea called," he said. "Told us she ran into Lyra at Sabbats."

I snorted.

"She thought she was helping," he insisted.

My stomach flipped. He was defending a woman who thought the worst of me without knowing me. A woman convinced I'd enchanted him. I wished it had just been jealousy over him defending an ex, that would have been a lot simpler.

"I have to go."

"Wait," he said.

I wasn't sure why I did.

"Talk to me," he said softly.

I imagined him running his hand over his jaw, the way he did when he was stressed—when *I* stressed him out. I bit my trembling lip and shut my eyes against more tears. I was getting so sick of crying.

He continued. "I know you felt like you didn't have a choice."

I took a shuddering breath. "Just because you don't agree with my choice, doesn't mean I didn't have one."

"Em—"

"Lyra's okay," I said. "You and Leander should know that."

I hung up before he could say anything else. There was nothing I wanted to hear from him. Not tonight. It may have been harsh not letting him get his piece out, but I wasn't in the mood. As angry as I was, I still didn't want to say something that would make it worse. Irreparable.

"*Reditus*," I said, waving at the river. Sound returned and I watched the water in the dark for a few more minutes. Finishing the bottle, I turned to go back inside, but three sets of glowing amber orbs stalled me.

I stared at them for a moment, but with a quick shake of my head they were gone. The cold drove me back inside just as I convinced myself the wine had my mind playing tricks on itself.

Chapter 12

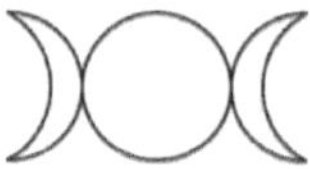

When we checked out the next morning, the woman had been replaced by a younger guy—Rafe, according to the name tag. He asked no questions when we turned the keys in and only gave us the obligatory goodbye any guest would have gotten.

It was almost nine o'clock and Lyra wasn't fully awake, even though she'd managed to sleep through the night. I fell asleep quickly but never managed to stay asleep for more than a few hours at a time, thanks to the eerie feeling of being watched. The wine headache didn't help any of us.

Earthshine Diner played into the town theme. It made the rumors Lyra wanted to be true that much more unbelievable. If there *were* werewolves in town, their choice of motifs was questionable.

We found a booth by the window, near a small couch occupied by two girls. One had an apron and a name tag for the diner and gave us a warm smile before returning her attention to her companion. The other girl was about the same age, with short silver hair and a large cut down the front of her face. It was still pink, fresh enough it hurt to look at. I turned away, not wanting to get caught staring, and focused on the gray winter morning outside.

Our vouchers were good for one hot breakfast each. I didn't think I could stomach anything too big, so I opted for oatmeal and green tea. We spent the time between ordering and eating on reviewing the route.

It would take a little over an hour to get to the border crossing from here. Martin lived in Elmswell Harbour, a small coastal town about two hours south of Halifax. If we didn't run into any problems, we'd be there in seven hours.

Yet another reason I wanted to get on the road.

Lyra wasn't thrilled with our quick departure. I wasn't sure if it was the wine hangover, waking her up before she wanted, or the fact that she hadn't met any werewolves that had put her in a sour mood, but I chose not to ask until she'd had her coffee.

As we ate, I noticed our server didn't stop watching Lyra. A stocky boy in the corner blatantly stared at Blythe while we settled the bill. I added honey to my takeaway tea and the woman at the counter gave me a nervous smile. They *really* weren't used to getting visitors this time of year.

Back at the car, Lyra put her coffee in the front cupholder and stretched, ending it with a loud yawn. She froze, then lowered her arms slowly, staring up the street. She frowned, zipping up her jacket, and headed in that direction.

"Where are you going?" I called after her.

"I saw something," she said, quickening her pace.

I caught Blythe's eye over the hood of the car.

She twirled her key ring over her finger. "We could leave her."

Sighing, I shut the door Lyra had left open and followed her. A beat later, Blythe fell into step next to me. We caught up to Lyra just inside the line of trees that made up the woods surrounding the town.

"Lyra?"

"It could be a wolf," she said.

"It's not even close to a full moon," Blythe reminded her.

"Everyone knows that's a myth," Lyra said.

"No one knows that," Blythe muttered.

Lyra waved a hand behind her as if to shush and moved further into the trees.

"Are you even sure you saw something?" I mumbled, trying not to spill my tea as we stepped through the branches and sticks covered by snow.

"Is she still drunk?" Blythe asked, shoving her hands into her pockets.

"She can fucking hear you," Lyra hissed over her shoulder. We walked another few minutes before she finally stopped, frowning around at the trees.

We leveled with her. "Is your curiosity satisfied?" I asked.

"I swear I saw something."

"Maybe werewolves can turn invisible," Blythe said.

Lyra let out a short, fake laugh. "It's a tad early for your cynicism," she said.

I turned back the way we came when Blythe's sharp intake of breath and Lyra's vise-like grip on my arm stopped me.

I spun back around. "Ow—what the..."

The question died in my throat.

A creature, black against the snowy ground, stood staring at us. From this distance, it appeared cat-like, but bigger and...eerier. It slunk towards us, moving from between two trees before stopping to stare again. My feet were frozen to the spot despite my brain screaming at me to run.

"It's like a tiny panther," Lyra breathed.

"Because Maine is known for its wild panther population," Blythe countered.

"Does it look like a fucking house cat?"

The creature prowled closer. A sleek black—except for a patch of white on its chest. A large circle with what looked like brush strokes sweeping from either side, crescents facing opposite directions. A familiar symbol...

I closed my eyes and let out a breath through my nose. "Lyra," I asked quietly, opening my eyes. "Did you cast the familiar spell?"

She was quiet for a moment and her grip on my arm loosened. "Possibly."

"*Possibly?*" Blythe hissed.

Lyra grimaced "I had a lot of wine, and Amity's book was *right* there."

"Seriously?" I snapped as Blythe let out a groan.

Lyra waved her hand at the creature as it watched our hushed argument. "It can't be that bad," she said. "I mean, look at it. It's cute."

"We have no idea what *it* is," I countered. "There's a reason no one uses those spells anymore." The cat creature cocked its head to the side as if it heard—and understood—me.

Mom and Wes had warned against doing any spell that might call a familiar. If cast with ill intent or selfish aims, the Otherworld could send something to match, and that was never good. A familiar called out of negativity breeds the same. I didn't think Lyra—drunk or not—would cast it with anything negative in mind, but I didn't want to know *what* her drunk brain came up with.

It blinked at me a few times, and I swore it smirked. Gray-black smoke began to roll off its back. Translucent at first, like mist off water, but then it solidified. On either side of the creature now stood two just like it. The three moved together, closing the distance between us.

The one at the center, its white patch round and missing the brush strokes, sat in front of me. The top of its head came to my knee. It looked up at me, eyes red to match the ruby hanging around my neck. The one curling around Lyra's legs had a white mark that resembled a waxing crescent moon on its chest and bright blue eyes. The one stopped at Blythe's feet had a waning crescent and black eyes rimmed with red.

"Cool." Lyra bent over and scooped up the cat. It nuzzled against her neck. "See, it's fine." She stroked the cat's fur and it purred loudly.

"Just because it didn't eat your face off doesn't mean it's fine," I said, trying to take a step away from the probing stare of the cat-thing in front of me.

Blythe had gone stone still under the cat's gaze. It moved closer and she flinched, taking a jarring step away from it.

"Make it go away."

"Try petting it," Lyra suggested.

"Do I look like a cat person to you?" Blythe bit back.

Lyra smiled over at her. "Do you want me to answer that honestly?"

Blythe shot her a glare.

"Put it down," I told Lyra. "And let's go."

Lyra frowned. "But they're ours."

I turned away from the piercing eyes of the thing in front of me. "There's no way we clear the border with them, so they stay." I didn't wait to see if she'd put it down as I took the path we'd came down, but I did hear her grumbling.

When we emerged back onto the main street, she was thankfully sans cat. Blythe unlocked the car, and I opened the back door and let out half a scream. The creature was sitting on the seat, staring at me with those red eyes.

"They're in my car," Blythe hissed, waving her hand at the creature like that would actually get it to move.

People in the diner were watching us through the window.

"Guess they don't want to be left behind," Lyra said, smugness more than a little irritating.

As more people came to the window to see what was stalling us, I realized we didn't have time to figure out a way to leave them behind without drawing more attention. They clearly had their own magic.

"You have one hour to figure out how to hide them from Border Patrol," I hissed to Lyra before climbing in the back seat. The creature moved for me and the one in Blythe's seat hopped into the back.

Lyra's familiar curled up in her lap as soon as she buckled in. As Blythe pulled away from the curb, the three of the creatures let out a sound like an eerie lullaby best forgotten.

Chapter 13

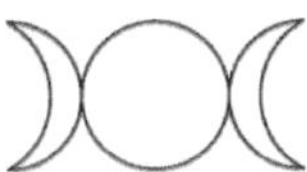

The crossing at Calais was practically empty when we arrived. We'd pulled off earlier to put a quick disruption charm on Blythe's license plates to keep them free of any recordings. Neither Blythe nor I had done the spell before, but Lyra was too busy attempting her own charm on the cat-things. So far, none of her known or new spells had done anything to help.

Otherworld beings had their own magic that was far more potent than ours. I would have been impressed if she'd managed to tint their fur, let alone hide them completely. Still, she refused to leave them behind. Instead, her plan was to enchant the agents into mistaking the creatures for suitcases.

Lyra and I were already using fake passports, and spelling the agents was risky—but avoiding detention because we didn't have any documentation for our supernatural strays was worth it.

Wiping my sweaty hands on my pants, I watched the gray minivan in front of us move up. The agent waved us forward, and I forced myself to fix my expression. Calm was what I was going for, bored would have been better, but the anxiety clawing at my insides made that impossible.

Blythe put the car into park and rolled her window down to pass over our IDs. I swallowed hard and pressed my thumbnail into the opposite palm to keep myself from letting my leg shake. I didn't want to fidget.

The agent said something that got a polite chuckle from Blythe before he asked her to roll down the window to the back seat. Lyra slid her hand over the console slowly, doing her best not to draw attention. Without direct contact, she would have to direct the spell another way, and this was never as successful. This had been a tremendously idiotic idea.

I glanced over at the creatures in the seats next to me and let out a gasp just as the window opened all the way that I tried to turn into a cough when the agent cocked an eyebrow at me.

He frowned but didn't comment. The cats had completely vanished—not concealed, not blending in with the black leather, completely gone. I resisted the urge to reach out and feel for them to make sure we hadn't just had some sort of shared hallucination.

After our passports cleared and the standard questions were answered appropriately, we were welcomed into Canada.

"What did you do?" I asked Lyra as soon as the whir of the windows going up stopped.

Lyra turned around in her seat and her gaze swept the back. "That wasn't me," she insisted.

"Then who—gah!"

All three creatures reappeared with a *pop*, one right in my lap. The one with blue eyes licked its paw like it hadn't just been interrupted by an international border crossing.

"Oh, aren't you just the cleverest little thing," Lyra cooed, reaching back to scratch behind its ears.

I caught Blythe's eye roll in the mirror as she merged into traffic.

○

Five and a half hours later and we drove under the large ornate sign welcoming us to Elmswell Harbour. Banners hung on the lampposts on either side of the street, advertising a celebration months early. "Home of Solstice Days," a festival held in June, and I could imagine the traffic it brought in. Summer fun combined with the haze of magic that hung in the air. It wasn't nearly as strong as Salem—due to the lack of family connections for me—but it was strong enough I knew this town was made by, and for, witches. And that drew mortals like moths to light.

Now, the coastal town was blanketed by snow and frost, empty and cold. The residents, no doubt, were bundled up in their homes with warm fires and drinks.

Even the three creatures were unusually still and quiet when we'd crossed the town limits. Not that they'd been excitable during the drive, but it was more unnatural the further we got.

The main strip had shops catered to summer tourism—closed for the season—like day tours out to Ascendant Island, haunted walks, outdoor fresh seafood stands, and bike rentals. These were mixed in with local businesses ranging from a law firm to a very vintage drug store.

We weren't the only ones out, but to describe the others as "traffic" was being generous. It was late enough I hadn't expected it to be busy, but the emptiness gave off the impression we'd stick out.

Lyra spent the majority of the drive in the back seat with the creatures and all the books. She wanted to know what kind of familiars the Otherworld had sent in response to her call.

Unfortunately, her research hadn't gleaned any answers. The cats—for lack of a better term—hadn't been hard to travel with. Though, once they went to sleep and I couldn't feel their stares, the drive was far more enjoyable.

Except for Blythe. The closer we'd gotten to Elmswell, the worse her disposition became. Now that we were actually in town, her dark mood filled the car.

The road split off at the end of the downtown strip and we could either wind further inland or take the coastal route. Blythe veered left and took us along the coastline. From here, we could see the boat slips for the local fishing community, a storehouse for shipping seafood, and a pirate-themed pub.

As the road continued, it became obvious what part of town we were headed to. Private boat slips—gated—and large houses. The road climbed upwards to a neighborhood dubbed "Ascendant Point." It was high enough to overlook the town below and the ocean.

A large iron gate at the top of the incline blocked the way. The rest of the fence was nothing special, but the main gate itself had metalwork of the constellations built into it.

Blythe pulled up and leveled with a small security box. It was small, black, and easy to miss in the dark if you didn't know it was there. There was no keypad, no camera, or speaker I could see. We sat there and let a couple awkward seconds pass.

"Blood sacrifice?" Lyra teased.

Blythe rolled her eyes with a sigh before rolling down the window. A bluish-green light came from the box as soon as she leaned slightly out of the window. It engulfed the space between it and the car, receding after a few heartbeats.

She leaned back into the car and rolled the window back up without a word. The gate swung soundlessly for us.

"Biometrics?" Lyra asked, leaning forward to rest her forearms on the console between the two front seats.

"Something like that," Blythe said as the gate closed behind the car.

Lyra opened her mouth to say something else, but then closed it after taking in Blythe's profile for a moment. "You good?"

"Fine."

"Really? Because you look like you're going to puke."

Blythe gave her a half-shrug in response, and I wondered if that meant she *did* feel like she was about to vomit. She looked paler than before, and I was about to ask why when my attention landed fully on the mansion Blythe pulled up to.

Mama's house was large, but this place was *massive*. It was the furthest back from the gate—not that the gated community had too many residents—and built into the rocky cliffs that edged this side of the point. Lights around the property showed off the pristine white of the outside and there were more windows than I could count.

It kept going, hiding the ocean from view behind it and spreading out to either side of the road. My best guess put it at double the bedrooms as Mama's, maybe triple. Whoever Martin Foster was, he was doing *very* well for himself.

Blythe turned into the long driveway and up to the garage, pulled down the visor and clicked the small button. The garage door furthest from the front door opened and she pulled forward.

"What the fuck?" Lyra whispered with a chuckle.

"It's late," Blythe said. "We should use the front door." She hopped out of the car with no other explanation.

I raised my eyebrows at Lyra.

"What the fuck," she repeated. We climbed out of the car with nothing else to do but follow her. The garage was large enough to fit six cars at least. In addition to Blythe's car, there were three others parked inside. A blue BMW SUV, a white Range Rover, and a small black sports car.

Pulling a practically drooling Lyra away from the sports car, I grabbed my bag out of the back.

"Do you know what that is?" Lyra hissed at me, peeking around me to ogle the car again.

"No," I admitted. "But can you freak out later?" I nudged her and jerked my chin at Blythe, who was waiting for us. She was far more tense than I'd seen her.

"Right." Lyra grabbed her own bag and made sure the cats were clear before closing the door. The garage closed silently behind us, as if having sensed our exit.

The front door was so tall I had to crane my neck to see the top of it, with frosted-over glass, and etched with an exact rendering of the night sky above us. A bright white spot streaked across the door, disappearing into the seam with the wall. A live rendering.

Blythe tapped her fingers against her leg and stared at the door. Shaking her head, she reached forward and pushed the small button.

The bell echoed through the house, and I felt it reverberate in my chest. Large, deep echoes like thunder to announce our arrival. It left a ringing in my ears.

Booming dog barks followed the end of the bell and all three cats hissed at the same time. Three pops and they vanished. Lyra raised her eyebrows at me but said nothing. I preferred they not be around for this. The three of us showing up was one thing; us plus unknown Otherworld creatures was another.

The ringing in my ears still hadn't stopped, and I pressed my palm to one of them to try to relieve it.

"What's up?" Lyra whispered to me.

I just shook my head, trying to shake the ringing out, and wiped my clammy hands on my leggings. Blythe ran a hand over her hair as if trying to smooth it. Lyra straightened next to me, brows drawn together at Blythe's back.

"How exactly do you know Martin?" Lyra asked.

"Hush." A command from the other side quieted the barking. Moments later, the door opened to reveal a tall man with salt-and-pepper hair, eyes so dark they could have been black, and a black silk robe tied at his waist. Two Rottweilers sat behind him, eyes trained on us.

The man's smile was ready for strangers but grew wide into a genuine grin when he spotted Blythe. He stepped forward and pulled her into a hug. She stayed stiff in the embrace.

"You're using the front door?" he asked, ending the hug but still holding her by the shoulders.

She nodded. "I didn't want to intrude on—" She stopped and glanced around him. "On anyone."

His smile slipped slightly. "You are never an intrusion," he said. "On *anyone*." He echoed her words with such an emphasis that I knew Lyra and I were missing something. He gave her a strong, affirmative nod before turning his attention to us.

"And who do we have here?" he asked.

Blythe shook his hands off and took half a step back towards us. "This is Em and Lyra," she said. "Friends."

He smiled expectantly.

"Hi," Lyra said with a half-wave. His smile didn't change, and I knew what he was waiting for. He wanted family names. But Blythe hadn't offered any, and I wasn't about to either. Both Lyra and I had family connections that would raise some questions I wasn't willing to answer just yet.

"Martin Foster," he finally said. "Please, come in." He stepped aside and we followed Blythe through the door. It closed on its own behind us. The high-ceilinged hall let out to an open living space with floor-to-ceiling windows overlooking a lighted backyard, devoid of snow, which looked like it dropped off into the ocean. In the daylight, I imagined, the view would be amazing.

His two dogs sniffed at our ankles as he led us through. He offered the couch with a sweep of his hand and took the chair across from it for himself. One of the large dogs put its head in his lap and the other curled up at Blythe's feet.

"So," Martin began, crossing an ankle over his knee. "No word from you in, what, almost a year? And now, here you are, in the flesh." He steepled his fingers and regarded the three of us.

Blythe crossed her arms and leaned back against the couch. I couldn't help the slight twinge of anger at how she'd downplayed her knowing Martin. She'd made it seem like an acquaintance at most, but that had clearly been a lie.

"Who was it, dear?" a woman said, sweeping into the room, a duster sweater wrapped around her, and a book tucked under her arm. Her graying hair was twisted into a loose bun at the base of her long neck. Her light green eyes took in the room and rested on each of us in turn.

"Blythe." Her voice was soft, but the curtness laced in the single word made Blythe tense next to me and the ruby sparked.

The woman perched herself on the armrest of Martin's chair and set her book on the side table. She draped an arm around Martin's shoulder.

"What brings you by?" she asked. "After, what, a year now?"

Blythe fisted her hands against her folded arms.

Martin put his hand on the woman's knee. "We were just getting to that, Selvina."

Selvina raised her thin eyebrows expectantly.

"We can stay somewhere else," Blythe said, voice small, not looking directly at either of them.

I hadn't thought of Blythe as timid until that moment. She'd slapped me and not been bothered, but these two asked a question and it was like she wanted to be eaten by the couch.

More bizarre, I had the urge to stick up for her. Against what, I didn't know, but my defensiveness was aimed at them.

"Of course not," Martin said. "You're my granddaughter and you're welcome anytime."

My mouth went dry and it took a lot of effort to not look at Blythe.

"You're a Foster?" Lyra hissed.

Selvina snorted.

Martin's hand tightened on her knee.

"Or not?" Lyra said, directing the question to the couple.

"She's an Osborne," Selvina said.

Blythe flinched like the name was a slap and the ruby sparked again. Like it had when we'd met and whenever she got too angry. Unable to stop myself, I turned to stare at the girl sitting next to me.

Blythe wasn't just a Blood Witch. She was an *Osborne* Blood Witch.

Chapter 14

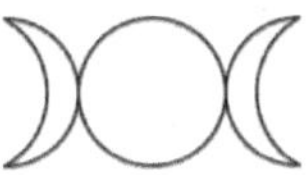

Blythe was suddenly too close to me. The dog's breathing was too loud. My breath wouldn't take and the tension swelled, making the room too small. There was no way this was real. It couldn't be.

"If this is a problem—"

Martin raised his hand to cut Blythe off. "It's not," he said. "We're just..." he paused to give himself extra time and glanced up at Selvina. "Concerned." With the amount of time he took, he probably could have come up with a better word to use. "You show up late and without warning, you cannot blame us for asking questions," he continued.

I could tell Blythe was struggling not to look at me as much as I was forcing myself to stare at her. "I just needed to get out of Salem for a bit," Blythe said, gaze falling to her lap.

"Of course you did," Selvina muttered. "What spell did you screw up now?" she added to Blythe.

"I didn't do anything," Blythe replied. Her voice was barely audible.

"You never do," Selvina said.

"Blythe thought you could help me," I said quickly. Processing could wait. Right now, I just needed to know if I'd wasted a trip. If Martin couldn't help me, I could leave Blythe—and everything her existence could mean—behind me.

His dark eyes moved to me. "Did she?"

"I have questions about memory modification spells," I told him. "She said you're the expert."

"And, you are?" Selvina snapped.

"Em," I offered.

Selvina's eyes widened, and Martin sat up a little straighter. His eyes grew darker as he glanced between Blythe and me, and a vein pulsed in his temple from how hard his jaw clenched. I opened my mouth to add my last name; since they seemed to care so much about family names, I'd have liked to see how they reacted to mine.

But I suppressed that urge. The Outliers weren't the Collective, but that didn't mean I wanted my whereabouts broadcast to either group right now. Not until I knew he could help me.

Martin glanced at Selvina for a moment. The woman's mouth was pursed in a firm line.

"You must all be tired from your travels," Martin finally said. "We can discuss this more tomorrow. Blythe knows where you can stay."

Blythe frowned at him, but that had obviously been a dismissal. Both Martin and Selvina stood and moved out of the room, though their hushed conversation carried over to us and I heard my name more than once.

We sat on the couch, none of us moving. A large family portrait hung above the fireplace behind the chair Martin had vacated: Martin and Selvina in the center, surrounded by who I assumed were their children and grandchildren, in front of a nondescript gray background. They had a large family. None of their smiles reached their eyes.

"So," Lyra started. "You're an Osborne."

Blythe stood and grabbed her bag, moving to the stairs on the other side of the living space. Lyra and I scrambled to follow her. Dozens of questions rolled around in my mind, but I clamped down on them until I could collect the chaos into coherent thoughts.

Those stairs led up to a long hallway and we moved past open bedroom doors. She didn't stop at any of them. Instead, we went up another set of half-stairs and came to a large room with a projector screen on the wall, overstuffed couches, and a wet bar with a mini fridge. Through that room, we found ourselves surrounded by four full-sized beds with twins above them like grown-up bunk beds.

The fulls were set up to have the foot of each bed pointed towards the center of the room; instead of a ladder, sets of block stairs built into the wall led up to the top bunks. At the far end of the room, a large window overlooked the backyard and the ocean. Lights from downstairs bled onto the clear grass.

Blythe tossed her bag onto a bed and went into the attached bathroom, shutting the door with a hard *snap*.

Lyra dropped her bag and flopped onto the bed closest to her. "That was fucking awkward."

I sank onto another of the beds. "Yeah." I glanced at the bathroom door.

"Congrats on the new cousin, though."

I glared at her.

"What?" she said, not even bothering to conceal the smile.

"Cousin's a stretch." I laid back and rubbed my hands over my face. My eyes hurt, my skin hurt, my brain hurt, and my stupid ears were still ringing. Attempting to process all this had wreaked havoc on my body. We weren't even sure she was one of *those* Osbornes.

Except I did.

The way the ruby responded to her, how my magic had reacted when I'd lashed out against her, and why she wasn't the biggest fan of the Boswells all made a lot more sense now.

Even with all that, cousin *was* a stretch. Our relation was centuries old. After the terrible family reunion that was Sebastian Charlevoix, I wasn't ready for any more cousins, no matter how distant they were.

I felt the stares before I heard the small meows. Groaning, I sat up and saw that all three cats had claimed the last of the four beds.

"Of course," I muttered. Pulling off my shoes, I tossed them to the side and stripped off my thick sweater to crawl under the covers. I pulled them over my head to block out the light and the cats. I didn't have the energy to deal with the creatures Lyra had drunk-summoned.

At some point, I heard the shower from the bathroom turn on, then off. A hushed conversation. That was the last thing I remembered before the dreams.

Amity was me as we ran through Old Salem. Lyra was in present-day Salem, also running. Blythe watched me run, the ruby crushed in her bloodied hands. Salem—old and new—burned.

○

It was either the sudden warmth or the red-eyed cat pawing at my chest that woke me. A toss-up, really. I sat up, clearing sweat from my forehead. Gently, I pushed the cat off. It moved to the end of the bed and curled up, eyes never leaving me.

Dim gray light peeked through the curtains not fully drawn over the window. Lyra and Blythe were asleep, the other two cats with them. Lyra's snuggled up next to her while the other one slept on the bed in the furthest spot from Blythe it could be.

I ran a hand through my hair, fingers catching on the mess of tangles my restless sleep had caused. Slipping off the bed, I went to the bathroom. My eyes were a dull red with large dark circles under them. No wonder Mama hadn't believed me when I said I'd been sleeping.

Under the warm water of the shower, I began to scrub away the itch the dreams left on my skin. I'd had bad dreams before—vividly bad—especially after mom died. All of those had drained me, but none of them stayed *on* me like this after waking up.

Even after the actual visions faded from memory, the lingering need to escape whatever ill fate the dreams had conjured stayed. It was like my cortisol production was dialed up to a thousand and all my body wanted to do was respond.

Only there was nothing to fight, nothing to run from. My own mind decided there were threats everywhere I went. I'd had enough to worry about, the last thing I needed was my brain making more up.

Wrapping my hair in a towel, I was glad to see my appearance had improved slightly with the steamy shower. What I wouldn't have given for one of Wes's mixtures right now.

By the time I forced myself out of the warm bathroom, Blythe's bed was empty, and Lyra's cat was trying to wake her up. She flopped over, swatting at the creature without opening her eyes.

After pulling on a clean pair of leggings and an oversized sweater, I found my phone in my jacket pocket. It needed a serious charge. I grabbed Amity's book and took it with me. Closing the door on the still-sleeping Lyra, I climbed onto the couch outside the bunk room and tapped Wes's name.

It was too early for him to be up, let alone answer calls, but I left him a quick message saying we'd made it okay and I'd call again later. The cat—who had followed me—hopped up and snuggled against my leg. I absently scratched it between its ears.

Cracking open the old book, I ran my fingers over the aged ink of the family tree inside. Mary Boswell and John Osborne, Amity's parents. Looking at it now, I wondered if the tree was missing a branch, one of a half-sibling of Amity's that was lost—or deliberately hidden.

"It's not him," Blythe said from the doorway.

I looked up and frowned at her. "What?"

She moved into the room and sat down next to me, pulling her legs under her. Her hair was damp, and the puffiness under her eyes had me wondering if she'd been crying. She sighed and held up her own book. The same one I'd seen on her shelf in her apartment with the Triple Moon symbol pressed into the front.

"John," she said. "It's not his line I'm from, technically."

"But, Osborne..."

She nodded and glanced down at the grimoire in her hands. She scratched at the stud in her nose before holding the leather-bound book out to me. I hesitated for a moment before taking it. Opening it slowly, I read the first page. Scrawled in the center, like a person would label a journal, was a single name: *Patience Osborne*.

"Who was she?" I asked.

Blythe hugged her knees, resting her chin on them. "John's niece."

I turned to the next page to find a family tree like mine. Written above Patience's name were her parents, Anne Osborne and Matthew Burroughs. From there were generations matching my own, one daughter after another. Amity and Patience were only the beginning. It didn't take long to count them.

"Thirteen," Blythe confirmed.

The universe's sick joke. I pinched my eyes shut and opened them again, hoping I wasn't seeing what I was, that this was part of the bad dream I couldn't wake up from.

"I didn't know John had a sister," I said, voice shaking a little. The next page was familiar, too—a different handwriting, but the same words. Isobel Jacob's prophecy, the words that set this all in motion.

I frowned at it. "Why would she record this?"

Blythe picked her head up to look at the page I was on and raised her eyebrows at me. "Because Anne thought it was about Patience and her line."

I'd been hit with a clay pot recently and that had been less of a shock. I closed the book and took a few steadying breaths to calm myself.

"You started without me?" a groggy Lyra said, walking out of the room and falling onto the lounge end of the couch, her hair a mess on top of her head. Her cat leapt up next to her and laid across her ankles.

"What'd I miss?" she asked through a yawn, looking between us.

I wasn't sure how best to explain to her what I'd learned. What it meant about—

"Dulvane," I breathed.

"Huh?" Lyra asked at the same time Blythe said, "Who?"

I met Lyra's gaze. "Why did Dulvane send you to Portland?" I asked her.

Lyra rubbed sleep from her eyes. "He had a vision that a powerful witch was at this club—well, he actually *unironically* used the phrase," she began, then dipped her voice low in what I assumed was an impersonation of Dulvane, "*den of iniquity*." She shrugged. "But you know how dramatic Seers can be."

Blythe let out a snort that sounded suspiciously like a laugh. I did—in fact—know that Seers liked their dramatics. Isobel Jacob was proof of that.

"But he told you Portland, specifically?"

Lyra shook her head. "He didn't give us like a GPS point or anything," she said. "He just made a big deal about getting to this witch or else horrible shit would happen."

I glanced at Blythe for a moment. "Then, why'd you end up in Onyx that night?"

"We did a tracer spell for magical anomalies and Portland popped like crazy, so off we went. Onyx was the third club we'd hit when we found you."

It was getting hard to breathe. "Portland is the only place the spell found?"

Again, she shook her head. "Salem lit up, too, but it's always a hotbed for power."

My mouth went dry. "Blythe," I asked slowly, "where were you on Samhain?"

Blythe looked between Lyra and me. "Sabbats," she said. "Friends took me out for my birthday."

My head swam.

"You were born on Samhain?" Lyra asked.

Blythe nodded.

"And you're the thirteenth generation," I said.

She nodded again.

"Patience..." I couldn't even bring myself to finish as nausea pinched my stomach.

Blythe hugged her knees tighter. "Anne's thirteenth daughter," she confirmed.

"Oh," Lyra said. She put a hand over her mouth and stared at the two of us. "Oh, fuck."

Blythe wiped a tear from her cheek quickly and I did my best to pretend I hadn't seen it.

"This is good, though," Lyra said, crossing her legs under her.

"How?" I choked out.

She shrugged. "I mean, between the two of you, Blythe is absolutely more the harbinger-of-war type, so you're off the hook!"

"Hey," Blythe shot.

Lyra winked at her, earning a half-smile and a watery chuckle.

Chapter 15

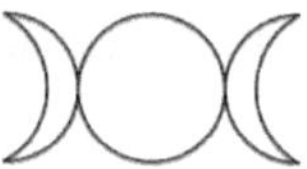

We found old movies to watch, and both Blythe and Lyra fell back asleep not long after the opening credits. I found it impossible to keep the churning thoughts quiet and sleep.

Two months ago, my life had changed forever. Changed due to a random choice. The Collective picked Portland because Blythe had hidden herself where they'd never notice her power. She'd embraced the world I'd run from. She accepted her magic, her history, and it had kept her safe from them, from hunters, from...me.

It could have been Blythe tossed into the Collective's sights. She easily could have been the one Jax, Lyra, and Leander found that night. She could have been the one to have her life upended because the Council put stock in Isobel Jacob's prophecy. And I could have been...

Dead.

It was that simple. Had they gone to Salem, I would be dead. The hunters hadn't used a spell to find me. They wouldn't have gone to Salem, not on Samhain. So, I would have died in that alley behind Onyx.

But Phoenix would be alive. Wes and Chad would be happy in their home. Ian would still have his memories, and Lyra wouldn't be on the run from her own family.

Wes taught me Nature had Her own way of doing things and we sometimes just got caught up in the flow of Her desires. There was meaning, a purpose behind it all, just not ours and we'd probably never see it. I'd been fine with that. Until now. Now, I needed to see the purpose—needed to have some kind of answer for why my life had gone so gloriously to shit.

I pressed the heels of my palms to my closed eyes, taking a series of deep breaths. Maybe I was wrong. There was no higher power determining anything and this was just the consequence of trying to control my own life.

Lyra let out a grunt and turned over under the throw blanket. I looked at her and the cat wrapped around her head. While I did miss the boring normalcy of my life before, it was hard to imagine a time when she wasn't there. Life before and life now were a running conflict in my own memory.

Truth was, I liked having her in my life. I liked having Jax—if he ever spoke to me again—around. I even found myself missing Sadiki's deep laugh. I wished there were a way I could have them in my life without any of the bad.

The movie credits rolled, and neither Lyra nor Blythe showed signs of waking up. I carefully slipped off the couch and grabbed my phone. Another call to Wes—and some fresh air—was due. Even one to Jax, now that anger and Riesling weren't fueling me.

The second-floor hall was quiet and my steps soft against the plush carpet. Even with that padding, however, I was nowhere near as silent as the cat moving next to me. It streaked ahead and positioned itself on the next set of stairs, keeping me from going down.

I tried to wave it out of the way, but it wouldn't move. It squinted at me but didn't let me by. I figured a less gentle nudge with my foot might work. It swiped back at me with a large paw.

"I want the Boswell girl out."

It wasn't just the venom with which Selvina spat my name that made me freeze on the top step, it was the fact that she knew it at all.

"We can't be overly hasty," Martin said, and I took a half-step closer to their voices. I didn't *want* to eavesdrop, but if they were going to throw me out before I had the chance to ask for help with Ian, I wanted to know.

"Hasty?" she echoed. "Blythe has done plenty of reckless things, but *this*?" She made a sound like a snort.

So, Blythe had told them who I was. She'd kept her secret from me but blurted mine out like it was nothing.

Selvina continued. "She's put a target on my family by bringing that girl here."

If they knew who I was, they probably knew the Council and hunters were both after me.

Martin cleared his throat. "Blythe is your family."

Selvina let out a harsh laugh. "She's barely yours, Martin."

No one spoke for a long moment, and I stepped back to go upstairs and pack.

"We cannot ignore the opportunity Emaleth presents."

I wasn't sure what set the itch on my skin: the way he used "opportunity," or that my last name wasn't the only thing he knew.

"Opportunity," she repeated, voice sounding like she was talking through clenched teeth. "Is that all you can think of? Your ambitions?"

"Keep your voice down," Martin commanded.

I swallowed and risked another half-step down. Peering around the wall, I could see them in the living room. Martin in the same chair as last night, a glass of amber liquid perched on the arm rest while one of his dogs laid his chin on the other.

Selvina paced in front of the fireplace, the other dog watching her from the floor in front of the couch. Her hair was slicked into a tight ponytail, and she wore loose black trousers and a black sweater.

"The girls will stay as long as they're needed."

I didn't like the sound of that any more than being called an opportunity.

Selvina paused her pacing and turned to face Martin, crossing her arms. "The Boswell curse will bring nothing but disaster," she said. "And I don't know if it's your stubbornness or pride that blinds you to it."

Curse?

He downed the rest of his drink. "Perhaps both."

She frowned. "What aren't you telling me?"

He shook his head.

She snorted. "More lies."

"Selvina, please, I thought we were past this." Martin stood and I ducked behind the wall as he walked to the drink cart. I heard the clink of glass as he poured another one. Whatever I'd been overhearing couldn't have been good if he needed two drinks.

"Why?" she said. "Your lies and affair with *that* woman are the reason we have to deal with Blythe in the first place."

"Enough!"

Glass shattered and I clapped a hand over my own mouth to stop the small squeak of surprise. One of the dogs whined and the hackles rose on the cat's back.

"They. Stay." Martin's voice was dangerous and sent a chill through me. The room darkened despite sunlight filtering through the windows.

"Brunch is ready, go get the girls," Martin said after a moment.

I tried to force my feet to move, not wanting to get caught by either of them, but something kept me rooted. The cat swiped at my ankle with its claws and the sting of the small cut brought my senses back. I rushed down the hall and sprinted back to the den.

For all I knew, Selvina had been close enough to see me round the second set of stairs, but I didn't look back to check. Closing the den door, I flung myself onto the couch, pulled a blanket over my head, and tried to steady my breathing.

○

Any other time I would have enjoyed the food they'd put out for us. Chad would have devoured it and asked for recipes. There was pumpkin and bacon quiche, spiced sweet potato hash with chorizo, green shakshuka with avocado and lime, a smoked salmon tart, lemon ricotta pancakes, and a sour cream coffee cake. It all smelled fantastic.

But I was too distracted to enjoy any of it. I was trying to fill in gaps of missing information and failing miserably. Why had Blythe told them who I was? What opportunity did Martin think I was? We were apparently staying as long as needed, but needed for what? And what *exactly* was the Boswell curse?

Blythe had acted like coming here had been almost painful. She'd been resistant at first even, but had this been the plan? Convince me to let my guard down so she could get me here to be used for some unknown purpose by her family? I hated not having all the variables.

I knew blurting out my burning questions during brunch wouldn't be smart. Unfortunately, I'd had too many mimosas, and questioning the three of them was sounding better and better with each drink.

Lyra poured me a cup of tea with a pointed eyebrow raise and I took my time stirring in a sugar cube. Once Selvina decided she couldn't fake the niceties anymore—not that she'd ever succeeded—she excused herself for an appointment.

Martin took a sip of coffee and gazed out over the yard towards the ocean. We sat in silence, and I had to physically bite my own tongue to keep myself from getting the answers I wanted. Drinking had been a stupid choice.

"Now," Martin said, setting his cup down. "What did you need my help with?"

Lyra nudged me under the table when I took too long to answer.

"Oh, uh, well." I took a sip of tea to steady myself. I was here for Ian. Maybe we could use each other. "I need help with memory spells."

He nodded for me to continue.

"Undoing one, specifically," I said.

He nodded slowly and put his cloth napkin on the table. "And why would you need that, if you don't mind me asking?" He glanced between Blythe and me.

I did mind, but I was also desperate. That didn't mean I was ready to give him all the information. The Collective had very strong feelings on having mortals too aware of witches. The exceptions to those feelings were rare, and until I knew what side of the coin Martin fell on, he got the bare minimum.

"I have a friend," I decided. "The Council took his memory of me."

"As punishment," he concluded.

I nodded.

He put his elbows on the table and steepled his fingers in front of him, looking me over. I tried not to fidget, but his stare was uncomfortable.

He leaned back after almost half a minute of wordless evaluation. "How long have you known this friend?"

I swallowed. "Almost eight years."

He crossed his ankle over his knee and tapped a finger on his leg. "Were you two ever intimate?"

My cheeks flushed. "No."

It was a fair question. Jax had said it when we first met. It was supposedly trickier when romantic feelings were involved.

He nodded. "Well, only a very powerful witch could truly erase memories."

I clung to the sliver of hope that gave me.

"It's more likely the memories have been put behind a wall of sorts, blocking them from surfacing."

"Can the wall be broken or removed or something?" I asked.

Martin nodded. "Usually there is no need, though."

I frowned.

"A witch's natural defenses will do it for them over time. How long depends on the power behind the casting and the power of the afflicted."

My heart sank. Ian didn't have natural defenses, not magically anyway. I knew the question needed to be asked, but I hadn't thought I'd have to reveal it so soon.

"What if—" I bit my lip, weighing the options. "What if they're not a witch?"

His eyebrows rose. "A mortal?"

I nodded.

"Well, that does change things."

"How?"

He picked up his coffee and leaned back in his seat. "A complicated question." He finished off the coffee left in his cup and checked his watch. "We will have to discuss this further later," he said. "Unfortunately, I do have a standing commitment I cannot be late for."

I frowned at the same time Blythe snorted.

"Please, do make yourselves at home," he said and stood, walking back into the house.

"Well," Lyra said, stirring her Bloody Mary. "That's not nothing."

Blythe poured herself more coffee. "Once he figures out what he can exploit, he'll be more than willing to help," she said.

"Runs in the family," I muttered, stabbing at a bit of uneaten quiche on my plate.

Blythe paused halfway through lifting her mug to take a sip. "What?"

I downed the last of the mimosa and cringed at the taste of warm orange juice. "You," I said. The carbonation and alcohol didn't sit well in my practically empty stomach.

Blythe set her coffee down. "And what did I do *now*?" she countered.

"You told him I was a Boswell," I said.

Her eyebrows arched. "No, I didn't."

I barked out a disbelieving laugh. "Then how does he know?"

Lyra ripped off a piece of pancake and shoved it in her mouth. "How do you know he knows?" she asked around the food in her mouth.

I shrugged. "I overheard him and Selvina this morning."

"So, you're spying on people now?" Blythe asked.

I shook my head. "Don't put this on me," I snapped. "You're the one who's been lying to us."

"Em," Lyra cautioned.

"You don't open with your family name either," Blythe pointed out. "Hardly call it lying."

"Fine," I said. "Then what's the Boswell curse?"

Blythe froze.

Lyra coughed on the bite of her pancake. "The Boswell what now?"

"Nothing," Blythe said too quickly.

"Your grandparents don't think so," I said, crossing my arms.

"Selvina's not—it's nothing," she repeated.

"See, liar." Anger didn't mix well with alcohol.

"What is your fucking problem?" Blythe snapped.

"My *problem* is you," I said.

"Maybe we should—" Lyra started.

"*This* is why I don't usually tell people I'm an Osborne," Blythe said before Lyra could finish.

I clenched a fist around the fork in my hand. "If there's a curse on my family, I have a right to know!"

"Whoa, Em, slow down," Lyra said.

"No," I said. Mimosas and anger had opened the floodgate, and it was all spilling out. Everything had been crap for months, and if this was why then I needed to know. If Blythe had caused all of it, I *deserved* to know. "What else are you hiding?"

Blythe's jaw clenched. "You Boswells never change."

"What the hell is that supposed to mean?"

"Hey, we really should—"

"It means that, no matter the truth, your family always makes themselves out to be the victims," Blythe said.

"Because of *your* family!"

Blythe let out a harsh bite of a laugh. "Fine. You want to know?" her eyes flared red, and the ruby sparked. "Your *perfect* family decided mine was disposable."

"That doesn't—"

"Amity cursed my bloodline," she said. "To save herself."

The silence that followed was so stark, it was almost like a spell had been cast over the table.

"And now Osborne daughters only get to live as long as their Boswell counterparts."

There was no way Amity would have done that. But then, doing horrible things to protect people was something we'd all done. I hadn't thought twice about hurting others to protect Wes. And I'd have to live with what I'd done to Alex, but what Blythe was suggesting was a deliberate torment that stretched generations. I couldn't—wouldn't—believe that.

"You're lying," I said quietly.

"Right, because I'm just an evil Osborne," Blythe said.

"Can we all please just take a fucking breath?" Lyra insisted loudly.

"Then why are you helping me?" I said, ignoring Lyra.

"Well, excuse me if I don't feel like dying because you can't get your shit together," Blythe said, standing up. "Feel free to leave." She stormed off without another word.

Breathing heavily, I slumped against the chair. "I can't believe her," I muttered.

Lyra didn't say anything, and I looked over at her. She was staring after Blythe with her brows drawn together.

She met my eyes. "You of all people should know how fucked up it is to be judged on something that has nothing to do with you," she said.

"Lyra, I—"

She pushed her chair back and followed Blythe before I could finish. I was left alone, stewing in my own head, with a table of ridiculously fancy food.

Chapter 16

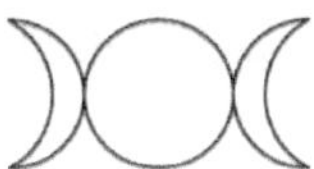

Winter sunlight streamed in from the two windows that framed the large fireplace, giving the space a slight gray tinge. Despite that fireplace being lit, there was a sterile coldness to the room. Hanging above the thick mantel was an old portrait. The man pictured had the same sharp chin and dark eyes as Martin.

His study was neat and organized. Bookshelves built into three of the walls were filled with books in varying stages of age. I'd been invited to sit in one of the stiff chairs facing his desk. Even so, I felt unwelcome.

I'd been sent to the office in high school once. Martin lacked the abundance of tweed Principal Harmon had worn, but that only made this encounter worse. Martin was a lot more intimidating.

The cup of tea he'd offered sat on his desk, still steaming. I wanted to hold it for something to do with my hands, but reaching forward would have been too much an intrusion. Maybe it was because he hadn't stopped watching me since I'd walked in, or because I wasn't sure what price he'd ask in exchange for helping me.

After our disaster of a brunch, Blythe had been avoiding me. I'd been avoiding her, too, but she was better at it. Even Lyra wasn't giving me much more than short replies. She'd thought I'd been too harsh.

And she was partially right. Everyone assumed the worst when they heard "Blood Witch." Leander had jumped to that very conclusion when we'd meet. Thea had said as much at Sabbats. Yet, here I was doing the same thing to Blythe because of her last name. I knew it hadn't been fair. But her keeping something like that from me wasn't right, either.

Nothing in Amity's grimoire had mentioned a curse by or against the Osbornes. I'd finally gotten ahold of Wes, who had been surprised to learn Blythe was an Osborne Blood Witch and even more surprised that there might be a curse associated with her. I'd heard him worried before, but not like after that call. He'd promised to look into it, and I failed to talk him out of it.

"Before we begin," Martin said, "I am a little curious how you and Blythe met."

I swallowed. Clearly, Blythe hadn't shared that with him while we'd been avoiding each other.

"Oh," I wanted to come up with a lie that didn't include the hunters or Emissaries she'd saved us from. "I was in Salem for New Year's," I said. Technically not a lie.

"Sabbats," he concluded.

I nodded.

"Well, I have to say, I'm glad you were able to get her out to have some fun."

I picked up the tea and took a sip to cover the nervous chuckle that threatened to come out. I successfully burned my tongue in the process. "Fun" wasn't the word I would have used for my first visit to Salem.

"I'm glad you found each other," he continued. "And to have her home is wonderful."

They stay as long as they're needed. His words echoed in my head, making me wonder how deep I wanted to get in with him. There had to be other witches who specialized in memory spells, and if I had to cross an ocean to find them, I would.

I took another—slower—sip of tea. Martin was right here though, and at least willing to hear me out. I owed Ian more than I could ever repay; getting over my own discomfort was the least I could do.

"Right," he said, rubbing his hands together. "I'm sure you'd like to get to it."

I nodded.

"Of course, and again I apologize for not being able to meet earlier, but I have clients that can be rather demanding of my time."

I almost asked what he did for work but caught myself. I didn't think I really wanted to know. "It's fine," I said instead. "We did sort of drop in unexpectedly."

He chuckled and picked up his coffee. "But not unwelcome," he said before taking a drink.

I mirrored him with my tea, not sure how best to change the subject.

He pulled out a worryingly thin file from one of the drawers and set it on the desk between us. "I was able to find almost a dozen cases of mortals having their memories restored after being spelled." He opened the folder. "That's over the last century. Prior to that, it gets difficult to find accounts."

Twelve over a hundred years wasn't promising, but it was something.

"These prove that it is doable, but..." He cocked his head at me.

I gripped the mug tighter. "What?" I asked carefully.

He took a breath. "All but two went mad."

The breath rushed out of me like I'd been hit. I started to ask, stopped, and tried to clear my throat and start again. With shaking hands, I took another drink to clear the fear lodged in my throat.

"Like 'mad' in the early nineteen-hundreds, or..."

His sad smile was the only answer I needed.

"Oh." I took a deep breath. "So, not impossible...just dangerous."

"Extremely," he agreed. He took another drink. "A lot of it comes down to the caster," he said. "An inexperienced witch could damage the memories."

"You can damage memories?"

He nodded. "It's why most witches won't deal with that kind of tampering," he said. "It might do your friend more harm to try to return them."

I glanced down at my hands.

"With a more experienced witch, there's a chance at a full recovery," he explained. "But finding someone equal to the task is difficult."

I set the tea back on his desk. "Knowing who did it will help?"

He raised his eyebrows. "I assumed it was Councilwoman Charlevoix."

I frowned. "How'd you—"

"As the selected leader of my own coven, it is my responsibility to deal with the Council on occasion," he said. "I like to keep myself apprised of their more...*interesting* goings-on."

First an "opportunity" and now an "interesting going-on." No wonder Blythe didn't like to admit she knew him. I'd hate to hear how he described her.

"You can be assured," he continued, "no one within the Collective will find out where you are from me."

As long as I was needed was a safe bet, though. His assurance aside, I was left with one issue.

"I don't know who the caster is," I admitted. "I don't think it was her directly, just her orders."

In truth, I had no way to back that up. It could have been anyone on the Council. It could have even been Kane making his own decision—though that seemed unlikely.

He nodded slowly. "Lenore does have a certain..." The corner of his mouth twitched into the start of a smile, but it vanished quickly before he went on, "...cruelty when it comes to those she perceives as a threat."

"Ian wasn't a threat," I said.

He gave me a placating smile. "I'll see if I can determine who the caster was," he said, closing the folder on his desk. "Once we know that, we can see about making a plan."

"Oh, okay," I said. "Thank you."

"Until then, it would be best if you girls stayed on the property. One Blood Witch draws enough attention," Martin advised.

I nodded. We didn't have plans to go anywhere, but something about the way he made it sound like a question without actually asking set me on edge.

○

Lyra had spread out on a lounger on the far side of the small pool in the backyard. The entire space—lawn included—was enchanted to keep the snow and cold away. The result was the temperature staying closer to an early summer day than one in January. Her cat curled up under her chair, enjoying the magical weather as much as the rest of us. The cat that insisted on following me padded over to its companion and laid down next to it.

Lyra had on a tank top, a pair of gold-framed aviators, and her hair was in a mess on top of her head. I moved a few notebook pages with her handwriting out of the way to make room on another lounger. She didn't look up from the book in her lap.

Tilting my face towards the winter sun, I closed my eyes and let it warm my face.

"You feeling less bitchy today?" she asked.

I opened my eyes to see her staring at me over a mug of coffee.

"I'm sorry," I mumbled.

She raised her eyebrows. "Not me you need to say that to."

I yanked my sleeves over my hands and stared at them in my lap. "She's avoiding me," I reminded her.

"Not for long," Lyra said. I looked up and followed her nod to the doors where Blythe stood at the threshold, arms crossed. She wore black leggings, an oversized sweatshirt, and her short hair was in a messy half-knot. Dark sunglasses covered her own eyes, but that didn't mean I couldn't feel the glare.

"What do you want?" she asked Lyra.

Lyra gestured with her coffee mug to the one lounger left. "Sit."

Blythe didn't move.

"It'll be worth it, promise."

She sighed but moved to the seat, pulling one leg under herself as she took it. Lyra raised her eyebrows at me, inclining her head towards Blythe.

I swallowed. "I'm sorry," I said.

She let out a snort.

"I am," I insisted. "I shouldn't have jumped down your throat." I pressed a nail into the pad of the opposite index finger. "But," I pressed my nail further into skin. "Are you sure there *is* a curse?"

She raised her eyebrows.

"Em," Lyra started.

I balled my hands against my legs. "It's just, I went through Amity's book and didn't see anything," I added quickly.

Blythe's face fell. "Nothing?" she asked.

I shook my head. "That's why you wanted to help," I concluded. "To see her book?"

Blythe picked at some lint on her leggings but didn't meet my gaze. "Maybe."

"Sorry to disappoint then," I said.

"You two are terrible at apologies," Lyra said. "Like, really fucking terrible." She rolled her neck side to side. "And you're both wrong."

"About what?" Blythe asked.

Lyra took a long gulp of coffee and set the mug to the side. She drummed her fingers excitedly on the book in her lap, which I recognized as Blythe's—or Patience's. Amity's was open next to her, like she'd been comparing them.

"It's not a curse and Amity's book does talk about it."

"The non-curse?" I clarified.

She nodded. "Basically," she explained. "The lines were bound, literally. Every time a daughter is born of Amity's line, so is one of Patience's." She held up the page with the family tree in Patience's book. "And like Blythe said, the death dates match up too."

I watched Blythe, but her expression only faltered a little. The news that our families had matching birthdays and death dates wasn't news to her. After all, we had the same birthday. Had our mothers? Did she lose hers the same way I'd lost mine? A fist clenched around my heart at the idea of it.

"Why would they do that?" I asked. "Even if there were hard feelings, that seems...weird."

Lyra grimaced. "See, I think that's why wires got crossed on *what* it was. The whole mirroring death thing was unintentional."

Blythe frowned at that. "Then what *was* the intention?"

Lyra nodded her head side to side as if she was weighing options in her own mind. "I think they were trying to invent their own version of the standard coven binding. Maybe. Probably. You know, motives are a little unclear at the moment."

"But they fucked it up," Blythe offered.

"Royally," Lyra agreed.

Blythe waved her hand at the book at Lyra's side. "Anything in there about coven bindings?"

I shook my head. "Just the sigil spell for the tattoo and an old unfinished one."

"Ah!" Lyra pushed her sunglasses onto her head. "Not unfinished, *incomplete*."

"What's the difference?" Blythe said.

Lyra flipped a few pages in both books and then held them each up in one hand. "Each of you had a piece of it," she said. "A third to be exact."

"A third?" I said, taking Amity's book out of her hands to reread the binding again. Now, it did look like it had ended perfectly, not the drop-off of an unfinished thought like I'd initially assumed.

"So, what, there's another orphaned Blood Witch out there whose life depends on Boswell here not being a total clusterfuck?"

"Hey."

Lyra shrugged. "Maybe." She scratched her head. "All I can say for sure is there is a missing part of the spell, probably in a third book."

"How do we find the last third?" I asked, closing Amity's book.

"Working on that," Lyra said, passing Patience's book back to Blythe. "But, since I have literally nothing else to do, we should have this binding issue fixed in no time."

Blythe let out a humorless laugh. "We've been trying break it the last few hundred years and got nowhere."

Lyra reached over to pat Blythe on the knee. "Ah, but none of them had what you do."

Blythe stared at Lyra's hand and then back up at her, a slight blush creeping into her neck. "And what's that?"

Lyra smiled, nodding her head to make her sunglasses flop back into place on her nose. "Me."

Chapter 17

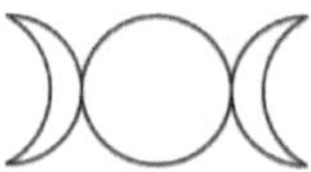

Threadcraft had everything from graphic sweatshirts to formal attire. We'd been sent to find something appropriate to wear for the new moon Esbat Martin and Selvina were hosting. None of the things Lyra had stolen in Salem were acceptable enough.

Martin approved of the outing, but he *preferred* if we kept to town and didn't waste our time in coming back to the house. He never flat-out told us what we could do or where we could go, but the tone was clear. I'd been in this position before and didn't like it now any more than I had then.

If Lyra or Blythe minded, they didn't say anything. Lyra was too busy enjoying her shopping break. We'd spent the last few days poring over the books for any hint at where the last piece of the spell could be. So far, all we'd figured out was the obvious, the third member of the Triple Moon Coven had to have the last piece.

Records, however, were spotty. All we really knew about Lydia Toothaker was that she had been a powerful Essencer and had disappeared from Salem about a year before Amity and Patience. Where she ended up—and where her book was—had yet to reveal itself.

I'd thought Lyra's new task would help distract me while I waited for Martin to get what he needed. The lack of answers from both parties meant it was hardly the diversion I needed. The Esbat, however, had drawn attention for Martin and Selvina.

Wes and I hadn't regularly observed like other witches. We'd occasionally hold one with just the two of us, but between his work schedule and my school they were rare. We had gone up north when I was twenty to participate in a blood moon Esbat his cousin hosted. I knew that had less to do with the celebration and more with keeping me extra hidden away during that particular full moon.

Still, I was curious to see how a full coven observed, although I had a feeling Martin and Selvina weren't typical hosts. Their rather strict dress code was the first hint.

Blythe found her dress first. Black velvet and styled to look like an oversized dress shirt. Instead of buttons down the front, there was a deep V-neck that showed enough of her elder tree branch and crescent moon chest tattoo that I knew Selvina wouldn't like it. Which I suspected was the reason Blythe had chosen it.

I'd picked out a simple black dress, but both Lyra and Blythe nixed that quickly. Lyra took over finding options and there were already about ten waiting for me in the dressing room.

Blythe sat on one of the chairs in front of the trifold mirror and curled her leg under her while she scrolled her phone. Lyra added another dress choice to the stack in my arms.

"Sofia says the hunters have cleared out, but there are a few Emissaries left," Blythe reported.

"I guess that's something," I said. The attendant offered to take the dresses off my hands and added them to my room.

"Is silk too much?" Lyra asked, holding up a thin-strapped dress.

"Yes," I said.

"Hmm." She put it back. "So, any update from Martin?"

I shrugged. "Not really. We're at a standstill until we can find who cast the spell," I told her. "And I get the feeling he's in no rush to do that."

"Shocker," Blythe muttered.

I turned to her. "Why would he want to drag it out?"

She set her phone down. "Did he ask for anything at your meeting the other day?"

I replayed the conversation with Martin in my head. We'd covered a lot, but I didn't remember him asking for anything outright. I shook my head. "No."

"Yeah, so he'll take his sweet time until he decides what he wants," she explained. "Then suddenly he'll have a solution, for a price."

"Great." I picked up the sleeve of a sweater dress on the rack next to me and ran my hand along the fabric. "Maybe I should just ask Lenore, get the same results."

Lyra shrugged. "Why don't you call Jax again?"

I dropped the sleeve. "What?" I said quickly. "I don't...I didn't..."

She put a hand on her hip and rested the other on top of the rack she'd been perusing. "Wolfe's Bend," she said. "I'm not judging, you have feelings or whatever."

I found the sleeve of the sweater dress again and focused on running my fingers along it instead of meeting her eyes. "How did you..."

"*Sonus removere* only works on outside sounds," Lyra said. "Not *your* voice."

Of course I'd gotten that wrong. I took a deep breath. "I didn't—I was pissed about Ian," I admitted. "I wasn't exactly nice about it, so I doubt he'd even want to talk to me right now."

Lyra laughed. "Yeah, okay," she said sarcastically.

"Who is this?" Blythe asked.

"My brother," Lyra said. "He and Em are...uh, a thing?"

I shrugged. Defining the relationship between Jax and I was the least important issue on my mind right now.

Blythe frowned. "Was this the Emissary you were making out with at Hinckley?"

Lyra and I both looked at her.

She grimaced. "I just—" She bit her lip and looked at her feet.

Lyra looked back at me. "Hinckley Woods?"

I stared at Blythe. "How did you...were you following me?"

Blythe sighed. "Sorta."

"Sorta?"

She nodded.

"For how long?"

She shrugged. "Day after our birthday."

"Are you kidding me?" I hissed.

"Hold on," Lyra started, turning to Blythe. "You've essentially been stalking her for months and are just now mentioning it?"

Blythe rolled her eyes. "I wasn't stalking."

I raised my eyebrows. "No, you were," I said as I thought back over the last couple of months to all the times I thought the ruby had been responding to my own stress. "Uncharted Tea." I remembered now, before Raven had shown up, the girl with the scowl and the red-streaked hair. "And my class."

"Alright," Blythe said. "We've established I was following you, can we get the fuck over it now?"

Lyra's lips pressed together like she was trying to keep herself from laughing. "She was following you for weeks and none of us noticed," she said before letting out a bark of a laugh. "Oh, someone is getting fired."

"I'm glad you're enjoying this," I grumbled. "Can I just ask why?" I turned to Blythe while Lyra tried to collect herself.

"I was looking for something to help with the curse," she said simply.

"Amity's book," I concluded. "What? You were planning on stealing it?"

She huffed out a breath. "I thought we were over that," she said.

I sighed. "Right, sorry."

She shrugged. "Besides, I scrapped that idea when *you* decided to take on hunters with some half-assed plan," she said. "Instead, I had to find a decent protection spell so we didn't both die."

Lyra—recovered from her laughing—and I looked at each other. No one had been able to figure out exactly how I had survived that night. Someone had floated the idea of a protective enchantment, but that was dropped when no one fessed up.

"That was you?" I asked.

She shrugged. "Don't make a big deal," she said.

"But you saved my life."

She sighed. "And if you don't find something to wear, it'll be a waste because Selvina will kill us both," she said. "You can call your boyfriend later."

○

Two hours later, we hung up our finds in the closet and I pulled out my phone. Lyra offered to call him instead and I almost took her up on it, but in the end, this was my responsibility.

She and Blythe left to give me privacy and I curled up on the large couch. As I stared at his name in the contact list, the cat appeared and leapt onto the seat next to me.

Staring at me with its red eyes, it cocked its head at me but offered nothing else. Taking a deep breath, I tapped his number.

The cat rubbed its head against my leg as the other end rang. I gave it a quick scratch behind its ears. Maybe he wouldn't answer.

"Hello?"

I swallowed. "Hi."

He let out a breath. "Is everything okay?"

I nodded and stopped scratching the cat's head. It laid it down on crossed paws, still watching me. "Yeah," I said. "I just—" I'd come up with a script in my head on the drive back to the house, but it had completely flown out of my mind as soon as I heard his voice.

"I'm sorry," he said quietly.

I frowned.

"I didn't mean to snap at you," he continued. "I was just worried."

I sighed. "I know," I said. "I shouldn't have snapped either."

"You have every right to be upset."

I clenched my fist against my leg. "I'm a little more than upset, Jax."

"I know."

"Do you?" I closed my eyes and took a deep breath. This wasn't why I'd called. Talking in circles about this didn't help anyone. "I want to know who spelled Ian," I said. Ripping it off like a Band-Aid was the best way to get this over with. I wasn't ready to be pacified; my anger was more than deserved, and that anger was keeping grief from taking over.

He didn't respond right away, and I could imagine him frowning. "That won't change anything."

I opened my mouth to argue but caught myself. If Martin's reputation was as widespread as it appeared, then I had to be careful how much I said or the Collective would be here within hours.

"Maybe not," I conceded. "But I need to know." I pressed the side of my hand to my eyes to stop the tears from spilling over. I needed to get the name of the witch—I could cry later.

He sighed. "It was the Council's decision."

I rolled my eyes. "You mean Lenore's."

"Either way," he said, "it doesn't matter. It's done."

The cat picked its head up and blinked at me.

"It does to me."

The cat let out a soft meow. I couldn't tell him why I needed it without potentially exposing where we were, so I just needed to give him another reason.

"And who else is going to get hurt if you know?" he asked slowly.

I frowned, running my thumb over the ruby. Power pulsed beneath my touch and the cat meowed again. Ian was the one who was hurt here. Who was Jax trying to protect?

But that was it: he was protecting the caster *from* me. He thought I wanted revenge and had seen what I could do when angry enough. He knew me better than I wanted to accept, the thought had crossed my mind more than once.

But now, with Blythe and the binding to think of, I couldn't exactly go on a revenge spree against the Council.

"Please," I said quietly. "I just need to know it wasn't some amateur hacking his mind to pieces."

Using Blythe's imagery might help sell it. Sounding like I was about to cry absolutely would.

He was quiet and I heard muffled voices on the other end. If they hadn't been trying to use the call to find me, they were now. If I didn't get the name from him, I'd have to wait for Martin, and if Blythe was right, I might not like that trade-off.

"Kane," he admitted finally.

I let out a long sigh. "Thank you." Although I wasn't sure how much of a comfort that was. It was better than hearing Sebastian or someone I didn't know, sure, but Kane hadn't exactly been a fan of Ian's involvement. I couldn't be sure he wouldn't have deliberately done more harm than necessary, especially if he was sure of the Council's protection.

"Come back," Jax said, and it sounded more like him than the Emissary I'd first met. "We can talk to the Council, help Ian." He lowered his voice as if he didn't want anyone to overhear. "Together."

My chest tightened, and for a split second I wanted to say yes to him. Wanted to believe it was that easy to fix and get my home back.

But I'd never have my home back. Not the same way it was before. They'd ruined it, and nothing I wanted from him—with him—would mend that.

And I wasn't the only one with something to lose. If they didn't know about Blythe and her potential connection to the prophecy, I had no right to expose her to them. Apart from sharing birthdays and death days, I didn't know the full extent of the binding. Whatever they had planned for me could mean something worse for her. Our differences aside, I wasn't willing to risk that.

"I can't, Jax," I said.

"Em, she's not going to stop."

"Neither am I."

"Em, please," he urged. "Sasha and Armin are still looking for you. Being exposed is dangerous."

"I can deal with them," I said, glad I at least *sounded* confident.

The hushed voices on the other side were getting louder. They weren't bothering to keep their attempts quiet. There was no point in keeping this up. Neither of us was going to get the conclusion we wanted.

"I'm worried about you," he said. "And Lyra."

"We're safe," I told him. "Promise." The cat stood and stretched, turning its ears towards the door. A few seconds later, I heard voices in the hallway.

"I have to go."

"Wait," he said. He either couldn't say what he wanted in front of the others or was just stalling.

"Goodbye, Jax." I hung up before he could say anything else. I'd gotten what I wanted but felt completely defeated. The cat slid off the couch and vanished with a soft *pop*. Helpful.

Chapter 18

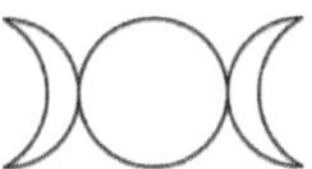

Even with only the one formal Esbat to compare it to, I thought Martin and Selvina had gone overboard. Swaths of black fabric were draped over most of the surfaces, the windows were turned to dark mirrors, and black candles lit the rooms and backyard. A large altar was set at the far end of the yard—overlooking the ocean—complete with a silver pillar candle, an ornate hand-held mirror, and a vial of blessing oil.

I stepped outside as the space was being cleansed and the earthy aroma of cedar smoke tickled my nose. Selvina directed the cleansing to ensure it was done to her satisfaction while Martin greeted his guests. They were dressed in all black as well: Selvina in a long, tight, solid dress with her hair knotted low against the nape of her neck; Martin in a black shirt, suit and tie.

Lyra wore a black halter jumpsuit and received an audible snort of disapproval from Selvina—which earned a warning glare from Martin no one missed.

I'd escaped reaction with my purchase. A solid black bodysuit style, with shorts that stopped at my upper thighs, lace overlay sleeves, and attached floor-length skirt with a long slit. I wasn't sure if it was approval or disinterest on Selvina's part, but either way, I was glad she wasn't paying me any attention.

Two of Martin's daughters arrived while we'd been out shopping and brought their families with them. They'd gotten older since the portrait had been hung. Blythe's mood darkened with their arrival, and we'd hidden away upstairs until we couldn't anymore.

I tried to stay out of the way as guests entered, not wanting to have to introduce myself or explain what I was doing there. Lyra slid up next to me, Blythe at her side.

"Your grandparents know a lot of people," I grumbled.

"The Fosters are like the Charlevoixs of the Outliers," Lyra answered for her.

"Hardly," a familiarly smooth voice said as Rez came to stand with us, Vadim with him. "Far less French." They were both dressed in black suits similar to Martin's, only Vadim had opted for velvet and Rez had forgone a tie and instead sported silver lightning bolt lapel pins connected by a chain.

"The fuck are you doing here?" Lyra said a little too loudly. Two older witches glared in her direction as they were led through the back doors.

"It is nice to see you too, malen'kiy yastreb," Vadim said, inclining his head to her.

"I didn't mean you, Vadim," she said. "I'm always thrilled to see *you*." Blythe frowned.

"But you," Lyra said, pointing to Rez. "Not so much." She crossed her arms.

Blythe looked between them. "You two know each other?"

Lyra turned to her. "*You* two know each other?"

Blythe nodded. "We're cousins."

Lyra blinked. "You're—you—you're a Foster?"

Rez nodded. "Martin's favorite grandson," he said.

Blythe snorted.

"From his first marriage," Rez added with a wink.

"Does Selvina know you're here?" Blythe asked.

He put his hands in his pockets. "You forget she tolerates me better than you," he said.

"She doesn't tolerate anything," I muttered, watching as Selvina ushered two of the grandchildren I'd met earlier up to a group of witches.

I glanced around to see the group staring at me. "Sorry, that was rude."

"But not untrue," Vadim offered.

I gave him a half-smile but wasn't sure why I'd said it. I'd been thinking it, sure, but usually I was better at keeping my thoughts to myself. A small tingle ran up my arms and I tried to rub the feeling away.

"Which marriage were you from?" Lyra asked Blythe.

Blythe rubbed the back of her neck. "None."

Lyra frowned.

"Her mother was unplanned after one of Martin's affairs," Rez explained.

I tried to keep up with the conversation, but the prick of being watched distracted me as I scanned the gathered witches for an unwanted stare.

Lyra let out a low whistle. "Gramps Foster got ar*ound*," she said, elongating the "ow" sound of the word in a sing-song voice.

I shouldn't have agreed to attend. There was something off, and I couldn't quite put my finger on it.

"Careful, Little T," Rez said. "Or you'll find yourself in trouble with the lady of the house."

Martin assured me the Council wouldn't find out where I was from *him*, but there were a lot of other witches here.

"How many times do I have to tell you to stop calling me that?" she snapped.

"You never minded before," he teased.

My heart beat faster, and I still couldn't find the source of the uncanny feeling of being watched.

Lyra snorted. "That was before you and Leander broke up."

My attention snapped back to the group. Lyra's eyes widened when she realized what she'd said as both Blythe and I stared at her.

"*That's* how you know each other?" I asked.

Blythe turned to her cousin. "You dated Leander Tsipras?"

Rez sighed. "You really felt the need to share that?"

Lyra shrugged.

Blythe smacked his arm. "Why didn't *you* tell me?'

"Do you divulge all your heartbreaks with me?" he questioned pointedly.

As Lyra and Rez continued to jab at each other, I tried to imagine Leander—uptight and obsessed with rules—with the club owner who had been more than willing to defy the Council to sneak us out. It didn't mesh well.

Their back-and-forth died down when a hush fell over the gathered crowd. Martin and Selvina came out to the patio, arm in arm, and the group parted to let them move to the black carpet laid out as a walkway to the altar. Everyone moved to form a circle on either side of the ceremonial space.

Vadim offered his arm with a smile, and I took it, thankful for the support to keep myself upright as my heels sank into the grass. I took a place between him and Blythe.

"Welcome," Martin said, voice magically enhanced so we could all hear him clearly. "Tonight, we celebrate the cycle passing as another month has gone by. We embrace the balance of light and dark," he continued. "Tonight, we welcome the darkness as a new phase begins."

He lifted the silver pillar candle and held it in front of him. Pulling out a strip of black cloth, he wrapped it around the candle in slow, deliberate movements. Once he was done, he returned the candle to the altar and stepped to the side.

Selvina took his place and snapped her fingers over the candle, lighting it. It flickered in an unfelt breeze. She picked it up and held it to the night sky.

"As the tides flow and a new cycle begins, we are thankful," she began. My magic hummed under my skin, responding to the words. I pressed the tip of my nail into the opposite finger to keep from reacting to the odd sensation. I took a quick glance at Blythe and Lyra, but neither seemed to be responding to it.

Selvina continued. "Mother Moon watches over us, ever constant, always changing, and we thank Her for Her light." She replaced the candle and began to unwrap the cloth. Martin stepped up to take it and wrap it around the handle of the mirror.

Once he'd finished, he moved to the side again and Selvina faced us, holding the mirror to look at the sky behind her. "Lend us your wisdom, your guidance, and your protection in the coming month. You are behind us at every step..." She took a step towards the center of the circle.

The magic in my blood hummed stronger, making my skin itch. It was harder to ignore now.

"...Watching, guiding, protecting each of us." With each word, Selvina took another step until she was in the center. She held the mirror high above her head and the surface glowed with a soft silver light. It grew, lighting Selvina and the immediate area.

A high-pitched ringing in my ears made me flinch.

"May the blessings of the Moon be with us all." At Selvina's words the mirror shattered, and the ringing got so bad it made me sway on my feet. Vadim put a hand on my back to steady me, frowning.

"Are you alright?"

I nodded, but that only made the spinning worse.

The shards of the mirror rose into the darkness and when they fell back down, they were no longer shards but mirror dust that settled onto the heads of the gathered witches.

The yard pitched again, and I tried to focus on what Selvina was doing—anything other than the rolling in my stomach and the heat coursing through me. She was saying something else. Again, motion.

"Come," Vadim said, taking my arm and leading me away. He took me inside the house and down a long hallway and opened the door to a bathroom.

"Take your time," he said with a nod and shut the door on me. I gripped the sink and took a few deep breaths. The dizziness had let up, but the ringing persisted—although not as intense—and my magic still itched to get out. My reflection betrayed my glowing eyes as they did when I used my power, but I hadn't...had I?

I ran the cold water and found a towel to pat the back of my neck, slick with sweat. The ringing continued to quiet, although it was far worse in my left ear than my right.

After a few minutes, it subsided completely, my body returned to a normal temperature, and my eyes stopped glowing.

My magic on the defensive, ringing ears, the shift of the new moon. The universe was warning me about something—or someone.

○

When I made my way back outside, the space had been transformed for a reception. The black fabric and window-mirrors stayed, as did the black candles, but the altar had been put away and round tables had been set up. A bar served the guests, and trays of hors d'oeuvres floated around.

I found Lyra and Vadim at a standing table near the bar with drinks. I maneuvered my way over.

"You good?" Lyra asked over the glass of dark liquid in her hand.

"Sure," I said.

Vadim slid a glass of water to me. "You are steadier," he said.

I accepted the glass and gulped down half of it. "Where's Blythe?"

"She and Rez got pulled away to play grandchildren," Lyra said.

I suspected that wouldn't last too long on Blythe's part. Downing the rest of the water, I glanced around at the party. The reception was filled with more witches than I thought called Elmswell home year-round, but I also didn't think this many people would travel for a monthly ceremony.

But then, Rez and Vadim had come from Salem for it, so maybe having an Esbat hosted by Martin Foster was a bigger deal than I realized. When I asked about it, Vadim explained that the honor of hosting was on a rotation among coven leaders. On bigger occasions—like Solstices—the covens would join together to throw the celebrations.

Eventually, my stomach had calmed enough to pick at a few of the food options, and Lyra grabbed me a black drink—a signature cocktail called a New Moon Kiss. It went down a little too easily.

Blythe found us after about half an hour, cheeks flushed, and anger radiating off of her.

"I'm going to yank all her hair out," she muttered as Lyra offered her the rest of her drink. It didn't take a genius to figure out who she was referring to. Selvina was across the yard talking with an older woman, one of her granddaughters—whose name I hadn't even attempted to commit to memory—at her side with a grossly fake smile.

"There's a hex for that," I said.

They both looked at me.

I shrugged and took a sip of the drink. Maybe it was the cocktail, the way Selvina judged every tiny little thing, the lingering energy of the new moon ritual, or maybe I just didn't like her, but if Blythe wanted help with a little hex, why not?

"Don't tempt me," Blythe said with a small smile.

Servers in all black with trays of drinks passed by and we all grabbed another round. We stayed on the outskirts of the party, swiping drinks and finger food as they came by. I kept an eye trained on Martin and Selvina as they moved through the crowd to talk with their guests.

Rez and Vadim seamlessly slipped into other groups of witches, either knowing them or being comfortable enough to get to know them. I was debating if I'd been there long enough to have paid my dues and sneak upstairs when Martin made a clear path towards us.

And he wasn't alone. There was a woman with long blond curls and black eyes, wearing an extremely deep V-neck black dress with a slight sheen to it and a long string of pearls around her neck. Next to her was a man with dark skin, cropped hair, and bone-white eyes, who wore a suit to match the woman's dress.

"Emaleth," Martin began, leveling with us. I grimaced at his choice to use my full name. "I wanted to introduce you to some of the other coven elders."

"Did you?" I said, annoyance coming through.

His smile held a warning. "This is Agnes Hewitt and Ambrose Varlett."

Lyra choked on her drink.

Blythe clapped her on the back.

Martin frowned at her but continued. "They are the heads of the Tenebris and Signa Covens, respectively."

"How nice," I said, wishing I'd tried to get out of there before this.

His gaze didn't leave me, and I had to wonder if I was about to find out the price of his help. "Agnes is a descendant of an original Boswell line," he said.

I took a drink to stall.

"Devaney's line," Agnes offered. "Distantly, of course, but not many can even claim that these days." She ran a finger down her pearls. She gave the information like flaunting it was a well-practiced habit. As if it was some kind of ticket to an inner circle that didn't exist. Not for me.

The more I learned about my own ancestors, the less I thought being related to the Mother Witch was something to admit.

"Martin mentioned you are a direct descendant of Amity," Agnes continued.

"Did he?" I asked, exchanging a glance with Lyra. The Collective and Outliers may not have been unified in their approach to practicing or handling some laws, but we already knew there was crossover among the elders, and I didn't need my whereabouts being leaked for clout.

"You were never here," Ambrose offered with a wink.

"Yes, of course," Agnes said. "Martin only thought to introduce us due to our shared ancestry."

"Distant," I reminded her.

"Not distant enough," Lyra muttered into her drink.

Agnes gave her a once-over. "You must be Castor's daughter," she said.

Lyra raised her glass in a mock toast. "Must be."

Agnes's smile was anything but friendly, worsening as her gaze fell on Blythe.

"You'll soon find how important it is that those with strong connections to the old—" she shot a glare at Blythe before she continued, "—inculpable, bloodlines keep—"

"Power," I finished for her.

She gave me a slight nod. "Your bloodline—"

"Which one?" I asked.

She looked at Martin and gave me a nervous chuckle.

"What do you mean?" Ambrose said.

I let my fingers linger on the ruby around my neck with deliberate slowness. "Did you forget who Amity's father was?" I asked.

"We don't need to get into that," Martin said.

"John Osborne was hardly *inculpable*," I pushed on, ignoring him.

Agnes swallowed while Ambrose's smile grew.

"I—"

"It was nice to meet you," I said before she could add anything else and turned back to the house. I wasn't about to get into it over whose bloodline had done worse things.

I'd used to wish I had more contact with my father's side of the family. He had brothers, sisters, and Lenore, of course. I'd wanted to know them at one time. But now, after everything they'd put me through and looking at the family Blythe *did* have contact with, I realized even if Lenore had known me from childhood, it wouldn't have changed anything.

We were Blood Witches, and that would always make us outsiders, even in our own families. We'd always be something *else*.

Chapter 19

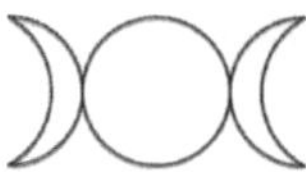

It was eleven in the morning by the time the cat pawed me awake and the vise grip on my head reminded me I had one too many New Moon Kisses. After washing the grogginess away with a quick lukewarm shower, I headed downstairs to find I wasn't the only one with a late morning. Lyra, Blythe, and Rez sat at the kitchen island—all looking extra tired—while Vadim was at the stove working over a pan.

I climbed onto the seat next to Blythe, and Vadim passed over a mug of something that looked like rose moon milk but smelled like cardamom.

"It will help ease the spinning," he said, nodding to the mug.

I didn't remember drinking that much, but it was obvious that magical mixologists were far better at disguising alcohol than mortal ones.

"Where is everyone?" I asked, glancing at the back doors. While I wasn't in any rush to see Martin after last night, I was surprised no one was around.

"Family brunch," Blythe muttered.

I wanted to ask why she and Rez weren't there but stopped myself when Lyra shot me a warning look behind Blythe's back. I took a drink to cover and found just the first sip soothing to my headache.

"You three made quite the impression last night," Rez said, setting his phone to the side.

"Don't I always?" Lyra teased.

Vadim divided scrambled eggs onto plates already set with bacon.

Rez shook his head with a smile. "Agnes, especially," he continued. "I think that was the first time she wasn't given the instant respect she thinks she deserves."

Blythe snorted.

"Uzhasnaya zhenshchina," Vadim muttered.

I rolled my eyes and immediately regretted it when my head gave a throb. The interaction with Agnes was why I wanted to avoid Martin while I could. I knew he wasn't thrilled with how I'd handled it, but I wasn't sorry.

Agnes hadn't done a single thing to earn respect from me; if anything, she'd done everything to ensure she never got it. Thinking you were worthy of respect simply because of who you were related to was something I could never get behind.

"No one cares what Agnes thinks," Blythe said.

Vadim passed each of us a plate and sat down on the other side of me with his own. He acknowledged the thanks with a nod.

"If you're planning on dismantling the Collective, you might have to start caring," Rez said.

I choked on a bite of egg. "If I *what*?" I sputtered.

They all looked at me.

"We're not dismantling anything," I said. "Why would you think that?"

"Does Charlevoix know that?" Lyra asked through a mouthful.

"You seem to have made them very angry," Vadim added.

"I—I just wanted to be left alone," I insisted.

"You've done a great job so far," Blythe said.

I shook my head. "Is that what people actually think? That I'm trying to stage some kind of coup or something?"

"Pretty much," Rez said.

"About fucking time," Lyra added.

"Just leave me out of it," Blythe mumbled.

"Perhaps they are misunderstood," Vadim offered.

I groaned and stabbed at a bunch of eggs. These rumors were starting because of that damn prophecy. I wished I could go back and smack Isobel Jacob myself.

○

Martin was so preoccupied with his family and gushing over their various achievements to have the time for the scolding I knew was coming. But when they left early Saturday morning, I no longer had a decent excuse to avoid him. I had the information we needed to help Ian, and that was worth receiving a lecture about my attitude. I was always apologizing for things that weren't my fault anyway, so it wouldn't be too hard to muster a fake one.

I caught him just after breakfast and he agreed to talk, leading me back into his office while everyone continued their conversations. Or—in Lyra and Rez's case—argument. She wanted him to try adding some kind of rhodiola mixture to the air flow in his clubs to help his patrons relax.

Martin closed the door behind us, and I picked at the fresh black nail polish I'd gotten done for the Esbat. The fire came to life without a word from either of us.

I turned to face him, and he smiled like a parent would right before telling a child he was disappointed instead of angry. I'd already worked out a decent apology, so I just needed the right time to use it.

Martin cleared his throat and leaned against his desk, crossing his arms. "I owe you an apology," he said.

My brain glitched. "You—why?"

He sighed. "I should not have introduced Agnes to you without warning," he said. "She can be rather..." He rubbed his jaw. "Brash."

I let out a half-laugh.

He smiled. "I should have made sure you even wanted to meet her," he continued. "I assumed, wrongly it would seem, that you might want to acquaint yourself with some of your kin."

I bit the inside of my cheek to stop myself from saying anything too harsh. "I've met enough," I said simply. "But I understand the assumption. Just a warning next time."

He nodded. "Of course. If there is a next time, I will ask first. Again, I do apologize."

"I appreciate that."

He uncrossed his arms and stood straight. "I'm glad we were able to discuss it."

I frowned. "Wait, that's—" I swallowed. "That's not why I wanted to talk to you."

He raised his eyebrows and leaned back against the desk. "Oh?"

I nodded. "I found out who spelled Ian."

He didn't hide his initial surprise well but recovered quickly. "May I ask how you accomplished this?"

"I asked a…" I wasn't sure how to describe what Jax and I were, especially to Martin. I also had a feeling he wouldn't be too thrilled to find out I was directly calling Emissaries while also hiding out at his house.

"A friend," I offered weakly.

"Well, then," he said, inviting me to take a seat in the chair in front of his desk. "Enlighten me."

I sat, instantly regretting it when he remained leaning on his desk instead of sitting as well.

"Kane Arriens," I said.

He frowned. "You're sure?"

I nodded.

He took a deep breath. "I am aware of Mr. Arriens," he said. "A powerful Igniter and one known for following the Council's orders without question."

Clearly, he *was* aware of Kane.

"I'll confirm with my own source to make sure you weren't misled. Then, we can begin work."

"I wasn't," I said. Jax wouldn't have lied to me, not about this. If either of us were being misled, it was him. I would never trust the Council—maybe with the exception of Selene—but I trusted Jax with my life.

He sighed. "I don't want to offend, Emaleth," he said. I really wished he'd stop calling me that. "But there is no way you can be sure of that."

"But—"

"Is your source part of the Collective?"

I nodded. "But so are thousands of witches."

"But thousands are not obligated to follow the orders of the Council," he reminded me.

"I know that." The ruby sparked under my sweater, and I tried not to react. The stupid thing was getting way too touchy when I got mildly angry. Some days, I wanted to just chuck it in my bag and leave it there.

"So, you will forgive me if I'd rather trust my own over someone who might be under orders to deceive you."

Swallowing my argument, I picked at my nail polish again. Mostly because as much as I didn't like the patronizing tone, he might have a point. I didn't want to believe that Jax would do that to me. They may be keeping him in the dark, too, and only telling him what they wanted me to know in case I called.

He'd defied their orders before to make sure I was safe, to help find Wes, and I couldn't imagine they'd be happy if they found out we'd had sex. There *had* to be some kind of rule against that. Keeping him on the outside could have been a punishment for him, and now they were using us both.

"I'm just worried," I said. "The longer Ian goes without his memories—"

Martin held up his hand to stop me. "There is no evidence that the length of time without memories has any effect on getting them back," he said. "The spell is done. It does not gain strength over time."

That made me feel better. Still, I wasn't a fan of sitting around doing absolutely nothing while Martin waited for someone else to tell him it was okay to help me.

"I understand your worry," he said. "Truly, I do." He smiled and put a hand on my shoulder. "And your restlessness."

Guess I hadn't hidden that as well as I'd thought.

"We will start as soon as we can. You have my word."

I nodded.

"In the meantime," he started, walking around his desk and sitting, "there is something you can help me with."

My gut twisted. This was what Blythe had warned me about. He'd want something for his help. But at least this meant he was going to help.

"I'm not sure how close you and my granddaughter are," he said. "Or what she has divulged about the connection your lines share."

The room got significantly warmer, and it had nothing to do with the fire. "A bit," I admitted.

He folded his hands on the desk in front of him. "It's something her family has struggled with for a long time."

Interesting that it was *her* family only. Pretty sure—based on what I'd overheard—Selvina was struggling, too, but I couldn't exactly point that out if I didn't want him to know his conversation was the reason I knew that.

"Unfortunately, it has driven many of her predecessors into an unhealthy obsession."

"I can see why," I mumbled.

He nodded slowly. "I do not want that for my granddaughter."

I found it hard to swallow. He was going to ask me to undo the curse—or binding. He thought I somehow had the answer. But, like Blythe, he was wrong. Lyra was the one who had discovered what Blythe's family had been missing, not me. And until we found that lost piece, there was nothing I could do.

"I need you to convince Blythe her preoccupation with the curse on her line is detrimental."

"I know," I said quickly. "And if there was anything I could do to help undo it, I would."

He shook his head. "You misunderstand," he said. "I want Blythe to live her life and let go of an aspiration that will result in failure."

I stared at him.

"This curse cannot be undone," he added.

"What?" I blurted before I could stop myself.

"It's an unfortunate truth," he said. "But one I need her to accept."

"And you think I'm the one to get through to her?" He clearly had no idea how much Blythe disliked me. Again, he should have been talking to Lyra, they at least got along.

He nodded. "As the other bloodline affected, you're the only one who could." He made it sound like he understood a lot more than he let on. He thought it was a curse that couldn't be reversed; if he knew it was a binding, would he still be asking me to make Blythe forget about it? Patience's book made it clear that keeping our lines bound could mean Blythe's premature death. If he knew that much, why wouldn't he want that corrected?

"I'm not sure that's…" I took a deep breath. "Are you sure it can't be undone?"

I wasn't a fan of his smile, one he'd give a toddler after explaining why touching a hot stove was bad.

He nodded. "I'm sure."

The ringing in my ears returned. Not as bad—or loud—as the night of the Esbat, but enough that it had me wondering why the universe chose that moment to warn me about the situation.

I nodded. "Okay. I'll try."

His smile widened and he clapped his hands together. "Wonderful." He stood and I mirrored him. "We'll meet again once I get confirmation that Mr. Arriens was the caster." He guided me out of the office, and we returned to the patio where everyone was still gathered. He poured himself a fresh cup of coffee and took a seat next to Selvina. When he caught my eye and smiled at me across the table, the ringing in my ears grew.

Chapter 20

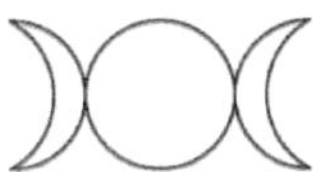

After what felt like hours, Martin finally excused himself from the table and left to get work done. Rez and Vadim left not long after for a meeting in Halifax—Rez with an invite for us to stay with him if we got sick of Martin and Selvina.

Finally, it was just the three of us. Lyra yawned with a stretch before standing.

"Where are you going?" I hissed.

She frowned at me. "To take a nap," she said. "If that's okay?"

I glanced at the doors to the house, closed after Rez and Vadim's departure. "I need to talk to you."

She sat back down. "Are you breaking up with me?" she teased.

"I'm serious."

She rolled her eyes but didn't argue.

"You look constipated," Blythe said.

I double-checked that I couldn't see anyone in the windows before I held my palms up and moved them in a circle around the table.

"*Removere audientis*," I said.

Lyra and Blythe exchanged a look.

The spell revealed nothing. We could have gone back up to our room, but somehow talking to them about this inside the house felt riskier.

"Em," Lyra said. "What's up with you?"

I turned back to them. "Martin asked me for something," I started.

Lyra leaned back in her chair.

Blythe raised her eyebrows. "Something bad?"

"Maybe."

"Spit it out," Lyra said.

I took a deep breath. "He wants me to convince you to stop trying to undo the curse."

Blythe frowned.

"Why?" Lyra asked.

I shrugged. "He says it's impossible and the obsession will ruin your life."

"Obsession?" Blythe snapped.

I held up my hands. "His word, not mine."

Lyra glanced at the house. "Does he know it's deadly?"

Blythe crossed her arms. "Yes."

"Then shouldn't he be kinda just as obsessed with figuring out a way to undo it?"

"But if it really is impossible..." I said.

Blythe shook her head. "Law of reversals."

I frowned; she was right. "So, why lie? Why would he want to keep us cursed?"

"Bound," Lyra reminded me.

"Whatever," I muttered.

"You think asking him would get us anywhere?" Lyra said. "I've been known to annoy things out of a few someones before."

Blythe flicked a crumb at her with a small smile. "He's got a lot more patience than I do."

I sighed. "Any chance you want to pretend you've given up on your life's mission?"

She shrugged. "No way he'd be convinced it was that easy for you."

"Good point."

Lyra glanced at the house again. "We know anyone else who's an expert in memory spells?"

I shook my head. My contacts in the magical community were lacking, to put it lightly. Wes was about it, and he'd even known of Martin. Other than that, it was Lyra...and Jax. Wes's cousin, Maggie, was sort of an expert in curses, but I didn't know her well enough to know if she had any other expertise.

Blythe huffed out a breath. "Technically, we don't need *him*," she said.

We both looked at her.

"He uses books just like the rest of us," Blythe explained.

I shook my head. "You said it yourself, messing with someone's mind is dangerous. I've never done it. Have you?"

She shrugged. "We get the spells we need and we can figure it out. It's not like there's a deadline."

There wasn't. Martin himself had told me there wasn't any evidence that time made the memory loss worse—or more permanent. I didn't even want to imagine how long it would take to get comfortable enough to try it, even if we had all of his books. On top of that, the Council—Lenore—would be watching him, so that could drag it out even longer.

"He's not willing to take my word on who spelled Ian, I highly doubt he'd lend me any of his books just because I asked."

Blythe's eyebrows pinched together. "Who said anything about asking?" she mused, glancing at Lyra.

Lyra tied her hair up. "Fuck yes, I'm in."

"In what?" I asked, glancing between them.

"He's going to be gone for a bit," Blythe continued.

My mouth dropped. "You want to *steal* them?"

Blythe shrugged. "Technically, we're not leaving the house with them, so not *stealing* in the literal sense." She waved at the house. "We just need to get into his office."

Lyra smiled. "See, not stealing, just a little breaking in." She cracked her knuckles. "And you've already done that."

"My house doesn't count," I said quickly.

"Whatever you say," Lyra teased. "We thinking now or later?"

Blythe shrugged. "House is empty right now."

"You two have lost it," I mumbled. "He's probably got some magical protections or something." I lowered my voice. "What happens when we get caught and he decides to turn us over to Lenore?"

"Em," Lyra said. "We're doing this. You in?"

I shook my head. "No. Not happening."

○

The too-loud click of the lock on Martin's door made me flinch. Even though I knew we were alone, I couldn't help glancing over my shoulder for someone—or something—to respond to the noise. We'd gotten this far without running into anything other than a basic lock that Lyra managed easily enough.

It was strange for him to have locked the office and not put up anything else if all of his books were in there. Unless it was to trick someone into thinking they'd successfully gotten in before the trap snared them. Or maybe he just honestly thought no one would try to take them from him.

I rubbed the ruby with my thumb and glanced down the hallway for what had to be the dozenth time.

"Would you chill?" Blythe hissed. "I can feel your nerves from here."

"Well, *excuse* me," I snapped back.

"We're in," Lyra said, replacing the pin she'd used to open the lock into her pocket and looked up at me, waggling her eyebrows. We'd all at least agreed not to use her spell on the door in case using magic to get in was the one thing that would set off alarms.

I rolled my eyes and nudged her forward, wanting to get in and out as quickly as possible. We filed inside and Blythe closed the door quietly behind us. I'd found the perfectly neat and organized office impressive before I'd been in, but now it just meant he would absolutely know if something was out of place.

I had to avoid looking at the portrait above the mantel where the dark eyes of his ancestor watched. Hurrying to the shelves across the door, I scanned the collection as Blythe went to the other wall and Lyra started on the desk.

It didn't take long for me to register the shelves weren't the ones I'd need. They were history tomes. I turned for the shelves directly behind his desk when I saw Lyra pull out the pins to unlock one of the drawers.

"Seriously?" I hissed.

She froze. "What?"

"I think he'll notice *that*," I said, gesturing to the pin.

She looked down at it. "You think?"

Blythe sighed. "Probably." She hopped off the low stool she'd been using to search the higher shelves. "If anything is spelled, it's the desk."

"See," I said.

Lyra rolled her eyes but replaced the pin and turned to the books behind her. Blythe and I went to opposite ends of the same shelf, and I started my search. There were a lot more history volumes there as well. Maybe he didn't even keep his grimoires in here.

The closer I moved to the center, however, the spines changed. More worn, obscure languages, and as I ran my hand across them, I could feel the difference. These were the ones we needed.

I pulled one out and let it fall open to the most used page. It was in Latin, and I recognized a few words. Most of the language I retained was for specific spells I used and the occasional remedy Wes taught me. The page in front of me would take some work to fully translate.

I forced my mind to focus on the words I did know, and my heart fell. A spell to extract dream memories. Something most likely written for Seers. I kept turning the pages, stopping whenever *memoria* jumped out.

"Anything?" I asked, setting the book down on the desk and pulling out a few pages of the notebook paper I'd brought. I copied a few of the options to translate later. I'd probably have to find substitutes for any extinct or non-native ingredients, but that was a problem for another day.

"Nothing useful," Lyra muttered, replacing the book she'd pulled. "You?"

"Maybe," I said, copying a spell onto the last page I'd brought with me.

"Blythe?" Lyra asked.

When she didn't say anything, I glanced over at her. She was staring at an open page of one of the grimoires. Lyra caught my eye and I shrugged.

"Blythe?" Lyra asked again, taking a step towards her.

"He—" she started, voice shaking.

I flinched as the ruby shocked me and I grabbed for it in case it did it again.

Lyra looked between us. "What's wrong?"

"He knew," Blythe breathed. She looked over at us. "He's known this whole time."

Lyra moved to look at the page and frowned down at it. Her eyebrows rose the higher she read. "Well, fuck," she muttered.

"What?" I asked, folding my copies of the spells and putting them in my pocket as I moved to stand on the other side of Blythe. It took me a moment to grasp what I was seeing. An aging page with a rough sketch of the ruby talisman that currently hung around my neck.

Osborne Binding scrawled at the top in bleeding ink. Below that, in the same handwriting, was the first part of the binding from Amity's grimoire, the second from Patience's, and the third—missing—part at the end. Completed from start to finish.

If that hadn't been enough, there were bright yellow notes stuck on the sides of the page with blocker writing—Martin's no doubt.

Three names: Ailís, Dahlia, and Blythe, the last three Osborne daughters. Arrows from their names connected them to three others. Geralyn, Grace, and Emaleth, the last three Boswell daughters. We all had the same birthdays and—in two of the three—death dates, just like Patience's book. Another set of arrows from my family's names pointed to two question marks. Only Dahlia and Grace had a third name connected to theirs. *Marnie.*

He'd known about me, mom, and grandma. He knew about all of us. And he—like Lyra—thought there might be a third bloodline caught up in all of this.

"Maybe he wasn't sure what it was," Lyra offered.

Blythe peeled the note off the page and held it up. "This is his fucking handwriting," she snapped.

"Okay, so he's a total dick," Lyra agreed.

"He could have helped end this years ago," Blythe said. "They could be alive right now." Her voice was shaking from anger, and I had to hold the ruby away from me to keep the heat from burning through my shirt.

"Having the spell and knowing what to do with it are different," I pointed out.

She glared at me. "You're defending him?"

"No, I've just learned that jumping to conclusions about people can end badly."

"I'm not jumping," she said. "He's been able to help me—us—for who knows how long and *chose* not to."

"Let's just grab a copy and we can work the why out later," Lyra said, searching the desk. "What kind of old person office doesn't have printer paper?"

Blythe ripped the spell out from the book.

"That works too," Lyra said as Blythe stormed out of the office. Lyra hurried after her.

I went to close the book but the page directly behind the one Blythe had taken caught my attention. Similar writing scrawled—not a spell—but an explanation. One that had my own anger flaring and the ruby reacting to me. Following Blythe's lead, I ripped the page out and put the book back. I didn't bother to lock the door behind me.

Lyra and Blythe were back upstairs, Blythe pacing the length of the bunk room while the cats and Lyra watched her. I walked in mid-rant.

"He didn't care that they died, he just let it fucking happen." She flexed her hands out of fists and then balled them up again. "How could he not care?"

"Because keeping the lines bound helps keep them in control," I said.

She rounded on me.

Lyra frowned.

The cats blinked in unison.

I held up the page I'd taken. "It's not just our lives that are bound," I said. "It's our power."

Chapter 21

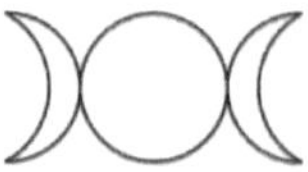

Dinner that night was anything but relaxing. After learning Martin was hiding things involving our lives and power, we agreed undoing the binding was the top priority. I'd need every ounce of my own power—and what was stored in the talisman—if I was going to help Ian.

There had been times when tapping into my magic had felt harder than it should. I'd chalked it up to lack of use, but with the page from the book, I now knew better. Neither Blythe nor I were at our full strength while the binding was in place.

Whatever our ancestors tried to do, they really had—in Blythe's words—fucked it up. Still, Lyra was confident that with all three parts to the spell she could get it to work. We were going to need a lot of supplies, however, and Blythe hadn't wanted to raid Martin's store cupboard in case he figured out what we were up to.

And so, after a couple days of planning, we were ready for a trip. We waited until both Martin and Selvina had left for their day's plans on Wednesday morning and headed to the nearest place we thought Martin wouldn't have eyes on us.

Lunenburg's old historic harbor was filled with vivid red buildings that stood out against the gray winter day. All the shops were just as vibrant and inviting. I would have loved to spend a day or two there to explore. Like Elmswell Harbour, it seemed to primarily be a summer destination, but I found myself liking the still beauty of winter.

The Amethyst Spellery was painted a deep purple to match the row of other colorful buildings around it. The only hint it wasn't a typical souvenir shop was the perfectly grimed-over windows. Flickering candlelight added an orange glow to the otherwise ominous aesthetic, and an iron sign hung out front displaying a cutout of a steaming cauldron. Iced-over wind chimes and crystals framed the door for both practical protection and enchanted embellishment.

Inside, it was warm; the overwhelming aroma of frankincense and myrrh hit me the moment we crossed the threshold. The air was heavy, and the room dim. It certainly played into those stereotypical mystic shop vibes. Perfect to attract a tourist or two.

The shop was remarkably well organized. Herbs were alphabetized, crystals had been thoughtfully displayed so as not to cancel energies, and they even had a build-it-yourself spell jar station with instructions for the intention you were looking for.

"Greetings, sisters!" A woman in a long black skirt, purple corset top, and layered sheer robes in multiple colors swept into the shop from a back room. The beads and long necklaces clanked together as she moved. Her eyes were heavily lined with purple, and her light brown hair was a mix of braids, jewels, and streaks of black.

"I am Amethyst. Tell me, what do you seek from the Spellery?" she asked, voice wispy and far away.

Lyra pulled the list I'd made from her back pocket. "Unbinding supplies," she began. "Agrimony, comfrey, nettle." She read down the list. "Blessed thistle, if you've got it."

Amethyst blinked at her. "You practice?" she asked, taking a step towards us.

"Frequently," Lyra said. "Oh, and fresh moon water would be good too."

"Any herbs I got are on the back wall," Amethyst said, jerking her thumb over her shoulder, airy voice gone. "Balm of Gilead will strengthen manifestation of intentions if you're dealing with a tough one." She handed Lyra a small shopping basket. "I'll see if I have any moon water left, don't tend to make much as mortals don't buy it often enough."

Lyra nodded. "Thanks," she said and moved to the back wall. While she and Blythe gathered the supplies, I wandered through the books. They had beginner guides on herbs, crystals, and spells. Some histories on witchcraft in Europe and the early North American colonies—U.S. and Canada. Blank bullet journals with sticker packs, labels, and the Wheel of the Year for starting your own grimoire.

I took one off the shelf to get a better look. It was good, especially for someone just starting out.

"What's that?" Lyra asked.

"Start your own grimoire," I said, holding it out to her.

"Cool." She took it and tossed it in the basket.

I raised my eyebrows.

"What?" she asked. "I think we've invented enough spells to need one." She held it back up. "And it has stickers!"

Blythe came around the corner and slipped a package of devil's shoe-string into the basket.

Lyra glanced at it. "Isn't that for *binding*?"

Blythe nodded. "But they used it in the original spell, so it can't hurt."

"Fair enough." Lyra ticked off a few things from the list. "I grabbed some hyssop and sulfur powder just in case."

Blythe grabbed a glass pillar candle and checked the price on the bottom. "Why sulfur powder?"

Lyra shrugged. "The Osbornes consider the Boswells enemies, so we might be able to use that to loosen the hold this thing has on you two." She picked up an obsidian tower and turned it over in her hands. "Who knows how generations of witches trying to undo this thing has changed it?" She set the tower in the basket.

Blythe replaced the candle. "So, this probably won't work," she muttered.

Lyra pat Blythe's cheek. "Relax, my little dark omen, I know what I'm doing."

Blythe frowned as I let out a snort. None of us knew what we were doing when it came to this. Not even Blythe who had been working on it for years. We were about to try a complicated, hundreds-year-old spell with nothing but two days' prep and Lyra's optimism.

"Are we good?" I asked.

Lyra nodded. "Just the moon water left."

A frail woman appeared next to us, and Blythe started. I took a step towards Lyra as the woman stared at us with mismatched eyes, one deep gold, one bright purple.

"With the thirteenth it will begin," she said, voice rough like she smoked at least a pack a day. "At their binding, the course is set—"

My veins turned to ice. Why was she saying—reciting—*those* words? Why now, here? Blythe's eyes had gone wide.

"The course is set," the woman repeated. "Strife...blood turns on blood..."

"Ma!" Amethyst cried, coming around the corner. "Not the customers!"

The woman grabbed my wrist with one hand and Blythe with the other, strength surprising given her stature. She stared between us at Lyra. "With the thirteenth, it *must* end." Her touch was too cold against my skin. And she was going off script. Those weren't Isobel's words anymore.

I tried to pull free, but she kept a hold. "Do not ignore the signs."

Amethyst pried her mother's fingers free. "I'm so sorry," she said, pushing her mother away from us. "She fancies herself a Seer."

I rubbed the spot where her hand had connected with my skin, a burning sensation irritating it. "A Seer?" I asked.

Amethyst let out a nervous chuckle. "Hasn't predicted anything in years...it's just brandy-induced rambles now." But her smile didn't reach her eyes and her voice was unusually high.

"They've returned," her mother said, looking the three of us over. "Don't you see it?"

"Sure, Ma," Amethyst said, leading her away.

Lyra frowned after the two women. I knew that look. I'd seen it before when she was trying to work something difficult out. I didn't like it. She shook her head and looked over at us. "Anyone else hungry?"

We checked out and Amethyst insisted on giving us a twenty-five percent discount as an apology for her mother and wouldn't be talked out of it. We headed back into the chilly winter day and agreed food wasn't a terrible idea. It was getting late, and we wanted an excuse not to have to eat with Martin and Selvina when we got back.

The Knot Pub wasn't far from the Spellery and served warm comfort food. I wasn't too hungry after the encounter with the Seer. No matter how much Amethyst insisted her mother didn't have her gift anymore, the timing couldn't be ignored. Unless she went around regularly spouting Isobel Jacob's words, her choosing the moment two thirteenth daughters were in the shop was not a coincidence.

I wasn't the only one who seemed to be unsettled. Blythe was quieter than usual, and even Lyra wasn't as talkative as normal. She ate automatically, as if her thoughts were distracting her.

I picked at my food and Blythe stabbed at the ice in her drink with a finger. We caught each other's gaze long enough I knew she was still thinking about it too.

Even as we piled back into Blythe's car, I couldn't shake the stupor. Something about hearing the words out loud like that rattled me more than I wanted to admit. They'd always been there in Amity's book for me to read and reread.

They'd been recorded by Mary Boswell and picked apart by the Collective for centuries after Isobel had spoken them for the first time. But that woman had taken it a step further. *They* had returned. What had she meant by that?

If nothing else, Isobel would have appreciated the dramatics of it all. That was the one thing all the varying accounts of the Seer agreed on. My family believed her desire to make a show of everything was partly to get back at Mary for a slight. The Collective believed Mary could do no wrong, so the words had to be true.

Either way, Mary had decided the vision meant her youngest would—knowingly or not—start a war if she was bound to any one coven.

Then, she faked Amity's death at the expense of Amity's unbound Triple Moon Coven. Amity's life for theirs. Only, it hadn't worked because the coven wasn't unbound. Had Mary known that? And had her actions been to protect Amity from her other daughters instead? Amity and Patience had both lived, despite Mary's interference. Had the third member survived too? Had the Triple Moon Coven really been destroy—

"Shit," I breathed.

Lyra looked at me in the rearview mirror. "What's up?"

I shook my head. "I just..."

But I'd...what? Thought of yet another *potential* meaning behind Isobel's words? What would that help? This was why Seers' words were rarely preserved. There was just too much room for multiple interpretations—usually, to suit a need.

"Nothing," I mumbled. I was giving myself a headache. Closing my eyes, I leaned my head against the cool window.

"*Circe*, back the fuck off dickwad."

I opened my eyes to bright light in the car, coming from the headlights behind us. The car was right on our bumper.

"Can't they just pass—"

With a crunch, the car rammed into us, jolting us forward.

"What the fuck!"

Another hit from the car and we skidded across the slick road, careening towards a ditch.

Chapter 22

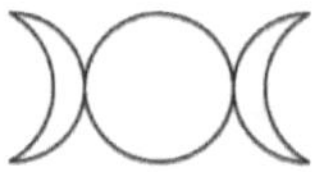

They rammed us again and Lyra tried to regain control, but I was useless. I wasn't sure what we smashed into, but it didn't give. My head smacked against the window and stars burst into my vision. My stomach lurched as the car rolled.

When it settled, we were upside down. My seatbelt kept me suspended. Blood dripped down my face, my head throbbed, and something smoky filled my nostrils. I pushed myself against the ceiling to stop the seatbelt from cutting into my chest.

"Are you okay?" I grunted.

"Ib nob dead," Blythe grumbled through what sounded like a hurt nose.

"Lyra?" I asked, turning as much as I could while still upside down. No answer. "*Lyra!*" Using one hand to keep myself propped up, I used the other to smash the button on the belt release. I crumpled out of the seat and onto the ceiling of the upturned car.

Crawling to Lyra, I checked to make sure she was still breathing. Her warm breath came out slowly against the back of my hand as I pressed it under her nose. I pressed two fingers to her neck to double-check for a pulse. It was there, and she groaned at my touch. That, at least, was a good sign. Her bloodied nose and the massive gash on her forehead were less so.

Blythe whispered something and I flinched at the crack that followed. She undid her own seatbelt and tried the door.

"Stuck," she confirmed.

I ducked back to my seat and tried the back door. It wouldn't move, but the window was cracked. Using the grab handle for support, I kicked at the window. It took a few attempts, and my head swam with each kick, but the glass gave and I crawled through.

Blythe followed moments later, and we both hurried to the driver's door and yanked. It took both of us a few really good tugs before it released, sending us both backwards into a snowbank.

My head spun again as Blythe hurried forward. Vision blurring, I blinked it a few times to clear it best I could, crawling forward to help her pull Lyra out of the car.

Her nose was definitely broken, thanks to the airbag, and the cut on her forehead looked deep. Her light hair was stained with her own blood, and I tried to keep the panic tightening my lungs from taking over.

But I'd been here. Seen this. Mom hadn't woken up.

Blythe cradled Lyra's head. "She's going to be okay, right?" she asked, voice cracking like she was about to cry.

I couldn't get air down and tried to nod. My head throbbed again. The snow should be cold. It was black. The wrong kind of black.

"Em?" Blythe's voice was distant. Why was she so far away?

I squeezed my eyes shut and counted. Down from one-sixty-nine by thirteen. Just like Stanley had taught me. Pick a number. Visualize it.

Voices.

My eyes snapped open at one-seventeen to see stars and wispy clouds floating above me.

"Are those the people who hit us?" Blythe asked.

I forced myself to sit up and the pain in my head made me want to puke.

"What do we do?" Blythe hissed, glancing down at a still-unconscious Lyra. There was something eminently wrong.

"...Or an enchanter, or a witch. Or a charmer, or a wizard—" Rhythmic recitations. "—or a necromancer. For all that do these things are an abomination unto the Lord; and because of these abominations—"

Hunters.

"We have to get out of here," I said, struggling to keep upright.

"How?" Blythe snapped. "Where?" She waved her hand to the empty road and forest around us.

"I don't know," I growled back.

My ears popped, and I wasn't sure that was a good sign. I started when something warm and soft rubbed against my hand. I glanced down to see the cat with red eyes looking up at me.

"What are you..." The other two cats had also appeared.

"I'm so glad the *cats* are here," Blythe said, trying to shoo away the one rubbing against Lyra.

I scooted next to them and slung one of Lyra's arms over my shoulders. "We head for the trees," I said. "Hide the best we can."

"You can barely stand," Blythe countered as she put Lyra's other arm over her shoulder.

"I'll be fine," I said.

"How'd they even find us?"

"I don't think these are Sasha's friends," I muttered. Hefting Lyra, we made slow progress and didn't manage to get far enough away to block out the words following us.

"...Or woman that hath familiar spirit, or that is a wizard, shall surely be put to death." Whoever they'd picked to read had one of those super creepy TV pastor voices that made my skin crawl. "Pray my Christian brothers," he continued. "Pray so that they will be rendered powerless."

I never thought I'd miss Alex and Sasha's direct approach to murder. They at least had the courtesy not to subject me to the religious shit.

Forms appeared in front of us, stopping us short. They came out of the trees holding torches. Literal fucking *torches*.

"Thou shalt not suffer a witch to live."

We backed away from the fire-wielding nutjobs. The cats hissed, hackles raised.

"Whosoever lieth with a beast shall surely be put to death."

"Give it a fucking rest," Blythe grumbled, but I could feel the fear rolling off of her. It did nothing to bolster me against my own pounding fear. Hunters blocked the route to the trees, more circling around, keeping us from the road.

Someone had to come by soon. It wasn't like this was a completely untraveled route. All we had to do was hope they'd stop. We dragged Lyra back to the car and leaned her against it. We crouched down and I closed my eyes and took a deep breath—the dizziness and nausea only getting worse the more energy I exerted.

The cats let out angry yowls that echoed across the snowy road. I watched as they continued the eerie call. The hunters paused at the noise.

"Stay strong, brothers!" the preacher called.

Two *pops* and the cats were gone, blinked away into the darkness. We were alone. It was getting harder to drown out the voices of the hunters, still spewing verses at us.

It was stupid and I knew it, but I didn't know what else to do. I closed my eyes and focused on the energies around me. Their heartbeats filled my ears as their blood pumped through their veins, bright flickers of what I could control.

I didn't need them all. Only enough of them to let Blythe get Lyra away from here, to safety. I found one, closer than the rest, and went to take it. The ground pitched from that little effort. I shook out the distraction and tried again. Swaying from the effort, I rested a hand against the car to keep myself steady.

"What are you doing?" Blythe hissed.

I didn't—couldn't—answer. I needed everything I had to focus. Crinkling my nose against the putrid vapor of gasoline, I snapped my eyes open, abandoning the attempt. They'd stopped reciting, and the harsh strike of a match against the sudden silence was louder than it should have been.

Flames crawled towards us as the preacher started his next verse. Blythe's eyes widened as the flames circled us, encasing us in fire. I pulled myself up with the tire and looked around; we just needed a way out. I would even welcome cars full of Emissaries right now.

Something sharp caught the side of my head and sent me stumbling backwards. A rock lay less than a foot away. As if my head hadn't taken enough damage tonight. Another rock came flying at us.

Blythe flung herself over Lyra's head in an attempt to save her from the stones. She was terrified and tears streaked her face.

It wasn't fair.

Blythe grabbed my hand and squeezed. Her blood touched my skin and her magic seeped through. The ruby burned, and my vision blurred red against the firelight.

Blythe's eyes glowed red as she stared at me. It was happening too slow and too fast at the same time. Blood rushed in my ears, and I swore I heard laughter.

The pain was gone, replaced by burning anger—not just mine. It sparked a flood of power deep in my core. Power I'd never touched before. Blythe was shouting. Hunters were laughing.

I placed a hand on the snow between Blythe and myself.

Scutum. Sciath.

The words came and the tug of magic followed. One a language I didn't speak, but the invisible barrier went up around Blythe and Lyra. A shield.

The hunters weren't laughing anymore. Taking a deep breath through my nose, I focused on the flames. The fire meant to consume us.

"*Ignem accipere,*" I whispered. An echo in a voice that wasn't my own filled my head. *Chun tine a ghlacadh.* A spell that gave me extra power from borrowed magic. The pull at my core tightened and the magic flowed, bright red through my veins, glowing under the skin on the backs of my hands.

I repeated the command in my mind. Both languages mixed together. Over and over, I thought the words. Magic flared. The fire surged towards me and away from them.

Power hummed through me, the ruby white-hot, and all I saw was red.

Pain seared in my fingertips, through my hands, up my arms. It broke me. The spells dropped. I dropped.

The stench of burning flesh assaulted my nostrils at the same time my brain registered what I'd done.

My arms burned, skin bubbled and peeled from my body. I screamed. There was no stopping it.

Blythe cried out in pain. Her own arms burned from my mistake.

The ground pitched and my stomach roiled. My magic abandoned me as my body succumbed.

Blistering pain erupted all over my body when something wrapped around me. Arms? Blythe screamed. A new voice—close. Yelling. Panic.

THE CURSED DAUGHTER

My ears popped, and everything went black.

Chapter 23

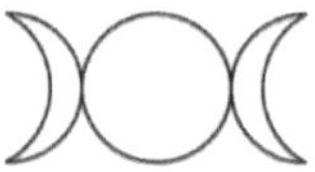

All I remembered was pain. Voices came and went. When I tried to sleep, my dreams were filled with yowling cats and burning flesh, waking me in feverish chills. I wished for the blissful healing coma the Collective had given me after I'd been stabbed.

I finally woke up after a full night's sleep to fully bandaged arms and a salve that made them itch like crazy, but I knew that meant it was working to heal the burns faster. Still, I wanted nothing more than to shower.

Blythe had also spent the last three days in pain, thanks to my stupidity. Lyra's concussion had been worse than I realized, and Martin had called for multiple healers from a few different covens to ensure no permanent damage. She was still out, but they were hopeful for a full recovery.

That did very little to make me feel better.

They'd let me move out onto the patio for fresh air, and even that was more effort than my body wanted to put in. Winded and sore, I managed to get comfortable on one of the lounge chairs and closed my eyes. The temperature was perfect, and the bright winter sun helped rejuvenate me after three days of delirium.

The cat came to curl up at my feet after a little while, and I opened my eyes to shuffling as Blythe came out to join me. Guilt twisted my gut at the matching bandages on her arms. The salves and magic of the healers would speed up the process, but it wouldn't leave us without scars. A reminder for us both of what was at stake if we were unable to unbind our lines.

Rez helped her into a lounge chair and her own cat jumped up to lay its head on her lap. She absently stroked it. After asking if we needed anything, Rez walked back into the house.

He and Vadim were the first to show up at the scene. Apparently, the cats' disappearing act had been to get help, and they'd arrived just in time to make sure more damage hadn't been done. He hadn't been nearly as friendly since we got back. And he had every right to be upset with me.

I swallowed. "How are you?"

She shrugged. "Could have been worse."

"Blythe, I'm—" I took a deep breath to stop the tears that wanted to come. I had no right to cry in front of her. "I'm so sorry. I had no idea—"

"What you were doing," she finished for me. It wasn't nearly as harsh as I deserved.

I nodded. "I'm not even sure what happened," I explained. "My magic, it...I don't know."

Blythe sighed. "You siphoned from me," she said. "Combine that with a whole lot of anger and adrenaline, and I'm surprised you didn't kill anyone."

I frowned. "I'm so sorry."

"Is this going to be a thing?" she asked. "You constantly apologizing? Because I don't have the energy."

"But—"

"You fucked up, you're sorry. I get it. Can we move on?" She scratched behind the cat's ears, and it purred loudly. "Lyra's what we need to focus on."

I opened my mouth.

"I swear to The Morrígan, if you say *sorry* one more time, I'll use that hair loss hex on you," she snapped.

I pinched my lips shut and nodded, shoving the urge to apologize again as far down as it would go. Hearing about the binding was one thing. Seeing what it did was completely different. How many injuries had I sustained over my life that I now had to wonder if Blythe had suffered them too? Did she share the scars from Alex's knife? How much had I unknowingly hurt her because of this connection?

"Stop," she said.

"What?"

"You're overthinking it." She closed her eyes and draped an arm across them. "I can practically feel the guilt."

"Sorry—"

She lifted her arm to glare at me. "Has Martin said anything?" I asked, trying to change the subject.

She shook her head. "Not yet, but I'm sure he'll be here any minute to tell us off," she said. "All about how we should have told him we were leaving, how we left town in the first place, and on and on." She let out a huff of a laugh. "Wanna make a bingo sheet?"

"I don't appreciate you making me agree with him," Rez said, walking back onto the patio, Vadim with him. He handed each of us a steaming mug and took a seat. "You know how much I hate that."

She snorted. "Agree on what?"

"On how monumentally senseless it was not to tell anyone where you were going," he said, crossing his arms.

"It would have made finding you easier," Vadim added.

Blythe sighed. "If I'd known hunters were going to try to kill us, we *probably* wouldn't have gone in the first place."

"And why did you go in the first place?" Martin appeared in the doorway, looking less the concerned grandfather and more the demanding coven leader. He wanted answers and expected to get them. I glanced at Blythe. We'd both been laid up and, without Lyra, we hadn't agreed on a lie yet.

Blythe, however, didn't seem intimidated with the shift in demeanor. She swung her legs over the edge of the lounger, the cat letting out an indignant meow at the sudden movement.

"Because we wanted to," she said.

Martin put his hands in his pockets and fixed her with a hard stare that gave me chills. She stared right back. Anger and frustration rolled off her in waves, and the ruby responded. I didn't dare move to adjust it and draw his attention.

"I asked that you stay within the town," Martin said. "That wasn't good enough for you?"

"I can do what I want," she snapped. "Unless there's some other reason you want to keep me here?"

"The only reason is that I worry," he said. "The three of you have drawn a lot of attention from the wrong people lately."

"It was a day trip to see the sights," she said. "What do you want me to say?"

He took a deep breath, his features hardening. "I want to know why you felt the need to sneak away."

"No one was home, that's hardly sneaking."

Except we totally had planned for no one to be home so that we could sneak off.

"Then why not wait until I could have gone with you?" he said.

"I'm not a child," she ground out through gritted teeth. "I don't need a babysitter."

"Clearly you do," he argued, stepping forward.

I caught Rez's slight movement as if to block Martin. His face was set and his anger directed at his own grandfather. I didn't like the tension that settled over the patio.

Blythe stood up. "I've been doing fine without you for this long."

"Someone told those hunters where to find you," Martin said, closing the distance between them. Rez fully put himself between the two, forcing Martin back half a step.

Vadim stood but held back, keeping his hands in the pockets of his black jeans and angling himself between Martin and me. He feigned nonchalance, but the twitch in his set jaw told me otherwise.

"Or we were just in the wrong place at the wrong time," Blythe said, crossing her arms. She flinched and uncrossed them, the bandages no doubt rubbing against the raw skin.

I scooted off my own lounger to interject, but Vadim blocked me and gave me a warning look. He and Rez were preparing for a fight.

"You've done plenty of reckless things in the past," Martin said. "But exposing yourself because you were bored is on another level."

"I wasn't—"

"And to risk both Emaleth and Lyra's lives as well?"

I frowned. *That* was absolutely not Blythe's fault.

"Your friend is severely hurt, and you'd rather stand here and not tell me—"

"Stop it," I interjected, moving around Vadim to stand next to Blythe. "It's not Blythe's fault."

Martin sighed. "Emaleth—"

"It's *Em*," I finally corrected.

He nodded. "I appreciate you trying to defend her, but you don't understand."

"It was my idea to go. It was my idea not to tell you, and it was my fault we got hurt."

He raised his eyebrows.

"I've been under house arrest before," I said. "I played that game with Lenore and her Emissaries. I won't do it again."

His jaw clenched.

"I'm the one they're after," I continued. "So, if having me here makes you uncomfortable, I'll leave. But I won't be told I can't come and go as I want." I took a deep breath. "Don't blame Blythe for everything you think goes wrong."

"I'm not blaming her," he said, some of his bite gone. "I just need her to be more careful."

"She's been nothing but careful," I snapped. "You want to be angry at someone for being reckless with Blythe's life, I'm right here." I was breathing heavier than the conversation merited, but I couldn't help it.

I was sick and tired of being told to sit and wait, to be careful, to not show my power. I was tired of being coddled. If Martin needed to go toe-to-toe with a Blood Witch to make himself feel more powerful, I was ready.

He rubbed his jaw and looked between Blythe and me. "You're not being held captive," he finally said. "But until we find out how the hunters were able to track you, please do not leave without letting one of us know."

I glanced at Rez who gave me a half-shrug.

"Fine," I said.

Martin inclined his head to me. "Thank you." He turned on his heel and walked back into the house.

Whatever strength I'd built back up after the last few days left me and I swayed on the spot. Vadim held me up before I could hit the ground and helped me back to the seat.

"Careful now, malen'kaya gadyuka," he said.

I nodded my thanks and took a few deep breaths.

"You didn't have to do that," Blythe said.

"Well, you won't let me apologize anymore," I said with a shaky laugh.

Rez smoothed his already slicked hair. "Is pissing off coven leaders a hobby for you?" he asked.

I shrugged. "It is now."

Vadim glanced at the doors Martin had walked through. "Mne sleduyet ostat'sya zdes," he said, without taking his eyes off the door.

I glanced at Blythe, who shrugged.

Rez checked his watch. "Derzhi menya v kurse."

Vadim nodded. "I shall check on the malen'kiy yastreb," he said, and left us alone. Rez straightened the dark blue sweater he wore. "Vadim will stay here," he said. "If anything comes up, he'll let me know."

Blythe rolled her eyes. "Didn't I just say we don't need a babysitter?"

Rez patted her shoulder. "It's not for you." He pulled out a set of keys from his pocket and handed them to her. "In case you need to get away fast," he said with a wink.

She shook her head but accepted the keys and gave him a hug—a little awkwardly to avoid the bandages. He gave me a nod on his way out.

The cat curled itself around my feet and I stroked its head. They were slightly less annoying the longer they stayed, and I could hardly shoo them away after they'd saved our lives. I wasn't about to buy it a collar or anything, but a few appreciative pets seemed appropriate.

Blythe sat back down and let out a slow, long breath. She'd stood her ground, but I could guess how she was feeling. Like we could sleep for another three days. I usually wasn't much for confrontation, but the more I was told to keep quiet and not stir things up, the less I was willing to do it.

Chapter 24

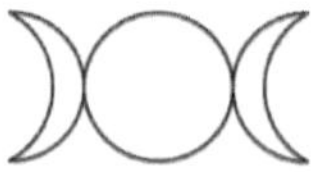

Lyra woke up the morning after our discussion with Martin. The healers stayed the rest of the day to monitor, but she successfully annoyed them into refusing to stay another night. They'd done their job, and she was pretty much back to her normal self. Although, she did admit to a few more dizzy spells than before.

We gave her as much of an update as we could when she asked why Vadim was there. He hadn't left us alone, except to sleep. He'd be at breakfast, reading outside while we spent the afternoon trying to come up with names for the familiars, and he'd appear if Selvina tried to talk to any of us.

Our plans to do the unbinding were put on hold, thanks to all our supplies burning with Blythe's car plus our ever-present shadow. I'd brought up the idea of asking Vadim to get what we needed instead, but Blythe didn't want Rez to know what we were trying either.

While he was a lot more supportive than Martin, she didn't think he'd sit back and let us try something dangerous. Especially not so soon after the attack.

That left only one thing for my brain to dwell on. How the hunters had found us. I knew they weren't with Sasha or Armin; the over-the-top religious drivel made that obvious. But they'd followed us from town and waited to attack. After everything, I'd learned not to underestimate anything when it came to hunters. Still, I had hoped Sasha was the only murderous zealot I'd have to watch out for.

I'd called to check in with Wes, but mostly to make sure there weren't any factions of hunters specifically targeting my family—other than the ones that were *already* targeting my family. It was hard to get around to what I was trying to say without giving him specifics. He knew me too well for me to flat-out lie, so I'd just told him we'd heard of hunters in the area and he should be careful.

He assured me they hadn't encountered anything like that. They'd settled into the house fine, Chad wasn't overly impressed with the kitchen, but they were good.

He hadn't managed to find out anything about the binding outside what I already knew. Clearly, my ancestors hadn't thought that part of the family history was worth sharing. So, the only thing we had was the page ripped from Martin's book.

Blythe had contacted Sofia and Devya, but no hunters had tried to get back into Salem after Sasha left. I hadn't thought they would. Sasha's hatred for me overrode any logic. Other hunters wouldn't want to piss off the Salem witches—not without a whole lot more resources than they could muster.

Lyra didn't feel the need to call anyone. Between the D.R.U.s looking for us, the Emissaries in groups, and the Council on alert, hunters weren't going to cause them trouble.

If only that had been enough for me. I needed to hear it from him. They were focused on finding me, and that meant they might not be watching out for anything else.

I snuck out to the backyard Monday afternoon, my cat—named Grace, after my mother—at my heels. Walking to the edge of the yard, I looked out over the ocean, soft waves disturbing the surface. Despite the magical climate, I pulled my sweater tighter around me as a phantom chill ran up my arms.

I tapped his name and held the phone to my ear, listening to it ring as I watched the late afternoon sun ripple over the water.

"Hello," he said.

My chest tightened. "Hi."

Jax was quiet for a few seconds. "Hold on," he said quietly.

I glanced down at my feet and listened to what sounded like a door closing on the other end of the line. "Hi," he said again. "How are you?"

"I'm okay," I answered. "How are you?"

He sighed. "Worried," he said. "I hadn't heard from you in a while and..." He went quiet and I waited while Grace rolled in the grass next to me.

Frowning, I pulled the phone away to make sure the call hadn't disconnected. "What?"

"I—we heard of some hunter attacks," he said. "I just thought...I was worried."

I couldn't stop the smile. "Nope," I said. "Just been busy."

"Yeah? Doing what?"

I laughed. "Nothing you need to *worry* about," I said, turning in a small circle around the grass.

He let out a chuckle. "You and Lyra being busy is cause for everyone to worry," he teased. I glanced down at my hand. The bandages had come off and the healing had progressed, but the scars were evident. He wasn't wrong.

Grace batted at my ankle on a pass by and I stopped to stare at her. She flicked her tail back towards the house, and I looked up to see Lyra waving at me through the window in the bunk room. I frowned at her.

"But you're alright?" he asked, voice softer.

I nodded. "Yeah, we're both fine," I said. *What?* I mouthed up to Lyra. She slid the window open. "Get your ass up here!"

Jax chuckled. "Tell Lyra I say hi," he said.

"I will."

"And Em?"

"Yeah?"

"I miss you."

A lump formed in my throat and tears stung my eyes. I swallowed, hard. "I miss you too." He ended the call first this time and I listened to dead air for a second before sighing and putting the phone back in my pocket.

Grace and I headed back across the yard to the house. Blythe and Vadim were already in the bunk room. Blythe curled up with her cat—Rhiannon, Rhi for short—on the large couch. Vadim had pulled a chair into the room and gave me a smile when I came in. Lyra pulled me inside and gently pushed me down onto the couch; obviously, I wasn't moving fast enough for her.

Her cat—Atalanta—was perched on the armrest of the couch, sitting proudly over the rest of us while Lyra shut the door. She moved to the front of the coffee table.

"Great, now that we're all here," she said. "We have a lot of prep to do before the full moon."

I frowned.

"Prep for what?" Vadim asked, crossing his arms over his chest.

Lyra put her hands on her hips. "You are only allowed in the meeting if you don't ask questions," she said.

He scowled.

"And you're not allowed to tell anyone outside this room what we're up to."

He shook his head. "Rez will expect me—"

"Those are the rules, Vadim," Lyra said, fixing him with a challenging stare.

He pursed his lips, clearly torn between his curiosity and his loyalty to Rez. "I will only agree to that if it will not put any of your lives at risk."

Lyra thought it over. "Fine."

"Seriously?" Blythe protested.

"We might end up needing him," Lyra said. "So, it's a compromise we'll have to deal with."

"Need him for what?"

Lyra rolled her eyes. "The binding—or, the unbinding."

"You still want to do that?" Blythe asked.

Lyra raised her eyebrows. "You *don't?*" she asked, nodding to our arms, scars matching under our sleeves. I pulled mine down further to hide them even more. Blythe grabbed a pillow and hugged it.

"We lost all the supplies," I reminded her. "You really think Martin's going to let us go back to Lunenburg for more?"

"No," Vadim said.

Lyra aimed a finger over her lips at him. She turned back to us and waved a hand at the table behind her. "What the fuck do you think I've been doing all day?"

I peered around her. Small piles of herbs were separated into sections, and empty tea sachets were stacked on the corner. The floor around the table was littered with empty tea bag boxes.

"Fun fact, local grocers do *not* carry sulfur powder," she said. "And I wouldn't suggest asking them for devil's shoestring if you don't want to be branded a freak." She put her hands on her hips. "But those were precautionary at best, so we should be good."

Blythe and I exchanged a look.

"You want to—" I rubbed my forehead. "You want to use tea bag herbs to try to unbind our lines?" I asked.

Lyra nodded.

"No," Blythe and I said together.

"Why not?"

"Every witch that has tried had every detail down to painstaking accuracy," Blythe said. "And it didn't work for them. But you want to, what, wing it?"

Lyra tapped the end of her nose with her finger. "But your ancestors thought they were trying to undo a *curse*, not a binding."

"Still," I said. "Not sure this is one of those spells you can modify and hope for the best."

She put her hands up on either side of her as if weighing things. "Modify this one or write a brand new one...risky either way."

I bit the side of my thumbnail. "Spell modification is dangerous," I reminded her.

"Apparently so is sightseeing." Lyra crossed her arms and looked at Vadim. "You want to chime in?'

He shrugged. "You have talent in spell work," he agreed. "This? This seems risky, even for you malen'kiy yastreb."

She shook her head. "Look, all spells are the result of trial and error at their core."

True.

"Not comforting," Blythe grumbled.

Also true.

"And," Lyra continued like she hadn't heard anything, "all the witches that tried before were working alone."

Blythe opened her mouth, but Lyra didn't give her the chance to throw in another argument.

"You have help, use it." She sat on the table, facing us. "The full moon is in three days, which will give us a boost. C'mon, what's the worst that could happen?"

"Death," Blythe said through a dark laugh.

Vadim shifted.

"Highly unlikely," Lyra said. She stood and took a deep breath. "I'm willing to try, but it's your lines that are bound, so it's up to you two."

I bit the inside of my cheeks. Having a full moon *would* probably make up for any of the herbs we were missing, or any stray ones Lyra hadn't separated well enough.

It also wasn't fair to keep our lines bound if we didn't have to. To either of us. With the Council and hunters after me, I'd be in more danger before this was over, and that would put Blythe in that same danger.

"That's not what you came here for," Blythe said, glancing down at her hands.

I sighed. "No, but Martin said Ian's memory issues won't get worse with time." I looked to Vadim for confirmation, and he gave me a firm nod. "So, I can wait a bit to work on this."

I'd come here with one problem to solve. Discovering another one hadn't been on the agenda, but as much as I loved Ian, he was safe for now. Taking his memories was the worst they could do to him. The Council didn't like mortals, but their laws dictated they couldn't harm mortals except in self-defense.

Blythe didn't look up from her hands. "Still…"

"Look, Lenore and the hunters aren't going to stop," I told her. "You don't deserve to get hurt again because of me." I took a deep breath. "But it's up to you."

She pressed her chin into the pillow on her lap and stared at the table of herb piles.

Vadim cleared his throat. "May I ask one question?"

Lyra waved her hand in a very "if you must" fashion.

"How do you propose to perform this spell without Martin finding out? He will want to attend the Esbat this full moon, no?"

Lyra nodded. "Which is where you come in."

He raised an eyebrow at her. "Oh?"

"We'll have to peel away for a bit to get this done. We'll need you to keep him from noticing.

He frowned at her. "You want me to distract him?"

"Yup."

He inclined his head to her but said nothing. I didn't know whether that meant he agreed to do it or he was planning on telling Rez about our plan so they could stop it.

Lyra turned back to Blythe. "Well?"

Blythe still had her mouth pressed against the pillow and hadn't taken her eyes from the table. She took a deep breath and met Lyra's gaze. "Let's do it."

Chapter 25

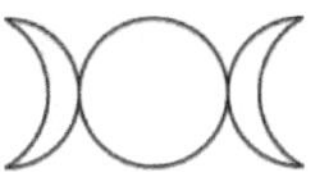

White and silver were the colors for the full moon Esbat, and Ambrose had gone all out. Entering the rented house was like walking into moonlight itself. White fabrics covered most of the surfaces, silver banners hung from walls, and everyone wore one of those colors. If this was the usual way a full coven celebrated an Esbat, I'd stick with my infrequent but casual ones.

The dress code had, once again, forced us into town to find something to wear. This time, we also had practicality to think about. We all found light silver pants and white tops. It was a tad matchy-matchy for Blythe's taste, but we reminded her we weren't looking to stand out and this would help.

We were saved the awkwardness of waiting for Martin to tell us we would be attending by the arrival of my own invitation. Apparently, I hadn't made as negative an impression on Ambrose as I had with Agnes. What came was an opulent invite that smelled of spruce and left white glitter everywhere.

I played the nice guest and let Ambrose greet me like we were old friends. After we exchanged a few words of small talk each, Vadim swooped in to draw his attention so that I wouldn't be asked to stand anywhere near the altar for the ritual.

Martin and Selvina drifted off to do their own greetings and we were left to plan the exit. The house Ambrose used for his Esbat wasn't in the gated community and that would make it easier for us to slip out. The issue was timing: too early and they'd be looking for us, too late and it would be obvious three witches were missing from the circle.

Lyra had scoped out the area as soon as the invite arrived with the address. There was an alcove in the cliffs less than a mile away that would serve our purpose. Vadim had dropped off our supplies earlier. He'd made it clear, however, that if we were not back by the end of the Esbat, he would come to find us and Rez would be informed.

I kept watching for any kind of cue to slip away. The invitation to make the circle outside was as good as any, but it seemed like we were still waiting for more people to arrive. Waiting was horrible. All it would take was for one of us to get caught in a conversation that took a little too long.

Blythe didn't struggle to look unapproachable. She'd found a spot in the corner and—with arms crossed—glared at anyone that got too close.

Lyra's strategy seemed to hinge on her being the person to start the conversation. She'd found a small group of people and was currently leading the chat.

I tried to keep to the edge of the party, make it look like I wasn't uncomfortable being there but not comfortable enough to talk to. I'd wanted to stick together, but Lyra thought having two Blood Witches in attendance was asking for attention as it was. The two of us standing together would be too good an opportunity for partygoers.

That probably had been Ambrose's plan. Prove he was better than the others by having us both there. First Martin, now Ambrose. I had no doubt it was only a matter of time before Agnes tried to display us like priceless art to try to get ahead of the other coven leaders.

The Collective regarded Blood Witches as something to be feared if left uncontrolled. The Outliers saw us as something to be used, collected. I hated either option.

Vadim slid up to me and handed me a small shot of vodka.

I frowned at it. "Should we be drinking before the ritual?" I asked.

He inclined his head. "No, but you're not attending the ritual."

"Good point," I muttered and took the shot. It was stronger than I thought, and I coughed past the burn as it went down.

"You are prepared?" Vadim asked. "For the spell?"

I nodded. "As much as we can be."

"I hope for your success," he said. "For her sake." He nodded at Blythe, who was still mastering the art of being completely unsociable.

I set the shot glass on the table behind me. "I know."

He smoothed his hair. "It took a lot for her to accept help."

I looked over at him.

"And I am glad you are friends."

I swallowed. "Me too." It was a weird version of friendship, but that's what it was. And I was glad for it. It would be impossible not to have her, or Lyra, in my life at this point. A little light in the bleakness, ironic as that was.

Ambrose stood before the gathered group and clapped his hands to get our attention. "Welcome all," he said. "It is now time to celebrate our Mother Moon, High Queen of the Night and Mistress of the Tides."

I caught Blythe's eye and had to turn away to keep from laughing. The Collective liked their rules; the Outliers liked their dramatics.

"Let us move into the night," Ambrose said, sweeping his arm to present the open door to the backyard.

"Good luck," Vadim whispered as he moved in front of me to file in behind the rest of the group. I took a deep breath before slipping away in the opposite direction to meet Blythe and Lyra at the front door.

○

The alcove in the cliffs wasn't as accessible as Lyra had thought. We parked as off the road as possible, made our way down a narrow trail—tripped a few times—and climbed down the rocks to get to our stash. Using the flashlights on our phones, we went about setting up the focus circle.

We estimated about half an hour before we were missed at the Esbat. I added another fifteen for Ambrose's flair. Still, that only gave us forty-five minutes. That wasn't a whole lot of time, considering what we were trying.

The waves lapped at the rocks below our space and the light from the full moon danced on the water's surface. I wasn't sure if it was the power of the moon or my own resolve, but I finally felt like this could work.

Lyra finished the circle with the chalk—enchanted to keep it from washing away until we were ready. After adding cross points vertically and horizontally within the circle, she added the four directional runic points.

Blythe and I each took our own chalk and added our own runes for intentions inside the sections. I'd really had to rack my memory for the little I knew about runes. Blythe was far more knowledgeable than I was with that kind of magic, but the spell called for us each to come up with our own. Runes that meant something specific to us, too, for they had to be personal to achieve the kind of binding—or unbinding—that the spell had been created for.

I'd chosen family and a combination bindrune for navigating change with grace. There had been—and would be—a lot of change in my life, and if I needed anything right now, it was help accepting that. I hoped it also had the added intention of navigating the change of not having our lines bound anymore.

My two went into the Northwest and Southwest sections while Blythe added hers to the Northeast and Southeast. After our runes had been chalked onto the rock, Lyra pulled out the small cast-iron cauldron with its stand and set it up in the center.

With a quickly whispered spell and a snap of her fingers, fire ignited under the cauldron. She added the bags of herbs and half a vial of moon water she'd stolen from Martin to the cauldron.

Once she was done, she stepped to the top of the circle, the Northern point. She nodded to us, and we stepped into the circle on either side of the cauldron. An eerily warm breeze swept into the alcove, the flames flickered, and the hair on my arms stood.

Lyra unfolded the page with the spell, cleared her throat, and then looked up at us, eyebrows pinched together.

"What?" I asked, not loving the look.

She shook her head. "Nothing," she said. "Just…" She frowned at the page. "Is anyone else getting the weirdest déjà vu?"

I glanced at Blythe over the simmering cauldron. She was watching Lyra with a strange expression. None of us said anything. Lyra shook her head again and went back to the spell. I tried to ignore the nerves that skittered under my skin because, truth was, I did have a sense that we'd been here before. Done *this* before.

"Okay," Lyra started. "Blood, please."

Pulling a safety pin out of my pocket, I opened it and punctured the skin of my thumb before squeezing a few beads into the cauldron. Across from me, Blythe did the same.

Lyra cleared her throat. "The offering has been presented," she began. The contents ignited into dark red flames and the heat warmed my cheeks. Once the flames died down, the mixture glowed a blood red, matching the glowing of Blythe's eyes—and my own, I was sure.

"Is that good?" Blythe asked.

I shrugged.

Lyra stepped forward and dipped her right index finger into the cauldron but grimaced when she pulled it back out. "Okay, that's gross," she muttered.

"Focus," Blythe hissed.

Lyra rolled her shoulders back. "Right, wrists up," she instructed.

Blythe and I lifted our hands, wrists facing up. Her right and my left. Lyra traced the binding sigil on each, then added a slash, cutting the sigil in half. A light tingle brushed my skin, running up my arm to my shoulder.

Something was happening.

Lyra pulled a red cord out of her pocket and nodded to our hands. We clasped them, right to left, and Lyra wound the cord around our bare forearms. It was warmer and heavier than it should have been. I took a deep breath as Lyra stepped back to her spot at the top of the circle.

Three sets of glowing eyes and soft meowing joined the soft wind and crackle of the fire. Our familiars had decided to join. I wasn't sure that was a comfort.

Lyra took a deep breath and began. "Diana, fill us with your essence on this night—"

Maybe we'd rushed into this.

"—cast your favor on our plight—"

Lyra hadn't actually spent that much time modifying the original spell.

"—unbind these sisters with your might."

She nodded to me, and I had to swallow a few times to find my voice. "Danu, we ask of this accord, you divide—" I flinched at the sudden burning under the cord. "—of the first plea, set aside—" My eyes watered and I had to take a steadying breath. "—unbind these sisters as previously denied."

"Hekate," Blythe began, "lend your wisdom to us daughters three—"

The urge to pull away was overwhelming.

"—accept this offer from the yew tree—"

Lyra emptied a bag of yew needles into the cauldron.

"—unbind these sisters for eternity."

"Maiden, Mother, Crone," we said in unison. "As we speak, so it is."

My head spun, Blythe's grip tightened, and the contents of the cauldron burst into flames, reds of all shades lighting the entire alcove. The heat left me sweating like the hottest summer, and I could have sworn I heard the cats hiss.

Pain surged up my arm. Red-hot tendrils glowed under my skin, racing up my arm. The cord burned away on its own. I couldn't hold on any longer, but Blythe let go first.

Blood rushed in my ears and my knees buckled, sending me to the ground. Sweat and blood dropped onto the rocks. The burning made its way to my chest. I clutched at it, wanting to scream.

The flames went out and the cold returned with biting ferocity. Sweat froze against the back of my neck and along my forehead, chilling me too quickly. My teeth chattered as I tried to force myself to stand. My legs wouldn't support me, and so I rocked back to sit, holding my spinning head in my hands.

Grace rubbed her warm fur against me, helping ease the dizziness. Wiping blood from under my nose, I looked over at Blythe. She wasn't any better off, shivering uncontrollably. My heart rate slowly returned to normal, and Grace bumped her head under my chin. I gave her a scratch behind the ears in thanks.

Lyra doubled over, hands on her knees and took deep breaths in and out. She pinched her lips together, shook her head, then hurried to the edge of the alcove and dry-heaved.

Chapter 26

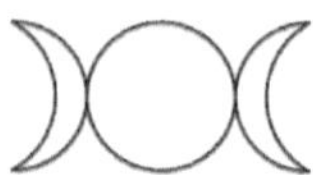

We made it back to the Esbat just as the group was moving back inside. We fell into the stream of people heading for the reception—another attempt to match, if not outdo, Martin's. Servers in white moved through the crowd with trays of canapés and other finger foods while bartenders in silver mixed signature cocktails that shimmered like moonlight on water. We swiped one each and pretended to be deep in conversation with each other, sipping as casually as we could.

It had taken us longer to recover, and Lyra had sped too much for comfort on the winding coastal road to get us back in time. The spot remover spell we'd tried on Blythe's shirt to hide the blood that had dripped on it only lightened the dark spots to pink. She'd turned it inside out and we just had to hope no one pointed it out.

Vadim found us before anyone else and slid over, drink in one hand, the other in his pocket. He took a drink and looked around the room as if nothing was off.

"Did it go well?" he asked.

I took an extra-large gulp of my drink. "Possibly."

He raised an eyebrow at me.

"Didn't have time to test it," Blythe said, her arms crossed over her shirt.

He glanced down at her. "Club soda," he suggested.

Blythe sighed, finished her drink in a gulp and turned towards the hall that split off from the main room.

"Want help?" Lyra offered.

Blythe shook her head. She stopped at the bar to ask for the soda and headed to the bathroom. Lyra frowned after her but didn't follow. The familiar prick of a stare filled my mind and I turned to see both Ambrose and Agnes watching us. I finished my drink and swiped another.

"I need air," I said, and we weaved our way outside. It was decorated very similarly to the celebration Martin had hosted. The colors were different, and there was less need for any other light than the full moon, but there were still some white candles for ambiance.

The fresh air and slight chill did make me feel better. I wasn't sure if I was still amped from the spell or if it was the drink, but it had been too warm inside. People were watching me—us, and I could feel it. But, at least outside, I wasn't as trapped. Or I could pretend not to be.

"Why was she bleeding?" Vadim asked, looking back at the house.

"You do know she's a Blood Witch, right?" Lyra said before taking a sip of her drink.

Vadim let out a heavy sigh.

"The spell got intense," I explained.

"How intense?" he questioned.

"Nothing we couldn't handle," Lyra said like she hadn't been dry-heaving over the ocean less than thirty minutes ago.

"More importantly, nothing you need to tell Rez about," I added.

Vadim frowned, and I knew that wasn't going to deter him. I had no doubt Rez would know what we'd attempted by the end of the night.

"Blythe was right, though," Lyra said. "We didn't test it."

"How are we supposed to do that?"

She shrugged. "You feeling particularly ragey at the moment?"

I shook my head.

"Could you?"

I frowned at her.

"I'm just saying, if you went all Blood Witch on someone's ass and Blythe, like, passed out or whatever, we'd know."

"That's a terrible idea," I said.

"I agree," Vadim added.

Lyra pursed her lips and glanced around before dropping her voice. "Do you feel *different*?"

"Than what?"

"Before."

I thought it over for a second and then shook my head.

"You sure?" she pressed.

I shrugged. "It's not like I knew it was there before," I reminded her.

"Right, but still, I feel like you should be able to sense...something."

"If I didn't before and I don't now, how is that a good test?" I asked. My scalp began to itch uncomfortably.

She frowned. "You're completely sure you feel normal?"

"I'm sure," I said, the itching in my scalp getting worse.

"Does that mean it didn't work?" She took another drink.

"I don't know," I muttered.

"There has to be *something*," she continued.

I bit the inside of my lip, trying to keep myself from telling her to shut up. We didn't need anyone overhearing us right now. I scratched at the itch that wouldn't let up.

"Perhaps it takes a while to work?" Vadim offered.

"I don't know," I repeated, getting more irritated by their questions and the damn prickling on my scalp.

"Like a lag? Not sure bindings work like that," Lyra said. "You think there's a lag?" she asked me.

"I don't know."

"But maybe *unbindings* do work like that." Lyra tapped her lips. "What do you think?"

"I don't know!" A few people turned to stare at my outburst.

Lyra raised her eyebrows and Vadim frowned at me. Anger burned in my stomach. Not annoyance, but hot rage.

"Okay, sorry," Lyra relented.

I glanced at the house and my vision blurred red and the ruby sparked in turn. "Blythe," I said, setting my drink down. We hurried inside and it didn't take long to find her. A small circle of other attendees gathered to watch the commotion.

Blythe and Martin facing off. Her fists were clenched, and his jaw was set. Martin was fully embodying the coven leader and not ready to back down. He stood straight at his full height and his dark eyes glowered down at her.

"You had no right—"

"To decide what to do with *my* life?" she bit out.

The closer we got, the more her anger clouded my own thoughts. We pushed our way to the front of the group, just behind Blythe. Lyra took a small step in front of me, ready for a fight. I hoped it wouldn't come to that.

"Performing a spell of that caliber as an amateur was incredibly irresponsible," Martin said. I knew he was choosing his words carefully. There was an audience, and despite the dislike in his features, he still wanted to appear the concerned grandfather.

"Well, that's me, isn't it? Your irresponsible Blood Witch granddaughter," she said. She was shaking, waves of hot anger rolling off of her. The ruby grew hotter, and my stomach ached from the effort to not start shouting at him myself.

"And Otherworld forbid I do something that might undermine your control," she added.

"I'm trying to ensure you don't make things worse," he said. "The Tsipras girl might be able to perform trivial spells, but this is bigger."

"Don't bring my friends into this," Blythe snapped.

Martin let out a harsh, humorless laugh. "You are showing your naïveté if you honestly believe that girl to be your friend."

"That's it," Lyra said, taking another step forward. Both Vadim and I moved to stop her before she could throw a well-deserved punch.

Unfortunately, Martin caught our movement and turned his own anger in our direction.

He pointed a finger at me. "You were supposed to keep her in check," he said.

I frowned. "I just wanted to help," I said pathetically.

He shook his head. "You've proved yourself as useless as your mother."

The flare of anger that warmed the back of my neck wasn't Blythe's. "What did you say?" I could hear my own voice deepening with power, even as the tears pricked my eyes.

"Your mother thought she could *help*, too," he said. "You've both been nothing but a thorn in my side."

The room was blurring red and I let go of Lyra, moving towards Martin.

"Em," Blythe warned, but I barely heard her.

Power rushed to the surface. "Don't you dare talk about my mom."

"Emaleth—"

"*You* don't get to call me that."

"You're both acting like children."

"Fuck. You."

His jaw clenched, a vein twitching from the effort. The onlookers were dead silent.

"Enough." His voice was firm and filled with his own power. The brightness of the room dimmed, and the people closest to us collectively took a half-step back. Black smoke rolled off of him and slithered towards me.

A tendril wrapped itself around my wrist.

Vadim moved.

My power moved faster. Martin made the mistake of forming the connection himself. His magic was easy to find, and I latched on. My veins burned red, and the smoke dissipated as if swept away by a breeze.

Martin didn't get to control this. Me.

His eyes turned pure black as his power came to his defense. He was the strongest I'd ever faced, and I knew he'd be able to throw me off. But this wasn't about winning, this was about forcing him to understand I wasn't going to sit back and let people like him run things anymore.

The world turned red, and the ruby burned. Sweat broke out along my forehead and neck and the floor pitched with the effort to take him. All I needed was one opening. His magic was darker than a starless night and wouldn't budge.

It swirled around my own, encasing it, constricting. My breath cut off as his magic suffocated my own. I wasn't ready to let go, not yet.

The darkness thickened until I could no longer see anyone but Martin. I pushed more power through the connection, trying to free myself from the cage he'd created. Something deathly cold wrapped around my wrist and sent ice scurrying through my veins.

My ears popped and I blinked into the night. I was in Martin's backyard, the light from the house flooding out from the living room. Vadim released my upper arm and stepped away.

"Wait here," he commanded, and in a swirl of darkness, he was gone.

The moon's light shone down, giving the grass a silver sheen. I pressed a hand to my chest where I felt Martin's magic still encasing my own. My lungs wouldn't fill, despite me sucking in as much of the fresh air as I could.

I'd attacked a coven leader. In front of everyone. Rumors couldn't be stopped now; they'd all know where I was by morning. I'd done some monumentally stupid things lately, but this was on a whole different level.

Chapter 27

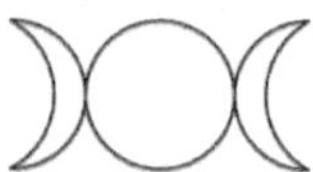

It took a minute for my head to stop spinning enough to focus on one thought. We had to leave.

I rushed inside and up to the bunk room, scurrying around to shove as much as I could into my bag. Grace appeared on the bed, staring at me as I frantically tried to cram everything in with no semblance of organization.

She let out a soft meow.

"Don't start with me," I snapped. I was struggling with the zipper on the backpack when Lyra and Blythe walked in, both looking a little shaken up.

I froze. "Is Martin back?"

Blythe shook her head and fell onto the bed.

Lyra shook her head. "So that was..."

"I know," I said, finally tugging the zipper closed. "But he was—he—I know that was bad, okay?"

"Guess this means the spell didn't work," Blythe said quietly from her bed.

We both turned to her. Rhi had her head in Blythe's lap, gazing up at her with sympathy.

I took a deep breath. "Doesn't look like it."

"There could be a lag," Lyra said like she hadn't questioned that theory less than an hour ago herself. "Like a twenty-four-hour waiting thing."

Blythe shook her head.

"We should have just left it alone," Blythe said. "For all we know, we made it worse."

I didn't want to agree with her, but I did. I'd never been able to sense her emotions like that before. Never fed off her anger like that. The ruby acted up around her, sure, but not *me*.

"He was right," she muttered.

"He's not," I said. "He just wants to keep you—"

"Can you stop bashing my family for two fucking seconds?" she snapped.

I frowned. "Your family is the problem here," I spat.

She stood up. "*My* family isn't the one who started this whole thing."

"You're going to keep bringing *that* up?" I said. "Martin is starting things now."

"I told you he was an ass."

"You said he'd want something for helping me, not that he'd try to use me like this."

"*Us*! Fuck, what is it with the Boswells thinking they're always the most important person in the room?"

"Why do the Osbornes always blame someone else for their issues?" I shot back.

"Because it *is*!"

"You—"

"Hey!"

We both turned to Lyra.

She pointed at me. "Your family has done shitty things."

I shifted uncomfortably.

She pointed to Blythe. "Your family has done shitty things."

Blythe crossed her arms.

"*My* family has done shitty things." She zipped her own bag shut a lot more aggressively than I expected. "All of our families are *currently* doing shitty things, so get the fuck over it and decide if you want to fix it."

I looked down at my feet.

She shoved her arms through her jacket. "Or—" She threw her hands up. "Just kill each other now and save me the headache of doing another unbinding spell." She tied her hair up. "Because I'm not about to waste my time if neither of you give a shit."

"Lyra, I—"

"I'll be in the car," she slung her bag over her shoulder and stormed out, Atalanta on her heels. Blythe and I turned back to each other, but neither of us spoke. Grace was perched on my bed, staring at Rhi like they were about to get into it. Blythe's arms were still crossed, and her face was set. I could see the slight resemblance to Martin in her clenched jaw.

"Can we get over it?" I asked quietly.

She shrugged.

I swallowed. "I'm willing to try."

She shrugged again. That was probably the only answer I was going to get tonight. We finished packing in quick silence, ensuring nothing got left behind.

Lyra and Atalanta were waiting for us in the car Rez had left. We loaded the bags and climbed inside.

"What about Vadim?" I asked as Lyra pulled out of the drive.

"He said he'd meet us there," Blythe said.

I frowned. "Where?" In the flurry of trying to get out, I hadn't actually thought about where we'd go before we could get to my house in Sandusky.

"Halifax," Blythe said, pulling a sweatshirt over her head. "Rez has a place."

"But, Martin..." I started.

"It'll take him a few hours to do damage control if he doesn't want the entire magical community to know about us," Blythe said. "By then, we'll be out of his reach."

I hoped she was right. Regardless, it was the best plan we had at this point. Trying to get to the border this late was risky, and there was still a heaviness set around my magic I couldn't shake off. If we got into another confrontation, I wasn't sure I'd come out of it.

I leaned against the window in the back seat and watched the moon as Lyra sped her way out of town. I felt numb after everything. The magic, the fight, yelling at Blythe. But in the silence of the car, my mind was able to conjure up the words I hadn't had the energy to focus on yet: *Your mother thought she could help, too.*

Had mom known about the binding? About Blythe? Why hadn't she told me? Why did it seem like my family had kept more secrets *from* me than for me?

○

The cats didn't stay with us for the drive, and I was grateful they hadn't tried to crowd in. Rez's loaner car was fast, sure, but small. We got into Halifax at about a quarter to one in the morning.

Blythe directed Lyra to luxury high-rise apartments near the waterfront. Lyra keyed in the code to the underground parking, and we found the slip assigned to the penthouse. In getting out, I had to shake out my stiff legs from the cramped back seat.

We collected our bags and found the nearest elevator, riding in silence to the top. The doors opened to an entrance foyer surrounded by windows. From this height, we could see almost all of downtown Halifax, the city still slightly lit up for the night.

Blythe knocked on the door and we waited. Rez had headed to Halifax over a week ago. What if he wasn't still there and had already headed back to Salem? If so, we'd have to figure something else out in a hurry.

Blythe glanced back at us for a moment before knocking again, a little harder this time. I bit my bottom lip. We could find a hotel room for a few hours until the airport ticket desk opened.

The door opened, and a tall shirtless man blinked at us. His auburn hair was a mess, and it was clear we'd woken him up. Definitely not Rez.

"Who is it?" Rez called.

The man looked us over. "Girl Guides."

Rez appeared at the door, tying a silk robe around himself. He frowned at us.

"What happened?" he asked.

"Martin," Blythe replied simply.

He nodded and opened the door to let us inside. The penthouse had curved windows that ran the length of the entire room we walked into. A terrace on the other side looked out over Halifax, wispy clouds moving by slowly. No curtains blocked out the night sky, and the full moon watched us.

It had only been a few short hours since we'd done the spell. Less since the fallout with Martin. Was he going to come after me? Was I on the run from the Collective *and* Martin now?

I rubbed my tired eyes.

"I told you my family was complicated," Rez said to the man. He didn't look pleased with the explanation and crossed his arms over his broad chest.

"I'll explain later," Rez insisted.

The man sighed but turned and headed down a hallway without argument.

Rez turned back to us. Before he could ask for any more details, there was another knock at the door. He went to answer it, and Vadim stepped inside. His silver suit had been replaced by black jeans and a black sweater under a black coat.

Vadim gave us a sympathetic smile, but he and Rez began conversing in Russian. I was too drained to even care enough to try to catch a word to look up later. They glanced at me more than once and that was really all I needed to know.

I didn't wait for an invitation and sank onto the couch. With how expensive it looked, I was surprised at the comfort. Every limb was sore, and fire burned under my skin. The headache I thought my brief nap during the drive had chased away returned in force.

I wasn't sure when I fell asleep, but I woke up lying on the couch with a blanket over me. Someone had taken off my shoes and set them on the floor. I hadn't slept long; the horizon was lightening at the farthest point, but the city was still dark.

Pulling the blanket around myself a little tighter, I moved to the windows and stared out. I'd overextended before, especially in the last few months. Tried too much too soon, but this was different. Whatever Martin's magic had done affected me on a deeper level.

Digging my phone out of my bag, I stepped out onto the terrace and let the frigid wind off the Atlantic burn my cheeks. I needed to feel something outside of myself. Sniffing against the cold, I tapped his name.

I counted every ring. He wouldn't answer, it was too early. I was ready to hang up when the ringing cut off.

"Em?" Jax said quickly.

The wind froze my tears as they rolled down my cheeks. I choked out a sob instead of words.

"What happened?" I could hear the concern in his voice, and that just made this all worse.

"I—" I barely managed that word. All I wanted was for him to wrap his arms around me and tell me it was all going to be fine. I wanted to *feel* him again.

"Jax, I messed up."

Chapter 28

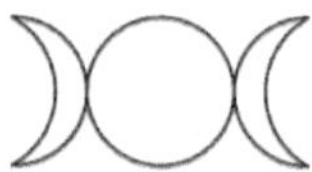

The smell of fresh peppermint tea and soft voices eventually woke me up. Soft sunlight streamed in from the large windows. Rolling over, I rubbed my puffy eyes and pulled the blanket back up to my chin, staring at the city. I hadn't cried myself to sleep in a long time. And that had been after half an hour of crying on the cold terrace.

Jax had listened to me. I hadn't—couldn't—fully explain what had happened. Even if I could have gotten the words out, telling him exactly why I'd called would mean he and the others would have been there in hours. And he hadn't pressed me to tell him more. Once he was convinced I wasn't in immediate danger, he just let me sob.

My body still ached, my eyes were sore, and despite the beautiful view, we were going to have to face what happened with Martin eventually. Not to mention, the failed attempt at unbinding the lines.

"Still have the jitters?" I heard Lyra ask in a hush.

"A little," Blythe said. "But not as bad."

They were quiet for a moment.

"And the headache?"

"Gone."

I could only avoid them for so long, and it sounded like anger hadn't been the only symptom we shared over the bond. Taking a few deep breaths, I pulled the blanket off and stood up.

Lyra and Blythe were at the kitchen counter. They looked around when I walked over. Lyra released Blythe's hand and cupped it around her own mug.

"You look like shit," she said.

I tried to run my hand through my hair but only met tangles. "Don't feel too great," I said, voice hoarse. "Where's Rez?" I climbed onto a seat at the counter.

"Out," Blythe said. "He and Vadim left early."

I nodded. "How are you?"

She shrugged. "A hot shower helps."

I swallowed past my dry throat. Washing off a bad night with an extremely hot shower typically worked. A cleansing bath with one of Wes's mixtures worked better.

"Bathroom's that way," Blythe said, jerking her thumb over her shoulder down a hallway to my right.

"We moved your bag to the bedroom," Lyra added.

When neither of them said anything else, I headed for the bathroom, the tears already coming again. I heard Lyra and Blythe resume their conversation as I shut myself in the guest room. With the shower turned on as hot as it could go, I let the bathroom steam up until it was warm enough to get through the chill on my skin.

I peeled off the clothes I'd fallen asleep in. I hadn't even been wearing them for twelve hours, but they stuck like they'd been on me for days.

The hot water felt nice on my sore body. I tried to scrub off the stubborn ick that stuck in my brain. Martin's magic had wrapped around mine and it was still there, squeezing my ribs and making it impossible to take a full breath.

The discovery that I could connect to other witches' magic was a recent one—and while I'd encountered strong magical defenses, this was different. Once the connections had been severed, there was nothing left. But not now, now it wouldn't leave.

Lathering the body wash for a third round, the lavender scent filled the shower and I closed my eyes, letting it soothe me. After rinsing off, I stood under the hot water as long as I could without someone coming to make sure I hadn't melted.

I dried off and braided my hair out of my face before finding my bag and grabbing a change of clean clothes. A piece of paper fell out of the leggings.

It was one of the memory spells I'd taken from Martin. The others were carelessly stuffed in around the other items of clothing. I smoothed them out against my leg. There was no hope in getting his help now.

Dressing quickly, I took the pages and headed back to the kitchen. This had been the plan all along, it was why we'd gotten mixed up with Martin in the first place. Get Ian back and get away from the Council. Everything else had been secondary.

Undoing the binding eclipsed all of that, and for a good reason. My life being tied to someone else's meant I'd had to put Ian's lost memories on the back burner. Last night proved why, but after our epic failure, I needed a win.

I had Martin's spells, my own books, and Wes could help with the Latin translations. I'd had a plan when I'd left Portland, and that had been derailed. Now, until we could work out what exactly went wrong with the unbinding, I needed something to occupy my time.

Lyra had moved from the counter to cooking at the stove. It smelled like French toast and made my mouth water and stomach grumble. Blythe watched her cook, arms crossed on the counter and chin resting on her arms. Neither of them looked up.

I set the wrinkled copies of the spells on the counter and cleared my throat. "Look, I know you're both pissed at me, and you should be."

Blythe eyebrows pinched together in a frown.

Lyra glanced at her quickly before looking back at me. "What?"

"And if you want to stay here and never talk to me again, I get it."

Blythe picked her head up. "Have you cracked?"

"But if you want to come to Sandusky with me, you can. I would like you to. I know I probably ruined—"

"Did you slip and smack your head in the shower?" Lyra asked, setting the spatula off to the side. She crossed her arms and leaned against the counter.

I blinked at her. "Uh, no."

"Then why do you think we're mad at you?"

I glanced at Blythe, whose eyebrows were raised at me.

"You're not?"

They both shook their heads.

"You really thought we were mad?" Blythe asked.

I shrugged. "Yeah. I mean, after Martin and the fight and stuff…"

Lyra licked syrup off her finger. "The Martin shit was badass," she said. "Could have timed it better, but still badass."

"So, earlier you were both so quiet, I guess I just assumed."

Blythe sighed. "You looked like complete shit," she said.

Lyra used a fork to beat the mixture. "Total shit," she agreed. "Like, you cried for…how long?"

I sank into the seat at the end of the counter. "A while," I admitted.

Lyra nodded. "We didn't want to overwhelm you first thing," she said.

"Oh." Tears pricked my eyes, and I was more annoyed by that than anything. "Thanks."

Lyra flipped over two pieces of toast and waved the spatula in my direction. "Sandusky was the plan, so I'm still down," she said. "Besides, a chill place to do some research on the binding would be helpful."

"And Martin will be looking for me in Salem," Blythe said. "So, I'd rather not be there when that happens."

I watched her face for a moment. "You sure?"

She nodded. "Like sunshine over there said, we'll need a chill place to do research and Salem is anything but."

"Oh, I'm *sunshine* now?" Lyra said with a smile.

Blythe shrugged before turning back to me. "And we still need to get your friend's memory back," she said waving her hand at the papers I'd brought out.

"That we do," Lyra agreed, pointing at Blythe with the spatula for emphasis.

I bit my lip and glanced down at the papers. "That would be really great," I said, voice cracking as tears for an entirely different reason welled up.

"You still feel like crap?" Blythe asked.

I pressed a finger to the inside of my eye to stop myself from crying again, surprised there were any tears left.

"It'll get better," she said. "Hex Witch magic lingers worse than anything."

I hadn't thought to ask what type of magic Martin had when we'd gotten there. But, as a Hex Witch, it made sense why he had a knack for memory spells. Typically, they were the ones called when minds needed erasing or changing.

They could get a bad reputation for it. Evil sorcerers in fairy tales or legends normally had their origins in Hex Witches. It stemmed from them positioning themselves close to those in power. Kings, queens, emperors, and in more modern times it wouldn't be unusual to find one higher up in mortal governments more than any other type of witch. Their kind of magic, though, would get into the system and linger like a bad cold.

Lyra put two pieces of toast onto a plate and passed it to Blythe. She added a few uncooked ones to the pan and the aroma of vanilla and cinnamon filled the space, making my stomach grumble more.

I felt lighter, despite the hex magic in my system. Knowing they weren't mad at me—and were not only willing to come with me, but also still wanted to help with Ian—gave me some hope that, despite Lenore, Sasha, and now Martin all vying for a piece of me, I still had friends.

○

We packed up what little I'd unpacked in the hours we spent at Rez's. Well, I repacked and actually folded all my clothes so that they fit into my backpack and be zipped up easily.

Rez offered us use of his private jet instead of spending the money on tickets to Ohio. I accepted before I knew that meant it was going to be a few hours before we could leave. Lyra and Blythe, however, seemed excited not to have to fly in cramped airline seats, so I did my best to hide my disappointment.

Even with Lyra supplying me with an herbal tea to try to keep the anxiousness to a minimum, I needed something to keep my mind busy. Attempting to translate the Latin in the spells I'd stolen from Martin was all I had with me. Rez had a small collection of language books in his place that I used, although the Latin one wasn't as comprehensive as I was going to need.

After two hours, I'd managed the first line and a half to an acceptable degree. Once I had access to the library in Sandusky, I'd have to double-check. Wes would be able to help too. Unfortunately, none of what I'd gotten so far made for a promising outcome to Ian's predicament.

Lyra set another cup of tea in front of me and cocked her head to the side. "Doesn't that mean love?" she asked.

I rubbed my sore eyes. "Technically," I groaned. I hoped I'd messed up that translation. If I'd gotten it right, that meant I'd stolen a spell to erase the memories of a past love. Everyone kept saying it was tricky retrieving memory spells, but I hadn't thought it would be this hard to *find* a spell in the first place.

My frustrations were interrupted by a firm series of knocks on the front door. Blythe hopped off her seat to answer the door as Lyra refilled her coffee. I mouthed the words of the spell over and over, trying to get my brain to click and give me the word I needed to get it to work.

"No," Blythe said.

I glanced up at Lyra before we both looked around at the small wall that separated the front entrance and the kitchen. Blythe's tone was never what I could call "friendly," but the way she spat that word out was concerning.

Lyra set her mug on the counter and moved to the door as I closed Amity's book and reapplied the concealment charm.

"The fuck do you want?" Lyra demanded.

I tucked the grimoire under my bag on the couch and rounded the corner to the entryway myself. Martin stood at the door, hands in his coat pocket, his dark eyes scanning the three of us.

"I was hoping to talk to you," he said. He sounded congenial enough, but that didn't stop my magic from rising.

"I said no," Blythe maintained, crossing her arms.

He inclined his head to her. "Not just to you," he said, gazing flicking to me. "We need to discuss what happened the other night."

I swallowed hard. Attacks—provoked or not—were a big issue in the Collective, especially on a coven leader, and I highly doubted the Outliers differed on that issue. But I didn't belong to *any* coven, so there was no one to help me, no one to come to my defense if I needed help.

"You plan on telling us why you lied?" Blythe asked.

Lyra finished a text on her phone and slipped the phone into her back pocket. "How'd you even find us?" she asked.

Martin gave her a condescending smile. "You insult my intelligence," he said.

Lyra rolled her eyes.

"Perhaps we should continue this conversation inside," he continued, taking a step forward. Blythe retreated further into the apartment and Lyra stepped up, ready to swing.

"Just let him in," I said.

His magic was still in my system, dampening my own, so if he wanted to force his way in, I wouldn't be able to put up much of a fight anyway.

Blythe hesitated but eventually moved aside to let Martin step into the apartment. Lyra—still poised to strike if necessary—followed as we moved into the living room. I faced him and crossed my arms.

He glanced around the space. "Is Reznor here?" he asked.

"You said you wanted to talk," I reminded him. "So, talk."

His eyes swept around the room one more time before he gave me a slight nod. "I would first like to apologize for my outburst," he started. "It was not my finest moment."

Blythe snorted.

I bit the inside of my cheek.

He cleared his throat. "When Blythe told me what you had attempted, I allowed my own fear to get the better of me."

Blythe and I exchanged a glance. "What were you afraid of?" I asked. "Unbinding our lines would be a good thing."

He shook his head slightly before catching himself and turning it to a nod. "That's what your mothers believed," he said. "But their attempts only made things worse." His gaze flicked to Lyra. "Now, there's no telling what your spell has further done to it."

"So, you attack Em?" Blythe said. "Not sure where that fits in."

"Again, my fear got the better—"

"You honestly expect me to believe this shit?" Blythe snapped.

His jaw clenched. "I was trying to keep you safe," he said. "Like I tried with your mother." He put his hands in his pockets. "You were both content until a Boswell got involved."

And there it was. Boswells were the problem, and I was starting to believe it. Mary, Amity, mom, and now me, we'd caused all the issues. I'd been raised to blame Isobel Jacob and her prophecy but, ultimately, the truth was the Boswell's reaction to the prophecy is what set all this into motion.

"Content?" Blythe repeated. "I haven't been *content* since my mom died." She crossed her arms.

"I just want to keep you safe," he said.

I took a breath. "What did our mothers do?" I asked.

He looked at me. "That's not important."

"It is," I insisted. "You said it made things worse. I think Blythe and I have a right to know what that means."

He shook his head. "I'm sure if they wanted you to know, they would have told you," he said.

I flinched as my magic flared, and a shock went through me when it hit Martin's block. "Considering they're both dead and we can't ask them, I'd like to hear it from you," I said.

"Since you know so much about it," Lyra added with a slight smirk.

Blythe looked between Lyra and me and I could see it click into place.

Martin cleared his throat. "They were operating under the assumption that your family was cursed," he said. "That won't help you."

I couldn't stop the smile. "So you lied to them, too."

His posture straightened. "I do not appreciate that accusation."

"Nice non-answer," Lyra muttered. "Just fucking admit it, you knew it wasn't a curse and decided not to tell anyone."

"Stay out of this, Miss Tsipras, it does not concern you," he said. "For all we know, your reckless flippancy has made the situation worse."

Lyra's eyebrows drew together in a frown.

"Don't talk to her like that," Blythe snapped.

"Blythe, please I—"

"If you don't know anything that can help us undo the binding, then leave," I said.

He stared at me. "You're seriously considering pursuing this?"

I met his gaze and nodded.

"I cannot allow—"

"It's not up to you," I said. "It's up to Blythe, and me," I nodded at Lyra. "And her. You lost any right to weigh in when you lied to us."

He took a long breath through his nose. "Your stubbornness is not a benefit," he said.

I shrugged. "Maybe not, but I'd rather be stubborn than used." I nodded to the door. "You can leave now."

"I will not be dismissed until I've said my piece," he said.

I sighed. "You're afraid of what will happen if Blythe and I get full use of our power, we got it."

"That is not—"

"You can leave on your own, or I'll have you removed." Rez walked into the room with Vadim just behind him. I hadn't heard them come in, although to be fair, they may not have used the door.

Martin faced his grandson and small swirls of gray magic rolled from his fingertips. My own magic tried to rise, hammering against the block of hex magic that kept it from surging forward. I had to grip the back of the couch to keep myself from swaying. I didn't need him to know that I couldn't defend myself right then.

His magic receded and he straightened his jacket. "I do hope you see sense," he said to Blythe and me as he moved to the door. "Before it's too late."

Chapter 29

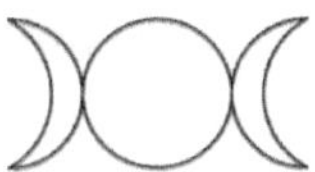

Rez insisted we get out of the apartment for some fresh air after Martin left. He assured us he'd send Vadim when the jet was ready. His idea came off as casual, but I had a suspicion he and Vadim wanted to discuss Martin without us around.

I didn't mind, though. Fresh air was a good idea. A headache had started not long after my magic had tried to fight its way through Martin's block, and I figured some crisp winter air might just do the trick to get rid of it. Or, at the very least, help the Tylenol work faster.

Lyra took us on a walk to Grounded Coffee Bar for warm drinks before heading to the waterfront for some sightseeing. Wrapping my gloved hand around my London Fog, I wished it had been hot enough to seep through the cloth and warm my fingertips.

A few other people were out—bundled up against the cold—walking their dogs or enjoying the brisk day. Occasionally we'd see a couple or a small posse of friends snapping a picture, but for the most part, we were saved from having to deal with large groups.

I squinted out over the sunny reflection on the water. The sunlight was not helping my throbbing head.

"You look like you're in pain," Blythe said.

"It's bright," I muttered.

Lyra glanced up at the sky. "I could probably come up with a sun blocking spell," she offered.

I shook my head. "Let's *not* mess with celestial forces."

She frowned. "You're no fun."

I shrugged and moved to a bench overlooking the harbor while Lyra balanced on the edge of the walkway over the water, arms stretched out on either side of herself. I took an extra-long sip of my tea and watched as she turned on her heel and reversed direction. Blythe tossed her small coffee cup into a bin and sat down next to me.

"Why don't you think they said anything?" she asked.

I looked down at the lid of the cup and turned it slowly, letting the small drip slide around the plastic edge. "I don't know," I admitted. I'd always thought mom and I were close. I'd only just turned thirteen when she died; maybe she thought I wouldn't have been able to handle knowing my life was tied to someone else's.

But she hadn't told Wes either. He'd been as surprised as I was. If she really thought I was too young to know, why hadn't she at least told him?

Thinking about this wasn't helping my headache.

Lyra skipped over to us, cheeks flushed with cold. "I see why Rez has a place here," she said. "Great views."

Blythe chuckled. "Ask nice and he might sublet."

"You think?"

I finished the last of my drink and moved to toss the cup away, but Blythe caught me before I could walk around the bench. I frowned down at her, but she wasn't looking at me. Her gaze was focused on something to her right. She slowly stood up, still holding onto my arm.

"Those yours?" she asked Lyra.

Lyra feigned stretching, but her head turned in the direction Blythe was looking. She nodded. "Unfortunately," she said, and my stomach dropped.

Lyra pulled her hair tighter while glancing behind her. "And they've brought friends." Her gaze flicked back and forth between the two groups. "They'll have at least two more up the street in case we get by them."

That would mean there were six Emissaries standing between us and the safety of Rez's apartment. I risked feeling out with my magic, sending it as far from me as I could with the hex magic still blocking it. Closing my eyes to focus on the places I couldn't see. Lyra and Blythe whispered a plan to each other, but I caught none of it.

Two energies up the street flickered like a dying flashlight, but that only confirmed it. Six well-trained Emissaries against the three of us. And I wasn't at my full strength. Our odds were shit.

I opened my eyes to Lyra looking at me expectantly. "All good?"

"Only sensed two," I confirmed.

"You're sure?"

I nodded.

"Okay then." She pulled her phone out and shot off a quick text before zipping it back up in her coat pocket. "We'll have about a ten-second head start if this goes the way I want it to."

"And if it doesn't?" Blythe asked.

"Then feel free to do what you think necessary," she said with a wink before moving a few steps forward, brushing by me. Blythe and I followed as casually as we could. We were halfway hidden by a group of dog walkers and a building with a giant "Beavertails" sign on it.

Lyra put her hands on my shoulders and stared into my eyes. "Give me a count of five, then run."

"What—" I watched her bright blue eyes turn red and her tanned skin lighten. Her blond hair turned dark, and she shrank a couple of inches. It was almost a perfect copy of me, had it not been for Lyra's signature smirk. I shook my head, ready to argue, but before words could come out, she bolted up the street.

I started counting in my head. Blythe took off in the opposite direction without warning, leaving me standing alone and with no idea where to go. I hit five, slid over the concrete planter, and sprinted.

Knocking shoulders with someone angry enough to shout after me, I kept running until I found a cross street. Heading up, I threw out magic to make sure I wasn't about to run right into someone I didn't want to.

I ducked into a side street and hurried up the incline, making my legs burn, the cold air stinging my lungs every time I tried to take a breath. I slowed when I got to the top of the street. I needed a sign, something that would help me get my bearings.

We just had to get back to Rez's place—an unspoken agreement that I intended to keep. Breathing heavily, I turned down the upper street in the direction we'd originally come from, keeping an eye out for any landmarks I might recognize.

Ducking into a stone breezeway, my steps echoed as I went further inside. I stopped to catch my breath and listened for footsteps following me. The cold wind whipping through it made me shiver. I leaned against the wall and took a few deep breaths.

"Trouble always finds you, malen'kaya gadyuka."

I jumped and let out a shriek when Vadim stepped out of the shadows.

"God, don't do that," I grumbled, pressing a hand to my already-over-acting heartbeat.

He extended his hand to me. "We need to go," he insisted.

I glanced at the entrance I'd come through but nodded and put my hand in his. He gave it a comforting squeeze.

Warm blood splattered across my face. Vadim's dark eyes went wide. He slumped forward and I reached to catch him. His weight brought me down, body crushing me. I yanked my legs out from under him and pressed myself against the wall.

He wasn't moving. His magic was gone.

Dead.

Chapter 30

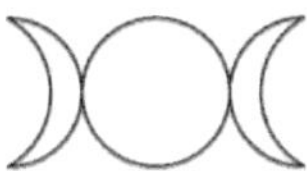

He—he—I—they—

Thoughts weren't working. Lungs wouldn't hold air. Blood and tears ran down my face. Vadim was gone. *Dead.*

Heavy footsteps.

Sasha replaced a gun into a holster around her thigh and strolled over to me. I tried to pull myself up the slick cobblestone and choke back the sobs. I needed to get away from her. My legs wouldn't work.

Why wouldn't my legs work?

She cocked her head at me. "You're not getting off that easy," she said, so calm. She'd murdered Vadim. Killed him and acted like we were talking about the weather.

She knelt in front of me.

I reached for my magic.

Her head snapped up and she stood, drawing the gun and aiming it at something behind me.

I didn't think, just reacted. I kicked her knee, earning a grunt and breaking her focus. Something careened into her with a loud thud, sending her sprawling. More hunters appeared behind her. One helped Sasha to her feet.

Flames flew over my head, heating the breezeway.

Dragged to my feet, I stumbled to get them to hold my weight. I reached for Vadim, struggling against the arms that held me.

"Em, we have to go," Jax said.

I shook my head. "We can't leave him!"

"He's gone."

"No—" I was sobbing again, trying to get free of him. "We—we can't—"

"There's nothing we can do for him now," he said.

I wouldn't leave him dead in the street. He deserved better.

"Just put her out," another voice said.

"Shut up," Jax snapped.

A shot echoed around the stone tunnel and hit the wall—too close to us. Jax pulled me around the corner. A car waited. Doors closed. Another shot clipped the side of the car. We sped away. I was going to puke. People argued. Jax's hand never left mine.

We parked, we were in a too-bright lobby, we rode an elevator with too-chipper music. The metal doors showed a blurry blood-and-tear-stained reflection. My stomach rolled and bile rose in my throat.

We were in a suite overlooking the harbor, not far from where the day had started on a much better note. Blythe sat on the couch in the main room, arms crossed and glaring at Kane, who stood with his hands clasped behind his back.

Her expression shifted when she saw me. "What happened?" she asked, hurrying over.

I shook my head. "They—" I swallowed. "Vadim."

She blanched.

"I couldn't...I'm sorry."

She pulled me into a tight hug, surprising me enough that it took me a moment to get my arms to move and return it.

When we let each other go, I glanced around the room. "Lyra?" I asked in a hush.

Blythe shook her head.

She wasn't the only one missing. There were only four Emissaries in the room. Kane, Jax, Sadiki, and Sebastian. There should have been two more. If they weren't back, that meant they were still looking for Lyra. Maybe she'd made it back to Rez's.

My stomach roiled and I shut my eyes against the fresh tears that were about to overflow. Blythe sank back onto the couch, and I dug my phone out. A soft song-like meow filled the room. Grace, Rhi, and Atalanta appeared next to her. Rhi put her head in Blythe's lap.

The Emissaries all moved as if the cats were a threat. The hissing they got in return brought them up short.

I moved into a bedroom off the main room, Grace sliding off the couch to follow me, rubbing against my leg before gliding ahead and taking up a spot on the large bed, watching the door.

Jax stepped in after me. Grace lifted her head off her large paws to watch his movements.

"Are you—"

I held up my hand to stop him from finishing. That's not what I needed right now. I could break down later. The phone had a large crack in the screen but lit up okay. I shrugged out of my bloodied coat as the line rang, and I used my free arm to wipe my face with my sleeve.

Jax put a hand on my shoulder, but I shrugged it off.

Rez answered. "Vadim should have had you back by now," he said quickly.

My voice caught. I tried to dislodge the lump stopping my words. A pathetic attempt came out, but nothing else.

"Em?" he said slowly.

I swallowed hard. "He's dead." I barely got it out, and though I did, it was so quiet I wasn't even sure he heard me.

Silence followed and my lip trembled. Rez cleared his throat. "Blythe?"

"She's...not hurt," I said. Telling him she was okay wasn't the truth. None of us were okay.

Movement on his end. "Where are you now?"

I glanced at Jax. "At a hotel, I think."

"Where?" he repeated.

I shook my head. "I'm not sure," I admitted.

Jax put his hand out and—after hesitating for a moment—I handed him the phone. I sat on the edge of the bed while Jax gave Rez the information he wanted. Grace nuzzled against me, her warmth spreading quickly.

Jax handed the phone back to me and I set it to the side. Was there any point to keeping it? We'd been found, again. Someone got hurt because of me, again. Someone was dead because of me, *again.*

I took a shuddering breath as tears rolled down my cheeks. I pressed the heel of my palm under my eyes to keep more from escaping.

Rez hadn't known we'd split up, which meant Lyra hadn't made it back to the apartment. She was still out there with hunters roaming the streets looking for me. If she still had her glamour on...

I stood and moved for the door.

"Take a minute," Jax said, stepping in front of me.

"We don't have a minute," I argued. "Lyra—"

"Leander will be back with her soon."

I shook my head. "She looks like me, and Sasha won't care about the difference."

He let out a long sigh and stepped aside. I hurried for the door, but Sebastian grabbed me before I could get out.

"You're not going anywhere," he said, grip tight on my arm.

"Let her go," Jax said.

Sebastian shot him a glare. "You don't have a say in anything anymore."

I ripped my arm free. "I'm going to find Lyra."

"You're staying here until we can get a clear transport back to Boston," Sebastian ordered, reaching for me again.

I sent a jolt of magic out, only letting it scrape the surface of his own. A warning. I didn't want to waste all my energy on him.

He took a step back from the shock and I reached for the door. Something yanked me away and I landed on my back, staring at the ceiling, air forced from my lungs.

"Charlevoix!" Kane scolded.

I rolled to my side and tried to catch my breath. Jax helped me to my feet.

Blythe jumped up from the couch and stood next to us. The cats hissed.

Sebastian stood in front of the door, arms crossed, and a smug smile on his face.

"That was out of line," Kane said.

"Councilwoman Charlevoix wants her back," Sebastian said. "I intend to deliver."

"You really think you can take her?" Jax said, taking a small step in front of me.

Sebastian inclined his head. "What's one Blood Witch against the Council?"

Blythe took a half-step forward, but I grabbed her arm and held her back. She glanced at me, and I gave her a warning shake of my head. If the Council didn't know about Blythe yet, we'd want to keep it that way.

Sebastian's smile was so arrogant, I sent a jolt of my magic into his system just to get him to stop. I didn't let it last long, just long enough to get me closer to the door. He backpedaled to block me.

The door slammed open, smacking Sebastian. Leander and a tall woman with auburn hair rushed into the room. I frowned, glancing over at Jax, but he avoided my gaze. Leander and Thea were flushed and breathing heavily.

"Where's Lyra?" Blythe asked.

Leander shook his head.

"They grabbed her before we could," Thea said. She looked at me. "They thought she was you."

It was like Martin's magic was suffocating me all over again.

Blythe fell back onto the arm of the couch. Jax rubbed his jaw.

"Looks like you all fucked up again." Rez appeared in the doorway, coming in behind Leander and Thea.

"What are you doing here?" Leander snapped.

Rez didn't answer but went straight to Blythe, putting his hands on her shoulders and looking her over as if to confirm she wasn't hurt. Tears silently rolled down her cheeks.

"We have Boswell," Sebastian said. "We should go."

"Sasha has Lyra," I said. "If you think I'm leaving without her, you're dumber than you look."

"She brought it on herself," he said.

"Sebastian," Thea interjected, clearly shocked.

"She chose to defy the Council," he continued. "And I, for one, will not disobey orders for someone like that."

My magic flared.

Leander swung, catching Sebastian's nose and sending him stumbling to the side.

Sebastian righted himself, clutching his jaw, and glared at Leander. He wiped the blood from under his nose and shook it off his hand.

"We are *not* leaving without my sister," Leander said through gritted teeth.

"You can stay," Sebastian said. "But I'm taking the Blood Witch and leaving."

He closed the small distance between us but froze before he could reach for me. He blinked too quickly and began scraping at his chest through his shirt.

"Touch her, and your life will be nothing but a living hell until the day you die," Blythe threatened.

We all looked around. She sat on the floor, crossed legs by the door—I hadn't even realized she'd moved—her hand hovering over the droplets of Sebastian's blood that had landed on the carpet after Leander hit him.

She flexed her fingers over the droplets and they moved, forming a dark rune on the fabric.

"You—you're—"

"Blythe Osborne," she said, eyes glowing red. "Blood Witch."

Jax caught my eye, and I gave him a small nod of confirmation. Add that to the list of things we were going to have to discuss if we survived the next few hours.

Kane cleared his throat. "I do not believe there's any need for that, Ms. Osborne," he said.

Blythe didn't move.

"While Lyra's choices were questionable," he said. "I do not believe the Council—Selene Tsipras, in particular—would want us to leave her in the hands of these hunters."

Sebastian opened his mouth to argue, but Blythe twitched her fingers and the rune began to glow, pain lancing his features.

"If they disagree, they will know the decision was mine alone."

We all waited for Sebastian to say something. His eyes flicked to all of us in turn.

Kane put his hands in his pockets and moved to stand in front of him. "I believe Ms. Osborne is waiting for your agreement," he said. "I wouldn't keep her waiting."

I frowned. I didn't like how calmly he'd accepted both the fact there was a second Blood Witch in the room and her name, like he was the only one not surprised.

"Fine," Sebastian bit out.

Blythe flicked her wrist and balled her fist. The rune dissipated and returned to nothing but drops of blood on the carpet.

Chapter 31

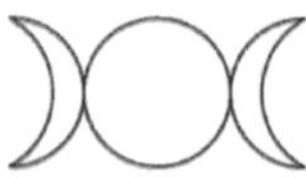

The shipyard was technically closed, but we saw more than the normal number of guards walking the length of the fence. And Blythe's blood location spell had led us there.

Rez pulled around the side of the yard and killed the headlights. He drummed his fingers on the steering wheel.

"They'll be in place in a minute," Jax said, securing his earpiece.

I ran the ruby along its chain, letting the hum of magic in it remind me that I wasn't alone. The power inside would always be with me. That was a small comfort as I watched the hunters make another pass along the fence.

Blythe turned around in her seat. "Ready?" she asked Jax, holding her hand out. Jax put his own hand in hers, palm up. She pricked the tip of his index finger with a safety pin. A bead of blood gathered, and she pressed the end of the ash tree twig to Jax's finger.

Once the tip was stained with blood, she gave him his hand back. Soft golden light filled the back seat as his magic healed the small prick.

Blythe wrapped her hand around the center of the twig, lips moving soundlessly, and her eyes glowed red as the spell took hold. Jax's blood shone under the bark of the ash but went dark in less than a minute.

"Did it work?" Jax asked.

Blythe nodded. She held her hand flat and laid the twig on it, ends facing the windows. "*Faigh*," she said. The twig spun until the tip that had absorbed Jax's blood was pointing at the warehouse.

"That confirms it," she said.

Jax tapped the piece in his ear. "Nothing from Leander yet."

I tapped my fingers against the seat. I'd agreed that walking through the front gate hadn't been a good idea, but waiting and trusting that the others were getting into place wasn't easy.

"How long do we give them?" Rez asked.

"As long as we need to make sure we don't all die," Jax said.

Rez glanced at him in the mirror, and I caught Jax's jaw flinching with the effort not to say more. Whatever happened between Rez and Leander clearly left an impression on both Jax and Lyra. I should just leave them in the car, Blythe and I could handle it.

A sharp knock on the window made me jump. Rez rolled down the window.

Rez frowned. "What?"

"Back's no good," Leander said. "They've got it too well covered."

"Shit," Blythe muttered.

Rez glanced at the gate in front of us and sighed. "Get in," he said.

Leander started to argue.

"Lyra doesn't have time," Rez urged.

Leander nodded and squeezed into the back with Jax and me. I had to climb into Jax's lap to make room. Rez's car clearly wasn't made for this many people.

"Is there another way in?" Blythe asked.

Rez shook his head. "Everyone, hang on."

"What?" Leander and Jax said at the same time. We didn't get an explanation. Rez slammed down on the accelerator, flinging us forward. Jax wrapped an arm around my waist as the gate got too close way too fast.

We crashed through the barrier arm, cracking the windshield. Rez sped through the front lot, sending hunters scrambling out of his way.

He hooked a right and screeched to a stop at the base of the staircase on the side of the building.

Blythe, Jax, and I tumbled out and Leander slid into the front seat.

"We'll give you as long as we can," he said and shut the door.

They flew off as the hunters recovered and went after them. We followed Blythe up the stairs, where she used Lyra's unlocking spell on the door.

The quietness inside was unsettling, and I shivered against the unnatural chill. The door had led us to one of many raised walkways above boats in various stages of repair. Each one of our steps intruded on the stillness, and it had me watching the shadows for movement.

Blythe used the ash twig, whispering the word to activate it. It pointed us forward at what looked like an office. Once we closed in on the room, I peered through the window. Lyra was inside.

She was handcuffed to a large filing cabinet and had a piece of duct tape over her mouth. Blythe pocketed the twig as Jax opened the door. I didn't want to think about what the door being unlocked meant.

When Lyra saw us, she shook her head and mumbled frantically. Blythe knelt in front of her and ripped the tape off.

"Ow," Lyra said pointedly.

"Are you okay?" Blythe asked.

"Other than you idiots walking into their trap, I'm fan-fucking-tastic."

"We weren't going to leave you," I said.

Blythe unlocked the cuffs and Lyra pulled her hands free, rubbing the red and irritated skin.

"I had it under control," she said, pulling herself up with the handle on the cabinet. She swayed slightly, and Blythe ducked under her arm.

"Clearly," Blythe muttered.

Lyra limped forward. "It's not my fault that toxin is a bitch."

I sighed. Of course they were still using that. They hated witches but weren't above using their creations for more murder.

I pulled out the four sachets and put them on the desk. After adding the fuse to the first one, I tightened the strings with my teeth to make sure it didn't move.

"You'll have thirty seconds max before they burn down," I said. "Try not to be around when that happens." I handed the finished herb bomb to Jax.

He took them. "You need to get out before they realize you're here."

"And you shouldn't?" Lyra asked.

He picked up a fuse and tied it in the second sachet. "We all took a dose of the antitoxin."

I stopped halfway through tying a knot on the third one. "They took his memory *and* his antitoxin?"

Jax wouldn't meet my gaze. Instead, he focused too intently on the finished bag in his hands. "Em, I—"

"Let's just get out of here." We didn't have time to deal with that particular betrayal right now. The Council didn't like mortals knowing about us, but they'd use them if they saw a benefit. A haunting similarity between them and the hunters.

Yanking the strings closed on the last sachet, I practically chucked it at Jax. "Let's get going."

I brushed by him to the door and pulled it open as anger surged through me. We moved back onto the walkway. Lyra—supported by Blythe—was regaining her steadiness quickly.

I rubbed my index finger and thumb together, drawing on the magic I would need to light the fuse. Jax caught up to me to give my hand a comforting squeeze and a nod before splitting off to head down a different walkway.

I didn't like splitting up, but with Rez's car smashed thanks to him using it as a battering ram, it was going to take an extra-long distraction to get us out of here.

Chaos broke out seconds later as fire erupted below us. The high-pitched whine of my bags followed by gunshots left my ears ringing, adding to the pandemonium.

"Guess backup is here," Lyra said with a weak chuckle.

The door was so far away—and without knowing where everyone was, we could be walking right into someone's perfect shot. Two figures ran up the stairs from below, right in front of the door.

"Around," I said, igniting the fuse on an herb bag and setting it on the walkway. We backtracked to the office and went around the other side to a different walkway, just parallel to the one we'd been on. There had to be another exit somewhere.

The two figures ran after us. My bag exploded, sending them tumbling over the railings.

Smoke and heat from the fires made it hard to see. My bags reeked of everything that should never be mixed, making it hard not to gag. My throat stung, and no amount of coughing would help.

A silhouette appeared in front of us and I froze.

"We're not getting out of here," Blythe said as Lyra sagged against the railing.

"Siphon me," Lyra said, breathlessly.

I didn't take my eyes off the approaching outline of a person but shook my head. "You're too weak."

"I'll be fine," Lyra insisted.

"She's right," Blythe said. "You'll probably pass out and I can't carry you."

I curled my fingers into fists. I might not be strong enough to take them all, but I could deal with one or two.

Someone's hand slipped around mine and I felt the slickness of blood just before it seeped into my skin, connecting me to someone powerful.

I glanced down at my own hand and then at Blythe. She gave me a nod and pressed her hand firmly against my skin. I'd siphoned from powerful witches before, but this was...she was *strong*.

The world burned red, clearing the smoke from my vision as I focused on the man in front of us.

I knew Blythe had already started moving to the exit. I couldn't explain how, but I was acutely aware of just how close she was to me.

I reached for the man in front of us and my magic clicked into place, quickly. I pulled it back almost as quickly, recognizing the connection.

Kane stepped forward, his hair disheveled and his shirt ripped open. I never thought I'd be happy to see him.

A hunter appeared on the walkway to our left, twenty feet away. But that wouldn't stop him from being able to shoot one of us. I sent my magic like a whip, taking their energy faster than I ever had.

Their arm twitched violently as they fought me. But they weren't able to fight long. They smashed their wrist against the metal railing until they were screaming in pain and the gun fell from their hand.

I turned back to Kane. "Where is—"

"Down!"

I ducked as he sent a torrent of flames to my right. Without a witch like Sadiki, there was no precision to it, and the heat singed the top of my hair.

The screaming wasn't something I'd forget soon, and the smell of burning flesh made my stomach churn.

I looked up to see Kane taking a shuddering step towards me. Time slowed as Armin appeared behind him, knife drawn and a vicious smile on his face.

"Behind—" I started, but the warning died in my throat the moment Armin plunged the blade into Kane. His eyes went wide, and a gurgle filled with blood left his lips stained. The flame on his fingers flickered and died.

Armin yanked the knife free. He let Kane fall to the side and stepped over him like he was nothing but trash.

I scuttled backwards on the catwalk, pulling my magic and sending it forward.

"Sasha has been waiting to get her hands on you," he said, pointing the knife at me.

Another herb bag exploded, letting out the putrid smell of sulfur into the air.

I faced Armin again and concentrated my magic into taking him. But I hit a wall. Even with Blythe's magic helping me, even with the ruby hot against my skin, it wouldn't penetrate. No mortal had ever been able to keep me out before.

"And just in time for her birthday," he continued.

"Not so fast, Armin."

He froze and a scowl crossed his face. Through the haze of herbs and smoke from Sadiki and Kane's fires stepped a slender woman with dark graying hair, a sharp chin, and an air of power I could feel.

She moved as though the fighting around us was nothing more than a slight inconvenience. As if the dead witch at her feet was of no consequence. She stepped up next to Armin, the collar of her black wool coat turned up and belt cinched at the waist.

"I need a moment with my granddaughter before you take her."

Chapter 32

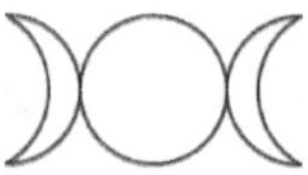

Using the railing to pull myself up on shaky legs, I watched as my grandmother took a few determined steps towards me. I resisted the overwhelming urge to run.

She clasped her hands in front of her and cocked her head at me as if assessing a new piece of art.

"You've been causing us all a lot of trouble," she said.

Armin watching our conversation, instead of trying to kill us both, did not make me feel better about anything.

"I just wanted to be left alone," I said, keeping one eye on Armin as best I could.

"That was never an option," she said. "You know that."

I swallowed. "You didn't want my mother," I muttered.

She let out a cool laugh. "Your mother wasn't foolish enough to tell my son her real name."

Armin chuckled.

Lenore took another step towards me and pulled the crystal dagger, once belonging to Raven, from her pocket. I took half a step away and Armin stood a little straighter.

"This is a special tool," Lenore said, turning it over in her hand. "It allows the user to take power from another witch."

Armin leveled with her. "We had a deal, Charlevoix," he snapped. "She pays for what she did to my son."

The heat from the fires vanished as it all crashed down on me. They had a deal. That's why I wasn't able to get through to take him. *She* was protecting him. She was helping him. That's how they'd found us in Salem, and now here.

She waved him off. "You'll get what's owed you," she said before looking back at me.

"And you want my power," I concluded, eyeing the knife.

She nodded. "I'd hoped to have you join my coven," she said. "But this will have to do."

I wrapped my hand around the ruby for comfort. I'd survived being stabbed before; maybe I'd get lucky again. Only I hadn't survived, not really. If it hadn't been for Blythe's protection spell, I would have died.

"And your *coven* is okay with you killing me?" I snapped.

She laughed. "Oh child, I don't have to kill you to have your power."

I frowned.

She closed the distance between us, leaving a curious Armin watching from behind her. "That poor girl didn't know the first thing about what she had. A drop of your blood, given willingly, will be more than enough."

I swallowed hard.

"A deal," she continued, "and your friends, your uncles, your lover, they will all be spared."

I glanced at Kane's body. "Not all of them."

She looked down at the body with no remorse. "Yes. Mr. Arriens's death is unfortunate, but there is nothing I can do about that now."

Lyra was right. She really was a bitch.

"It's a simple choice," she went on, placing the crystal dagger in my hand. "Your power for their lives."

Everything had gone disturbingly quiet. My breath and my heartbeat were the only things I could hear. Lenore was too close, the powdery amber of her perfume more stifling than the sulfur.

"We'll even give your mortal his memories back."

I pursed my lips, trying not to let that last promise break me. Ian was everything, and I should have been willing to do anything for him. He'd do it for me, but staring at the dagger...I couldn't. My power was who I was. I'd be giving up everything I had come to be.

The gentle thrum of magic in the ruby under my hand reminded me that it wasn't just *my* power I'd be giving up—giving her. It would also be of those who came before me.

And the binding was still in place. There was no telling what that would mean for Blythe and her power. A decision I would not make for her, no matter how much I wanted Ian back.

I let out a breath through my nose, dropped the ruby, and prayed to whatever Goddess was listening that I wasn't making a terrible mistake.

"No."

Her jaw tightened and she huffed out a long sigh. "Martin said you were stubborn," she said. "Very well."

She raised her hand and I flinched. But when she flicked her index finger, she sent the knife soaring through the air, right into Armin's throat.

His eyes went wide with shock as he scraped for it. Without looking at him, she crooked her finger again, pulling the blade free. It landed at my feet with a thud, wet blood coating it.

Armin fell to his knees, trying to stanch the flow of blood from his neck. He took a few shuddering movements towards us, trying to form words.

Lenore clasped her hands in front of her once more and looked at me like I was the naughty grandchild that messed up the living room furniture.

I wasn't about to be next. I let my power surge forward and connect with hers. Had she been ready for it, I never would have gotten through so quickly.

She gasped and clutched her chest as my magic snapped into hers. But that was as far as I got before meeting resistance. Martin had fought back and left a lasting impression, but Lenore was too powerful to even get as far as I had with him.

"You're an insolent child," she snapped through gritted teeth.

"Go to hell."

Her lip twitched in contempt as her own magic came to her defense, forcing me to grasp the railing to keep from passing out. My vision tunneled and the walkway pitched, but I wasn't about to let up.

"*Nostri sanguinis...*" the words came out in a pant. The ruby's heat was too far away. Dream-like. "*...viribus meis.*"

Bile rose in my throat.

But I could see the fight on her face as well. I was getting through. Just not fast enough. Unconsciousness was coming for me, and then I'd be completely at her mercy.

Fisting my hand around the ruby, I risked closing my eyes. I focused on the power humming in the gem. A force that was mine to wield. It vibrated under my hand, sending ripples of power to my core.

I repeated the words over and over in my head.

Lenore let out a scream and my eyes flew open. She clutched the railing to keep herself upright—glaring as her magic came for me, attacking harder than before.

I couldn't breathe. This fight would kill me. It would kill me and Blythe. And *she* would win.

"Up here!"

My focus slipped enough for her to gain purchase and send me crumpling to the walkway. Hot, rough metal dug into my hands. My own blood dripped from my nose, and I lifted my head enough to see her disappear into the smoke as if she were never there.

Sasha and three others took her place within seconds. She stared at her father's body, rage contorting her features. Her eyes found the crystal dagger lying beside me. She let out a horrible scream and charged.

I wasn't able to get up in time. She kicked my chest, sending me to my back. She was on top of me. She raised her arms and swung down with the crystal knife.

I caught her wrists and held them, keeping her from driving it into my body. Armin's blood dripped off the tip onto my face. She struggled against my hold, pressing harder against it.

Arms shaking from effort, more blood dropped onto my face. Sasha's. I should have been able to take her then, but after what happened with Lenore, I didn't have the energy. My focus was solely on keeping her from driving the blade into my chest.

She leaned forward, putting more of her weight into her attack. My muscles burned and I tried to kick her off, but it wouldn't work. My hold slipped and the knife tip came down.

I heard it connect with the ruby. Crystal on crystal. Sasha put every ounce of her strength into shoving the knife through the gem, into my chest; she was determined to end my life. The blade pieced through the ruby and an unseen force hit me like a punch.

A horrible screech filled the warehouse that made every hair on my body stand. Pain erupted in my ears. Metal creaked and snapped.

In a blast of burning air and blinding red light, Sasha was thrown backwards. I sucked in a few deep breaths of air before rolling over and pulling myself up.

Blood dripped from my nose, and I pressed a hand to my ear to stop the pain, only to find it covered in blood as well.

Sasha rolled to her feet, brandishing the knife and coming for me again. I stumbled backwards, trying to draw on the magic of the ruby, but it wouldn't come.

I braced my hands on either side of the railing to hoist myself up and kicked her with both feet. She hit the side of the railing and tumbled over, disappearing into the smoke.

Clutching my burning side, I pulled myself towards where I thought the door was. My whole body was numb, my ears ringing with pain. I couldn't breathe through the smoke, the heat, the sulfur, the burning flesh. I just needed to make it out the door.

The walkway collapsed in front of me, and I grabbed the edge of the broken metal before I could fall. Rough edges sliced into my hands and the strain made my arms shake. I wasn't going to be able to hold on.

My fingers started to slip. Letting out a groan, I tried to pull myself up but had no strength left to give. I'd survived Lenore and Sasha, but I wouldn't survive this.

I closed my eyes and tried to remember something happy. Just one day that hadn't sucked. I wanted to be happy when I went. Mom's face swam into my memories. Laughing, singing along with the music. Her red eyes bright as her warm smile stretched from ear to ear. I tried to remember what her laugh sounded like, tried to force it through to drown out the sharpness of breaking metal and screams.

"We're not dying yet." I opened my eyes as Blythe skidded to her knees on the broken walkway above me. She gripped my wrist at the same time Leander wrapped his arm around the other. Together, they pulled me up.

My face pressed against the walkway, and I choked out uncontrollable sobs. Leander hauled me to my feet and helped me limp to the exit. Metal screeched on metal as more of the catwalk broke apart behind us.

Blythe slammed through the door at the top of the stairs, and I gulped down the sulfur- and smoke-free air.

The black SUV was waiting for us at the bottom of the stairs. The back door flew open and Jax jumped out. He hurried over, and between him and Leander they were able to get me into the back seat.

Blythe jumped in the front and sped off before I could do a headcount to make sure everyone got out.

Jax's warm magic caressed my hands as it sought something to heal. Pins and needles pricked my palms as the cuts stitched back together under his touch. His magic continued up my arms, looking for more injuries, but there was nothing else he would be able to fix. Not now.

○

Blythe drove us to one of the private hangars at the airport like she'd been there before. She parked the car next to a jet with the stairs down and ready for us.

Leander and Jax helped me out of the car, and we headed inside. Lyra, Sadiki, Sebastian, and Thea were already on board. Lyra jumped up from the small couch and pulled me into a too-tight hug. She swayed a little, but that also could have been blamed on my own unsteadiness.

"You're alive," she breathed.

I nodded. "You too."

She let out a watery chuckle. Blythe moved by me to help Lyra back down to the couch. They both had cuts and ash-covered faces, but otherwise I didn't see any major injuries. Small favors.

Blythe caught my eye, and her sympathetic smile made my bottom lip tremble. I wanted to collapse right there and never get up again.

"We've been cleared for wheels up in ten," Rez said, walking into the main cabin from the cockpit. He gave me a once-over. "Bathroom's in back," he said simply before pouring himself a drink.

The door closed, and in the dampened silence everyone stared at me. On shaky legs, I made my way to the back and found the bathroom door.

Jax caught my hand before I could escape inside.

"What happened in there?" he asked quietly. I was way too aware of Thea watching us and I wished I could just not be stared at for five seconds.

"Em," Jax pressed.

I shook my head. "I need a minute," I said.

"Let me help."

"Please, Jax," I said. "Just give me a minute."

He removed his hand and stepped back. I shoved my way into the bathroom and locked the door behind me. I stood still for a second before doubling over and vomiting into the toilet.

Once my stomach had emptied itself, I rinsed my mouth out with water and clutched the side of the sink, staring at myself in the mirror. There was a bottomless nothing inside, and it threatened to sabotage every attempt at breath. Ripping the necklace free, I stared down at it.

Cracked into three pieces and only held in place by the silver setting. Pitch black stared back up at me. The red of the ruby was gone. The magic no longer hummed. Every generation's magic, gone. Mom, grandma, Amity. Everyone. The connection to the daughters that came before me was lost.

And I was left utterly alone.

ACKNOWLEDGEMENTS

Writing a novel is not an easy task. Writing a second one had more ups and downs (and pizza deliveries) than I want to admit. But the experience of getting the story from start to finish is not a solo one. Without the support I received from family and friends at every step of the process this sequel would not be what it is today.

My sister, Colleen, helped me work through my self-dug plot holes by translating all my ramblings into coherent thoughts. My first readers once again provided invaluable feedback on a less than perfect draft and helped polish the rough edges.

I want to thank my wonderful coworkers for their overwhelming encouragement. Their celebration when my debut novel was released and their excitement as I went through draft after draft of the second novel helped me keep the motivation to see this project though to the end.

As always, more than the author is involved in taking a story from notes to a fully fleshed out novel. Thank you to The Scribbler Editorial Team who ensured plot holes were filled and the world was as good as it could be. The Team at Blue Pen Books did an amazing job with the cover design and was a joy to work with for the entire process. And once again I would be lost without my marvelous editor Kate Murray Thiebauth who makes fixing all those little mistakes an incredibly fun process.

Finally, I will never be able to thank my fantastic parents enough. They continue to support me and encourage me in my writing journey as they have my entire life. You will never know just how much I appreciate you both.

ABOUT THE AUTHOR

E. O'Meagher has long been drawn to the idea of creating worlds with their own rules. After spending her childhood escaping into the fantasy realms of her favorite books, she now develops such worlds in her own work.

Raised in Western Montana, she currently calls Southern Maine home where she revels in a good rainy day on the beach. She loves exploring and spent two semesters studying abroad in Ireland as part of her university program. She enjoys traveling by train, exploring lighthouses (both haunted and not), rainy days, wandering through a forest, and a good cup of tea on a chilly autumn day. She holds a Bachelor of Arts in Creative writing with a minor in Irish Studies from the University of Montana.

***The Cursed Daughter* is the second install- ment in The Lost Coven Trilogy.**
Find her on Instagram and TikTok (@omeagherstories) and visit her online at w ww.omeagherstories.com.